TWO GUN PUBLISHING

THE ADVENTURES OF THE LONE RANGER

JOHN PAULITS

For information, please contact twogunpublishing@outlook.com

In association with Two Gun Publishing.

9798766894049

Chapter 1

Bryant's Gap

The harsh, shimmering Texas sun beat down on a slow-moving troop of six Texas Rangers. Collins, their guide, had gone ahead to scout safe passage through a canyon hemmed in by a lofty range of rock. To the left and right of the canyon entrance, trackless expanses of rough, difficult to navigate ground strewn with rocks and scrub stretched for miles. Bypassing the canyon would slow the Rangers' pursuit to a crawl. The Rangers, three days on the trail of the fearsome Cavendish gang, were worn out. They had food for two, perhaps three, more days. Any delays or detours would allow Butch Cavendish and his dozen murderous hirelings free license to continue their depredations against the innocent forces of civilization trying to tame the West.

Captain Dan Reid, leader of the Rangers, pulled rein. The others in his troop halted and went for their canteens, as Reid's brother, younger by a dozen years, guided his horse alongside.

"Collins has been gone quite a while," the captain's brother remarked.

"We need to know whether Cavendish passed through this canyon. I suppose a gap through those rocks isn't easy to locate. If Collins doesn't find one, we're licked."

"Cavendish must have found a way through."

"Doubtless he knows the trail better than we do. What is this place, I wonder?"

"Collins referred to it as Bryant's Gap, so there must be a gap… wait. Is that…?"

"Yes, I see him. Let's hope he found what we need."

Collins, a half-breed Mexican, took his time approaching.

"What did you find, Collins?" Captain Reid asked. The other Rangers clustered around to learn whether they were going forward or returning home.

"Good news. At the far end of the formation there's a narrow split in the rocks. Room enough to pass through, one by one. I went to the other side and saw a cloud of dust in the distance. I figure Cavendish knew about the gap—it's not easy to find—and supposes you don't, so he's in no hurry. He didn't count on your hiring me, though. Lucky you did."

Reid's squad capped their canteens and remounted. Collins led them into the narrow bowl of rocky ground, the jagged cliffs surrounding them mostly hidden in shadow. A stream gurgled somewhere ahead, and only the occasional squawk of a buzzard and the jangle of the Rangers' equipment broke the silence. On they rode in single file as the walls around them narrowed, closing in on what Collins assured them was a navigable fissure in the enveloping rock.

"We'd better fill our canteens at the stream," Collins suggested. "Don't know when we'll have another chance."

The Rangers mumbled assent. The brutal heat made a full canteen a valuable commodity. The Rangers dismounted next to the stream, which flowed out of a cave and wandered a short distance along the rock wall before disappearing underground.

Their canteens replenished, Captain Reid ordered them to remount. He took the lead, their objective obvious in the distance where the canyon walls narrowed to the point of a V. Collins fussed with the saddle of his horse and allowed them to go on ahead.

One minute later, all hell broke loose.

A rifle shot began it. One Ranger fell. Then a fusillade of bullets rained down on the Rangers from the walls of the canyon. Horses reared and spun in terror from the sound of gunshots echoing off the rocky walls. A second, then a third Ranger fell. The three remaining Rangers scrambled to control their horses and dismount to seek safety, and when they succeeded getting to the ground, their horses joined the other rider-less horses stampeding across the rock-strewn ground in panic back the way they had come.

Crouching, the Rangers fired their pistols at the rifle bursts coming from the cliffs above them. The barrage from the walls maintained its deadly rhythm as the Rangers searched in vain for cover. A fourth Ranger fell back as if struck by a battering ram. Now, only the captain and his brother remained in the fight.

Captain Reid cried, "If we can reach the cave…"

Then, he fell. Still the rifles' bullets pummeled the fallen Rangers. The captain's brother felt a lance of fire go through his left arm. His right leg exploded in pain. A crushing blow struck his temple, and he crumbled. Bullets continued to find the bodies of the Rangers until three rapid-fire shots from the rim of the canyon brought the massacre to a halt.

A voice called out, "Collins. Collins."

The treasonous guide stepped from the safety of the cave.

"Cavendish?" he called back.

"Yeah. Check them."

Collins made a circuit of the canyon floor, stopping briefly at each body. A few of the Rangers he merely glanced at, the number of bleeding bullet holes offering silent confirmation of their deaths.

"You got them all, Butch," he shouted.

"Good. We're leaving now. Montana says there's a cavalry unit somewhere in the area, and we *don't* want to run into them. We can't wait for you to make your way up to us. Meet me in Corbin City. I'll pay you off there."

Collins didn't like waiting for his pay. He'd done what Cavendish ordered.

"Wrap a gold piece in something and toss it down," he called up at the empty air.

He got no response, cursed, and went looking for his horse.

*

Hours later, the sun sank behind the steep walls of the canyon, leaving it in twilight. One Texas Ranger, the captain's younger brother, stirred, wakened by the drawn-out screech of a mountain cat hunting somewhere near the canyon entrance. The sound stirred the survival instinct in the badly wounded man, and he lifted his head to survey the scene. He recalled the gunfire; the canyon. Why was no one there to help him? He hadn't the strength to call out. Another noise. The cry of a buzzard. The gurgle of the stream reached him, and he recalled the cave where the stream originated. Lying in the open much longer would sign his death warrant, he knew, either from a hungry puma or the next day's blistering sun. With painful strokes, using his uninjured arm and leg, he dragged himself, inch by painful inch, across pebbles and outcroppings, toward the sound of the life-giving stream. Five painful motions forward and he rested. Another five, another rest. He drew near the cave. Only a few more prolonged efforts…But then, the Ranger blacked out.

When he awoke, night had fallen, but the clear music of the flowing water guided him forward. When he reached the stream, he dipped his face into its darkness. With his right hand he removed his red neckerchief, dampened it, and ran it across the nape of his neck and the top of his head. It felt wonderful. His left arm throbbed, his head ached, but he felt no pain in his leg. He realized he'd been shot there but hoped the wound was minor. He lowered his head again, drank deeply from the stream, and rested for ten minutes. Rejuvenated for the moment, he crawled forward to the cave wall and struggled into a sitting position where, in the meager moonlight, he saw the wide, still-spreading dark stain soaking his pant leg. He hadn't stopped bleeding. The torturous trip to reach the cave had done his wound no good. A wave of nausea swept over him, and he slumped sideways, unconscious and likely to remain so.

Night deepened and the temperature dropped. Only the occasional howl of a hungry predator penetrated the dark silence of the canyon as the desperately wounded Ranger lay next to the flowing stream, his fingertips touching the water.

The sun rose next morning on five, still bodies littering the canyon floor. As the sun edged its way over the rim of the canyon, a lone, buckskin-clad Indian, his black hair drawn into a tight war-knot behind his head and held in place by a red band circling his brow, trotted into Bryant's Gap on a sturdy, powerful, paint horse. The Indian knew of the stream and so did his horse, who moved unguided toward the cool water. The Indian reined up and stared at yesterday's havoc. He dismounted and allowed his horse to proceed toward the water on its own.

The Indian knelt next to each body, one by one, and offered a silent prayer. Only once before, in his youth, had he seen such carnage. He rose after inspecting the body of the fifth Ranger and heard his horse whinny in the distance.

"Scout find something," he muttered and walked forward. The Indian's horse stood a few feet inside a cave alongside a man lying next to the stream flowing from the cave. The faint rise and fall of the man's chest caught the Indian's eye. He turned the Ranger over and found an ugly gash on the side of his head, a bruised, purple patch above the man's left elbow, and a pant leg soaked with blood. He put his ear to the Ranger's chest.

"Him need much help," the Indian mumbled, rising. From his saddlebags he took some roots and herbs he always carried, as well as a coffee pot. He quickly gathered what little wood he could find and built a fire. As soon as the water in the coffee pot boiled, he dropped in some of the roots and herbs. He slipped his knife from the sheath on his belt and went to work on the Ranger's leg as a distant explosion of prolonged gunfire came faintly to his ear. He put the distraction aside and concentrated. When he removed the bullet from the leg, the Ranger moaned, and the Indian took that for a good sign. Using the skills he'd picked up in his time traveling the Texas plains alone, he patched the wound in the Ranger's leg using the remedy he'd brewed. He found no bullet in the arm. It had either passed through or the wound had come from ricocheting rock. He wrapped the arm, again soaking the bandage in the concoction he'd boiled. After dressing the Ranger's head wound, he prepared breakfast. By then the distant gunfire had stopped. Using the Ranger's own neckerchief, he bathed the man's head and neck. It would be up to the man, himself, now. The Indian could do nothing but let the wounded Ranger rest and pray for him to regain consciousness.

The Indian repacked his saddlebags as his horse

roamed nearby in search of its own breakfast. With a small spade he started in on what he knew would be a long, gruesome morning in the hot sun—digging five graves.

*

When the Indian saw the Ranger's eyelids flutter, he moved nearer the injured man. He had tended the white man's wounds for three days in the shaded but brutally hot cave, bathing the Ranger's face with cool water and pressing the soaked neckerchief to his lips, hoping to force some life-sustaining water into the man. Repeated changes of the poultice soaked in the mixture the Indian had brewed staved off infection. Keeping close watch on his patient, he brewed a second concoction, dropping six small, green leaves into the boiling water. He'd spent hours searching for the one plant he knew of whose leaves produced a drink that might bring the Ranger back from the edge of death.

"You awake," the Indian stated.

"Where am I? Who are you?" the Ranger asked in a cracked voice. "The others? Where are they?"

"Me fix something you drink. You feel better then." He poured the boiling water into a battered tin cup, careful to keep the leaves in the pot. "Wait, me help you sit up."

The weakened Ranger took the cup as a child might take medicine from its mother. He sipped.

"You drink it all, you feel better," the Indian repeated.

"There were six of us. Six Texas Rangers."

"Someone ambush you from top of canyon. Me find place they shoot from."

"Butch Cavendish and his gang. The other Rangers?"

Tonto looked away. "All killed but you. You lone Ranger left alive in canyon when me find you."

"The only one?" The Ranger lowered his cup. "All of them gone? My brother… ow long have I been here?"

"You sleep more than three days."

"Three days! It's not possible."

Three days me sit with you," the Indian repeated.

"Their bodies. Are they out in the sun? The heat, scavengers…"

"No, me bury. Make five graves."

"He had a family," the Ranger said softly. "A wife and a son."

"You drink medicine. You need food. Me go find rabbit for dinner. Sleep good for you."

"I've slept long enough."

"No! You not move! Leg need more time to heal. Here bullet me take out of leg." He handed over a slug.

The Ranger inspected it, then tossed it into the stream.

"Cavendish," he said, his jaw tightening. He stared at the Indian. "You look… familiar. What's your name?"

"You remember! Me Tonto."

"Tonto, yes."

"You save me many year ago when Indians on warpath destroy my people village."

"I recall the day. I was thirteen. The Texas Rangers…"

"Me twelve when Rangers chase away warpath Indians, but my village destroyed. Many killed. My family killed."

"My brother was in the group of Rangers that day."

"You find Tonto hurt and take me to him. Him good man. You good friend to Tonto."

"And now, you've been a good friend to me. You called me something then."

"Me call you 'Kemo Sabe'. It mean trusty scout. There guns of Rangers. Me bury badges with them."

The Ranger looked at the pile of weaponry and pulled an elaborately tooled, double holstered gun belt from the pile. He moved revolvers aside until he found the two ivory-handled weapons he wanted.

"My brother had these guns especially made by the Colt Company when he was promoted to captain two years ago. He gave up his .45s for these .44s so he could use the same bullets in either his carbine or his sidearm. He was proud of them. Here, feel the balance."

Tonto inspected the guns.

"Them plenty fine, but not same size, Kemo Sabe."

The Ranger smiled. "No. One pistol has a slightly shorter barrel. My brother believed it would allow him to draw it more quickly from his holster. The longer barrel adds accuracy at distance." He noticed a black garment buried deeper in the pile.

"This vest?" he said.

"Me find on ground."

"I recognize it. My brother's. It was so hot he slung it over his saddle blanket…"

The Ranger's emotions welled up.

"You rest. Me hunt. Have more to tell you. Me be back soon."

The Ranger, clutching the black vest to his chest, lay back and closed his eyes, wondering how the tides and eddies of his life had brought him to this point.

Chapter 2

Butch Cavendish

Six shots rang out clear, crisp breaches in an otherwise sultry, quiet Texas day. After each shot, a tiny ping sounded as the bullet took another tin can off the fence post. Daniel Reid, clad in his Texas Rangers' gear, smiled as his thirteen-year-old brother did not miss.

"How many is that?" he asked, putting his arm around the boy's shoulders.

"Eighteen. What's the Texas Ranger record?"

The older man laughed. "I don't think they keep records of such things."

"Well, if you had a record, I'll set a new one when I join."

"I'm sure you will, but you've got a whole lot to do before you get to that point."

The boy looked up to his brother the way few younger brothers did. The only thing in life he wanted was to become a Texas Ranger. Like his brother.

"In a few years, you'll be heading East for school."

"I know. I know."

"Just as I did. You'll enjoy it. You can only learn so much here on the ranch. I had a wonderful four years. You will, too. You'll come back when you're twenty-one and when you do…"

"When I do, I'll join the Rangers!"

"Yes, you will."

"In your Ranger company. You'll probably be a captain by then."

"Let's not get ahead of ourselves. Go again. I'll set up six more cans." The boy reloaded and holstered his revolver. When his brother returned from setting up the targets, the boy faced the fence.

"Watch," he said. His right hand flashed to his side, and the gun seemed to leap from the holster. Six shots cracked and six tin cans went flying.

"Twenty-four," the boy said, twirling his revolver and slipping it back into his holster. "I can do it left-handed, too. Let me show you."

His brother laughed. "You are something. *Uh oh*!"

Both man and boy raised their heads as if sniffing the air.

"Three shots!" the boy cried.

"The Rangers want me. It must be the renegade Indian band I told you about. I have to go. You stay here. Linda might need you."

The boy watched his brother race to his horse, mount, and gallop in the direction of the shots. The boy considered. When he left the house twenty minutes earlier, Linda had been busy baking bread in the kitchen. He reloaded his revolver and walked toward his own horse.

Twenty-five minutes later, following his brother's trail, the boy came upon a small Indian village razed to the ground, flames spouting from a handful of crumpled tepees. The Rangers were nowhere in sight. The boy brought his mount to a halt. In the distance he picked out an apparent dust cloud but heard no gunfire. He climbed down from his horse and walked slowly through the demolished village, the breeze carrying the smoke from the dying fires away from the boy toward the north. His brother had told him about a band of renegade Indians in the area, and when the boy asked why they would attack their own people, he recalled his brother's description of them.

"They refuse to conform. Anyone who doesn't think their way is the enemy, red man or white."

The young boy counted seven bodies as he walked, arrows embedded in them. Then he passed the smoking ruin of a tepee and had to turn away. Three charred bodies, one obviously a child, lay twisted in the conflagration. A shuffling sound made him draw his gun and turn. An Indian boy, about his own size, crawled from beneath a blackened heap of buffalo hides, coughing harshly. The boy's face and clothing were smeared with soot. Their eyes met and the Indian froze, proudly got to his feet, and stared at the boy, who holstered his weapon.

"I'm a friend," the boy said.

The Indian sank to his knees, and the boy hurried to him.

"You're hurt." The broken shaft of an arrow extended from the back of the Indian boy's thigh. "And you've been burned. Let me get you some water." He ran to his horse and returned with a canteen, which he held to the other boy's lips. The boy drank greedily.

"Give it here. Let me clean your face." The boy removed his red neckerchief and doused it with his canteen. Gently, he sponged away as much of the soot as he could. "My brother will be back soon. He'll know what to do. Do you speak English?"

The Indian boy reached out and put his hand on the other boy's shoulder. "Kemo Sabe." Then he touched himself on the chest. "Tonto."

"I'll get you out of the sun." He ran to his horse for a saddle blanket. He found two long sticks and two large rocks in the ruins of the village and with them made a flimsy lean-to. He gestured the Indian boy inside.

"I hear them coming." He called his horse over and mounted to get a higher perspective of the land. The Rangers were in view. Returning to the lean-to, he put the canteen down beside the recumbent boy and waited. He repeated to himself a familiar mantra. His brother would know what to do.

*

The years passed; the younger brother went to the East for school. When he returned to Texas, he joined his brother's company of Texas Rangers and rode with him for four years. One day, the Cavendish gang moved into their area. Before long and after frequent fights with the gang, the Rangers set out after the Cavendish gang, and

Collins, their guide, led them to Bryant's Gap.

*

Butch Cavendish, a thirty-five-year-old drifter, joined the Confederate army in late 1861, but when the promised pay did not materialize, he and three other rebel soldiers he had befriended during his brief enlistment deserted. The four like-minded men put the Confederate cause to their own use, raiding arsenals and storage depots in Texas, then taking their booty to Louisiana and, once, as far as Arkansas, to sell to other Confederate units desperate for supplies. But when April, 1865 dawned, they were out of work, so they took their war wealth home, Cavendish to his wife and fourteen-year-old son. There was money to be made after the war as cattle, ignored during the long struggle between North and South, roamed the rich, Texas grasslands, available to anyone willing to do the work of rounding them up. Hard work, though, did not appeal to Cavendish, not after the easy pickings of the previous few years. After a tedious, domestic six months, he rounded up his three deserter friends, and they took to preying upon the weak and helpless. New towns rising up on the plains offered easy targets, like flimsy banks and express offices, begging for a Cavendish withdrawal. Wagon trains heading west through Texas toward Sante Fe were easy quarry for his gang, which soon grew to a dozen men. Solitary homesteads became the easiest targets of all. The Texas Rangers, formed to protect the range from marauding Indians when U. S. Cavalry units were few and far between, set out after them. Rangers fell to the bullets of the Cavendish gang. The Rangers caught an occasional member of the gang, but Cavendish recruited replacements with little trouble. Cavendish's son Garth, now nineteen, rode with his father's gang, learning, as his father often laughed, a valuable trade. Both the gang members and the Rangers knew one another's tactics well and made use of what they knew to establish a stalemate between them as their inconclusive battles dragged on. Casualties mounted. In the spring of 1870, the gang raided an army depot. Coincidentally, a squad of Rangers had camped at the depot for the night. After killing the two army guards, Cavendish attacked while everyone slept, wiping out a half-dozen soldiers and five Rangers. Thereafter, the U. S. Cavalry as well as the Texas Rangers made it their number one priority to bring the gang to justice.

"Collins!" Cavendish called out, two months after the murderous raid at the army depot. "Over here." The gang camped in the hills five miles from the nearest settlement.

Collins had been a local scout for the cavalry as well as for the Rangers, especially with Captain Reid's patrol, but became dissatisfied with the pay he received. Cavendish knew of Collins' reputation as a scout, and when he learned of his growing dissatisfaction, he sent an emissary to offer him a job—lead the Rangers into a trap for more money than he'd earn in two years with the army or the Rangers. Collins, feeling especially slighted by the Rangers' treatment, jumped at the chance.

"You've decided on Bryant's Gap?" Cavendish asked. "You know the area better than anybody. Is it the best spot?"

"It's the *perfect* spot, Butch. You line your men along the top of the canyon. Once the Rangers enter, there's no way out. I'll tell them there is," he said with a laugh, "but it won't matter. Once they're inside, they ain't coming out again. There's a stream in the canyon, and I'll suggest they dismount to fill their canteens. They'll suspect nothing. Reid, the captain, trusts me. I've told you about him. I know him; I've worked with him before. Once they've entered the gap, and relax around the stream, they'll be off guard and you'll have plenty of time to pick them off."

"Reid trusts you, eh. Good. It's a shame he don't pay you," Cavendish chuckled.

"But you will."

"I'll pay you plenty, you get them Rangers into the canyon. We're taking the bank in Bremertown tonight, so they'll be out after us tomorrow morning."

"I know. I'll have the Rangers on your trail first thing. It takes a good two days to get to Bryant's Gap, but you'll have a big head start on them. Don't worry. I'll get them to the gap. You be there waiting."

"We'll be there, all right. See that you are."

That night, the Bremertown bank fell, and next morning, Collins led six Texas Rangers west on the trail of the robbers—toward Bryant's Gap.

Chapter 3

The Lone Ranger

"When me take bullet from leg, me hear far away gunfire," Tonto said. The Ranger had rested and eaten a good dinner. He and Tonto sat in the moonlight next to the stream. "Me learn cavalry catch up to Cavendish gang. Have big fight. Many killed. Here newspaper from Corbin City. It tell of fight."

The Ranger eagerly took the newspaper while Tonto lit a torch. The Ranger nestled the torch into the soft ground along the stream and held the paper near it. The headline read: CAVENDISH GANG CUT DOWN. CAVENDISH ESCAPES WITH FOUR OTHERS. The story told of how a second group of Texas Rangers had joined forces with a small cavalry unit and encountered Cavendish and his dozen men. Nine bodies lay slain at the end of the battle, seven of them members of Cavendish's gang.

"He's escaped again, Tonto."

"Maybe him not rob and kill any longer."

"Very little chance of that. He knows my brother led the patrol of Rangers he ambushed here. We fought gun battles with Cavendish more than once and as recently as last week. I hoped we were about to end his reign of terror, but darkness fell, and he and his gang got away. Two Rangers died in that battle, and my brother swore he wouldn't stop until Cavendish faced justice. Then came the Bremertown bank robbery, and Collins led us here to Bryant's Gap. I'm going to fulfill my brother's pledge, Kemo Sabe, but I cannot let Cavendish know who I am. I have no family, but he might go after my brother's wife and son."

"What you do?"

"He knows I rode with my brother. Now, he thinks I'm dead."

"There only five graves. Him know someone escape."

"Tomorrow, we'll make a sixth grave, my grave. It's the only way I can go after Cavendish and keep my identity a secret."

"That not easy. People see you. Them talk. Him find out soon you not dead."

"I'll wear some kind of disguise…"

"Maybe you wear mask. It easier than disguise."

"A mask, yes."

Tonto reached for the black vest, which lay next to the Ranger.

"Me make mask from brother's vest."

"Yes, yes. I'd like that, Tonto."

"You change name, too?"

"A name. For what I need to do, I won't need a name. You said something when I awakened. What was it? You said I was the lone Ranger left alive after Cavendish's attack. That's how I'll be called from here on. I'll be the Lone Ranger."

"That good. Me help you."

"You?"

"Me have no family, too. All bad men need be stopped."

Through both of their memories flashed the sight of Tonto's burnt Indian village.

"I'll be glad for your help, Kemo Sabe."

"You rest now. Tomorrow, me make grave. In day, maybe two, you strong enough to ride."

"I'll need to find a horse before I can do any riding."

"Me know where find band of wild horse. Them plenty fine. It not far from here."

"All right. I'll rest one more day. Then we go to work."

*

The daring attack on his band, and the loss of seven of his men stunned Cavendish. He, his son Garth, Montana Jenkins, Razor Gilliam, and Shark Lawson managed to flee the attack and take refuge five miles off in a cave; one of several caves, canyons, and deserted hunter's cabins the gang knew of. The cave was large enough to accommodate both the men and horses.

"Don't," Cavendish commanded. "Keep 'em

saddled. We'll split up the goods here and separate. Those Rangers don't give up. I'm afraid they won't wait till dawn to take out after us. Lay low and in two months, we'll meet up again. Things will have quieted down by then. Garth and I'll go south and find some one-horse town to settle in for the time being. You hombres pick your direction but stay away from each other and away from anywhere you might be known. The Ranger patrols will be looking for a gang, not individuals. Two months from today, show up in Coldstream." Coldstream was a growing town twenty-five miles south of Corbin City. "We'll get to know the bank there and make a withdrawal to start us off again."

Garth laughed, and the other men mumbled their agreement. Cavendish emptied his and his son's saddles bags onto the ground and split their haul into five piles as the others knelt close, keeping a wary eye.

"All even?" Cavendish asked wryly. "Any problems, talk now." A long silence passed as Cavendish's eyes challenged each man to impugn his fairness.

"It's all even, boss," Montana said. He was generally the spokesman for the gang and the only member of the gang to wear two guns. "We'll be sitting real pretty for a while. I like the plan."

Razor Gilliam, a grubby man of small stature, who sported a long scar down the left side of his face, a scar he received in a fight with a barber whose haircutting talents displeased him, grunted acceptance.

Shark Lawson, so named due to his strangely large

front teeth, said, "I'm happy."

"Be dark in an hour," Cavendish said. "The Rangers and soldiers'll be busy burying bodies and cleaning up the mess they made. We got a little time, but not much, not enough to wait till tomorrow to move out. Those Rangers are the ones I'd most like to deal with. Soldiers usually stay close to the fort, but the damn Rangers—they can be anywhere."

Shark said, "I'd like to put a bullet in the head of every Ranger in Texas."

"When they find the six bodies in Bryant's Gap, it won't make them very happy either," Garth Cavendish added with a laugh.

"Collins," Cavendish said. "I forgot about Collins. Well, if he meets up again with us, I'll settle with him. He'll hear about how they came after us, so if he's got a brain in his head, he'll lam out for a while."

Razor walked to the mouth of the cave. "Nothing in sight, boss. What say we have a meal and then travel? You're right about the Rangers. I don't trust them either."

"That's what I said we'd do," Cavendish barked. "Garth, start cooking and make it quick. Razor, stay there. Keep watch."

*

Tonto and the Ranger left Bryant's Gap after digging a shallow hole into which the Ranger tossed his badge. He removed a chain from around his neck, a chain holding a small, round medal.

"What that?" Tonto asked.

The Ranger handed it to Tonto.

"There writing on it."

"My brother gave it to me the day I became a Texas Ranger, but now that career is over, and this should be buried here, the place where it ended."

He took the medallion back and dropped it into the empty grave. After refilling the hole, he bowed his head for a moment.

"May they rest in peace, Tonto," he said softly. "I will see they did not die in vain. Cavendish," he muttered but said no more.

The Ranger, wearing the mask Tonto made for him and clad in his black, bullet-torn pants and tan shirt, both newly washed in the stream, rode double behind Tonto, who took them in a direction the Indian had not traveled during the time he had nursed the wounded man. Half a mile from Bryant's Gap, they came upon a grisly sight—a human body mauled and partly eaten by a mountain cat. The Ranger dismounted and approached the remains. "That might have been me if you hadn't happened along, Kemo Sabe." He studied the undamaged boots on the corpse. "This is Collins," he said in disbelief.

"Him man who lead you into ambush?"

"It is." The Ranger stood gazing off to the right, deep in thought.

"We go now?" Tonto asked.

"No. No, we'll bury the man. No one should…" He shook his head.

Tonto dismounted and retrieved the small shovel he'd used to bury the five Texas Rangers. Taking turns, they made a grave, rolled Collins' mangled body into it, returned the dirt, and covered it with as many rocks as they could find. They climbed back aboard the Indian's paint horse and set out.

An hour later, the men dismounted on a wide, grassy plain in the shade of some large rocks near the entrance to another canyon whose walls were twice the height of Bryant's Gap.

"This where me see many wild horse. Them like grass in canyon… you hear?"

The two men walked to where they could gaze out onto the plain, where they saw a distant cloud of dust rolling in their direction and with it an ominous, thunderous rumble of destruction.

"Buffalo!" the Ranger cried over the increasing din of the approaching herd. "A band of horses never made a noise like that. Some kind of stampede. We need shelter." Tonto rushed over to Scout and gave him a smart slap on the rump, sending him into the safety of the canyon. Then he and the Ranger scrambled up the nearest rock formation as high as time permitted.

A band of wild horses, led by a large white stallion, tried desperately to keep ahead of an unending sea of storming buffalo on their trail.

"I see what's frightened the horses," the Ranger said into Tonto's ear. "I wonder what frightened the buffalo."

The lead horse knew its destination—the canyon whose narrow entrance would stop the buffalo herd. When the white stallion reached the canyon opening, it reared high, front legs pawing the air as if encouraging the other horses to make for shelter. The two dozen horses following behind their leader managed to get inside the canyon, and a moment later, the buffaloes' pounding hooves made the land tremble. Only exhaustion would finally halt their stampede. The stallion stood at the canyon entry, repeatedly rearing, its forelegs thrashing, as the buffalo thundered by. At the rear of the buffalo herd ran a male of tremendous bulk. Unable to keep up and angry at being left behind, he jounced to a dusty halt and eyed the stallion as he pawed the ground, shook his massive head, and bellowed in anger as the clamor of the departing buffalo subsided. Panic-stricken but unwilling to cede the buffalo entry to the canyon and access to the herd he led, the horse reared and whinnied. The buffalo had no interest in the horse's theatrics and charged. A horn scraped along the elusive horse's side, leaving a thin, jagged, red trail as the stallion's sharp, heavy hooves tried desperately to drive the buffalo back. The buffalo retreated, bowed his massive head, and charged again. This time the horse felt the sharp point of a horn enter muscle. The horse screeched and struck out even harder with its hooves. Then it fell to its knees. The buffalo retreated once again, snorting and pawing the ground in anger.

"Tonto, I have to save that horse. It's fighting for its life and deserves to have it." The Ranger, ignoring the dull ache in his wounded leg, leaped from rock to rock to the ground. The buffalo, about to charge the horse and give the death blow, paused, distracted by this new antagonist. The Ranger, wearing his brother's guns, drew and fired six times. From the corner of his eye, the Ranger saw the brave horse struggle to its feet even as blood from the buffalo's second charge flowed slowly down its left flank. The buffalo staggered from the impact of the Ranger's bullets, and the Ranger took his other gun and with his left hand fired six more times. The buffalo bellowed in pain and tumbled onto his side. Tonto appeared at the Ranger's shoulder.

"Me no let it suffer," the Indian said. Walking forward, he put two bullets into the buffalo's head.

The Ranger approached the white stallion, who took a few steps back, eyeing him with suspicion.

"Easy, big fellow. I'm here to help."

The weak horse fell to its knees again, and the Ranger went to it and ran his hand along its flank.

"We need to stop the bleeding, Tonto."

"Me know what to do." He tracked down Scout and returned with his saddlebag and canteen.

For an hour Tonto worked on the horse, and the Ranger helped clean its wounds and calm it. Tonto brewed the same concoction he'd used on the Ranger to keep infection away.

Satisfied they'd done all they could for the brave stallion, the Ranger said, "I'll tend to the horse, Kemo Sabe, while you scout the canyon for us."

The Ranger knelt beside the horse, gently stroked its neck, and spoke softly to it.

"Canyon empty," Tonto reported. "Other horses gone. There must be way through, not like canyon where Cavendish attack you." The Indian paused a moment, then said, "You Lone Ranger. White horse lone, too."

"He's beautiful, isn't he? I'd love to have a horse like him."

"Him wild horse. Hard to ride."

"I know but he seems gentle at the moment."

"Maybe him know you save life."

"We'll stay here and nurse him, Tonto. If he recovers, and if he allows, this horse will help me catch Cavendish."

The sun had moved between two of the low, craggy peaks of the canyon, into a position where its rays fell squarely on the wounded animal lying peacefully near the Ranger. The sunlight shining on the white horse made it seem to glow like a creature from another world.

"Sun make horse shine like silver," Tonto said softly.

"Silver. Yes, Silver. That would be the only name for him." As the horse lay on the grassy ground, the Ranger continued to run his hand along its neck. "Get well, Silver. I hope we'll do a lot of riding together."

*

The horse nickered softly and got to its feet. The Ranger's eyes went to its wounds to check for bleeding, but Tonto's medicine had done its job. The horse looked through the canyon entrance and neighed loudly as if calling to his vanished herd, but getting no response, it swung its head back toward the Ranger, shook its mane, and walked a short distance to where a small spring had formed a pond of clear, cold water. The grass was fresh inside the canyon, untrodden by the rampaging buffalo. The horse drank deeply from the pond, then leisurely grazed.

"Tonto, I think he'll heal quickly here in the canyon, if he chooses to stay."

"Him not look like want to go anywhere," Tonto said, grinning. "Me fix dinner."

*

The Ranger and Tonto set up camp inside the canyon and hoped for the best with Silver. For the next four days, the Ranger bathed the horse's wounds twice daily, and on the rare occasions when Silver left the canyon, he followed him outside, hoping the horse had not chosen to go in search of his herd. But the horse never strayed far or stayed outside for long. On the fifth day, the Ranger managed to get a rope around the horse's neck and walk with him inside the canyon, taking the rope off whenever he sensed Silver's discomfort. He spoke to the horse many times a day to get the powerful stallion used to his sound of his voice.

Using up most of the money the Ranger had with him, Tonto visited Corbin City twice, bringing back food supplies, a used saddle and bridle, and the latest edition of the newspaper. The issue of the paper, the *Corbin City Bugle*, following the one he'd read detailing the attack on the Cavendish gang informed him of the names of the gang who'd fallen and who'd escaped, as well as the name of the Ranger and soldier who'd lost their lives.

"I knew the Ranger who was killed, Tonto. Frank Meredith. Like my brother, he had a family. Cavendish *must* be brought to justice."

"Any news of him in paper?"

"No. Only that he escaped and hasn't made a move since the attack."

"Maybe him hurt."

"No, I don't think so. The story says five of the gang rode away as soon as the shooting started. He's probably decided to lie low for a while."

"Maybe him travel somewhere far."

The Ranger nodded. "It's possible, Kemo Sabe. We'll have to be alert to any news of him and his men."

The next day, the Ranger threw the saddle onto Silver's back. The horse reared defiantly, and the saddle slid to the ground before the Ranger had a chance to secure it in place. Every few hours, the Ranger tried again to saddle the powerful animal and failed. Finally, however, on the fifth attempt, as the sun sank, casting weird canyon shadows across the ground, Silver accepted the saddle without complaint. The Ranger buckled it loosely beneath Silver and left it on all night, hoping to get the horse used to it quickly.

Tonto already had breakfast going when the Ranger awoke. He and the Indian ate eggs and bacon in silence as Silver stood off grazing.

"I'm going to tighten the saddle and mount him today, Tonto."

"Oh, him no like that."

"We'll see."

Breakfast over, the Ranger approached the saddled but unbridled horse. He spoke softly into the horse's ear as he ran a patient hand along its neck. He tightened the cinches and, taking a step back, grasped the saddle horn, lifted his left leg to the stirrup, and pulled himself into the saddle. Silver did a pirouette of anxiety and swished his head around, trying to get a good look at the strange weight on his back. The Ranger continued to talk softly and stroke the animal's neck.

"Lead him around, Kemo Sabe," he called to Tonto.

Tonto put the rope around Silver's neck and walked with him, the Ranger continuing his soft treatment. After ten minutes, he dismounted.

“A good start,” he said, smiling widely. “Once I get the bridle on him and ride with him for a while, we’ll be best of friends.”

“Horse like you.”

“And I like him. I can’t wait to see how he runs.”

“How your leg?”

“Good as new, Tonto, thanks to you. My arm, too. As soon as Silver is used to having me on his back, we’ll ride into Corbin City.”

“You wear mask?”

“Yes, but we’ll go at night. I want to get a look at the town and make sure neither Cavendish nor any of his men are hiding out there.”

“That good. Me think Silver get used to you pretty quick.”

“I’ll put the bridle on him tomorrow and take it from there.”

Chapter 4

The Corbin City Jail

The fresh supplies Tonto purchased in Corbin City provided another hearty eggs and bacon breakfast for the two men. Silver paced the canyon floor nearby with Scout at his side, both horses stooping to graze whenever the spirit moved them. Suddenly, Silver's head lifted from the grass, and he neighed softly, scraping the ground with his right hoof. Tonto and the Ranger came alert.

"Look, Kemo Sabe," Tonto said. A shadow, clearly of someone wearing a cowboy's Stetson, snaked along the jagged entry rocks of the canyon. The sun, low in the early morning sky, gave the shadow enormous length but kept most of the canyon in shadow. Tonto pointed to a dark recess in the rocks behind the Ranger, who quickly slid into it, out of sight.

From Tonto's left came a voice. "You, Indian. Don't make any sudden moves."

Tonto turned to see a young man, perhaps twenty years old, pointing a revolver at him.

"What you want?" he asked. "Why you point gun at Tonto?"

"I want food. I want any money you have. Give it to me or else…"

A shot rang out and echoed from the canyon walls. As if it were alive, the gun flew out of the young man's hand, and he screeched in pain and surprise as he clamped his gun hand under his opposite arm pit.

"You shot me! You shot me!" the man squealed.

The Ranger stepped forward, a silhouetted figure, .44 in hand.

"You're not hurt," he said. "I simply shot the gun out of your hand. Get it, Tonto."

The man inspected his hand. "I'm not hit but it hurts like the devil." He rubbed the front and back of his hand energetically.

Tonto lifted the damaged gun from the ground and bobbed it up and down. He broke it and spun the cylinder.

"Kemo Sabe," he said. "Gun empty. Have no bullets."

The Ranger's eyes went to the young man's cartridge belt, which lacked bullets along its entire length. He holstered his own revolver.

"You could have been hurt," he said to the young man. "Sit down. Make yourself some breakfast. What's your name?"

"Clement. Clem. Clem Hanson. I can really make myself a meal?"

"Me wash cup in pond, give you coffee," Tonto said.

The man knelt over the small fire Tonto used to cook.

"Are three eggs too many?" he asked, looking up as the Ranger approached the fire. "You're wearing a mask!"

"Don't let this mask concern you. It's on the side of the law. Take as many eggs as you wish. As much bacon, too."

"Gee, thanks!" It took only a few moments for Clem to scramble the eggs, cook the bacon, and down the results.

"Now," the Ranger said when Clem finished, "why did you try to rob us?"

"They're after me. I'm sorry. I couldn't help it. I've been running for days. I'm hungry. I have no money. On top of that, I can't leave the area."

"Slow down," the Ranger suggested, offering Clem a friendly smile. "Start at the beginning."

"I live with my mom—she hasn't been well lately—not far from here. I work in the livery stable in Corbin City. Or I did until…" He made a fist and struck himself in the leg. "How could they think I had anything to do with outlaws? I've lived here my whole life."

"You're going too fast again," the Ranger said.

"All right. All right."

"My mother felt ill a couple nights ago, so I went for Doc Johnson. He wasn't in his office, but someone passing by told me he'd gone to Rance Loober's place to deliver Mrs. Loober's baby. So, I started out for Rance's. It's about a mile or so out of town, south. When I was halfway there, I saw a group of, I don't know, about a dozen riders coming my way. I didn't like the looks of them, but they passed me by without comment."

"Did you recognize them?"

"Only when they were by me did I think of the Cavendish gang, and the moment I did, a troop of cavalry and some Texas Rangers rode out of nowhere and started firing. I could hear bullets whizzing, so I lit out as fast as I could go. I found the doc, and when he finished up with the new baby, I took him to see my mother. He gave her some powder to dissolve in water. But that's not to the point. Later that day around supper time, the sheriff rides up to my house and tells me I'm under arrest for being a member of the Cavendish gang! He says the Rangers and soldiers described me to a T. I told him he was crazy, but he insisted I had to go with him. I thought he was playing some kind of sick joke. He knows me. He's always known me—since I was a boy. Well, I made like I'd go with him. He never drew his gun on me, and as we walked to his horse, I grabbed his pistol and pushed him. I made for my horse where my gun belt was hanging, mounted up, dropped his gun on the ground, and rode like the wind. I was barely out of my front gate when he started shooting at me with his rifle. Thank the Lord it was a single shot piece. I fired back but only up in the air, hoping he keep him from reloading. I hoped he'd run for cover. He ran all right. Back to town for a posse, and they've been trailing me for days."

"All of your bullets are gone," the Ranger pointed out.

"They had me cornered a few times. I couldn't run far because I'm worried about Ma. I shot all my bullets trying to discourage them. I never shot at them, I swear! Only in the air. Now I have no bullets, no food, I haven't seen Ma for days. I hope Doc's been looking in on her."

"Your running away may have convinced them you *are* part of Cavendish gang. He and four others ran, too, and haven't been captured."

"I'm not part of any gang! Running was all I could think of to do. I made a stupid decision, I know, but I was scared and there was no time to explain things while bullets were flying. Now the sheriff wants to arrest me! That's a stupider decision than mine!" Clem's voice rose in panic. When he settled himself, he said in a soft voice, "I just want to go home."

"What you think, Kemo Sabe?" Tonto asked.

"I think the young man needs help."

"What we do?"

"I have a plan," the Ranger answered. "Listen."

*

The Ranger spent much of the day on Silver's back, first walking him within the canyon, then cantering him out onto the plain. The white stallion took direction well, pleasing the Ranger greatly, and as dusk fell, the Ranger, Tonto, and Clem sat around their small fire, heating beans and roasting three buffalo steaks Tonto had cut from the buffalo which had attacked Silver.

"That is one beautiful horse," Clem commented. "You say he just let you capture him?"

The Ranger repeated the story of the buffalo stampede.

"Wow! I saw that dead buffalo outside. Critters'll have that picked clean before long." He spooned some beans into his mouth. "I'm really nervous about tonight."

"It's the only thing you can do, Clem," the Ranger said. "We've talked about this. The sheriff has to be more reasonable than you've described him."

"He didn't seem reasonable when he tried to take me in."

"Don't get yourself wound up again. Perhaps he felt pressured to do *something* because of the terrible gunfight so near his town. Dealing with Butch Cavendish is enough to turn any man's head."

Clem shrugged and ate in silence.

When they finished, Clem said, "Here, let me do that," and he gathered up the tin dishes and cups and took them to the pond.

"You think your plan work, Kemo Sabe?" Tonto asked quietly.

"It should, unless the sheriff is a madman," the Ranger replied.

"You want me start to town now?"

"I think you'd better in case you can't find the doctor right away. Clem and I will travel slowly to give you time."

"Me go."

Clem, on his knees at the pond, watched Tonto saddle Scout and ride from the canyon. The plan was underway. He brought the dishes back, and the Ranger stowed them in his saddlebags.

"Mount up, Clem."

Corbin City, a town of some fifteen hundred souls, was originally founded as a waystation for travelers heading to Arizona or Mexico. It prospered and continued as a reliable hub for shipments to and from the area. Two stage lines and three shipping companies headquartered in the town. A number of small cattle ranches grew up around it, the plentiful grass in the area fueling the town's growth. The one main street in Corbin City had a stretch of stores, two saloons, the *Lucky Deal* and the *Silver Nugget*, a church, and a small jail containing two cells, one facing the other across a small aisle. The jail was the Ranger and Clem's destination.

"Let me do the talking when we go in," the Ranger said. "I'm sure I'll have to explain my mask."

"Why *do* you wear it?"

"I have good reason to keep my identity a secret." He offered nothing more.

"Suppose the sheriff won't listen." Clem's nervousness at carrying out the Ranger's plan sounded clear as a bell in his voice.

"Don't worry."

Clem gave a profound sigh, and the men rode on.

There were only a few splashes of light interrupting the darkness along the main street.

"They're the saloons," Clem said. "We better circle behind the buildings. We'll cause a commotion if anyone sees us. The jail's at the opposite end of town." He led the way.

A dim light came from the window of the jail.

"Sheriff Hosh usually stays out of the way and waits for trouble," Clem said.

"And when it comes?"

"He's always done his job good from what I've seen of him." They dismounted and tied up at the hitch post in front of the jail. The Ranger raised a cautionary hand toward Clem before stepping up onto the plank sidewalk and peering through the small window to the right of the door.

"The sheriff seems to be alone. Give me your gun belt."

Clem hesitated but finally obeyed. The Ranger slung the belt over his left shoulder and walked in the door, Clem a step behind him.

"What the…!" the sheriff barked. He'd been leaning back in his desk chair and nearly toppled over.

The Ranger drew his .44. "Don't draw, Sheriff. We're here on friendly business."

"Can't be very friendly if you're wearing a mask

and drawing down on me. And you, Clem Hanson! You're in more trouble than you'll ever get out of."

"He's not, Sheriff."

"What! Who are you?"

"Who I am doesn't matter. What you might be interested in is the fact that I'm looking for the Cavendish gang, same as you."

"To join up, most likely."

The Ranger smiled, shook his head, and said, "No, and you're mistaken about Clem, too. He's no more a member of Cavendish's bunch than you are. Here, he's taken off his gun belt, you see, and turned himself over to you. Does that sound like the act of a cold-blooded killer?"

"He shot enough bullets at us to make him look like one. Besides, he's been identified as riding with the gang and running when the shootout started."

"Were you there, Sheriff?" the Ranger asked.

"'Course I wasn't there," the sheriff snapped.

"Tell him your story, Clem."

Clem started at the beginning and as he spoke, the Ranger holstered his revolver.

When he finished, the sheriff said, "Mighty odd circumstances."

The Ranger said, "You know the names of the gang, Sheriff. There were twelve of them. Your newspaper listed the seven dead and the five who escaped. Where do you think Clem fits into that bunch?"

"By gad, he was seen with them!"

"He's explained that."

The door opened and Tonto entered, leading an older man dressed in a white shirt and string tie, black pants, and a bowler hat. He carried a small black bag with two handles.

"What are you doing here, Doc?" the sheriff asked

"Indian said it was an emergency. Clem!"

"How's my ma?"

"I stopped in today. The powders I gave her have done her good. She's mighty worried about you. She thinks the sheriff is an ass for taking out after you, and so do I."

"Now, we already had this discussion, Doc…"

"And we're gonna have it again right now," the doctor argued, his voice rising. "The boy was coming to get me that afternoon. He ran into those outlaws on the road. The people who identified him to you didn't know who he was. Why would you think…? *Ugh*, you're a damn fool, Sheriff."

"Don't get personal, Doc. The lieutenant with the soldiers…"

"You already told me about him. He wanted the ones who got away. Did you go after Cavendish and the other four murdering scoundrels? No, you took out after a boy you knew your whole life. The lieutenant didn't elect you. The lieutenant doesn't pay your salary. You seemed mighty impressed with the stripes on his shoulders."

"He came at me pretty loud to go after the one who rode off alone," the sheriff answered sheepishly.

"Who says you gotta listen to him?" the doctor thundered. "You got your own brain. What you ain't got is sense." He turned to Clem. "You work all week at the livery, Clem?"

"Sure, same as every week."

The Doc looked back at the sheriff. "You want me to go and find Smitty and let him tell you Clem worked the whole week alongside of him at the stable? Last week, the week before, and the month before that? I'll do it. I'll go right now."

"No, no, no."

"So, are you gonna drop this nonsense?" the Doc went on. "Clem's mother needs the boy. He's all she's got, and there you are chasing him all over creation."

"How about this one?" the sheriff said, pointing at the Ranger. "Look at him. Torn pants, torn shirt, looks like blood on them. He drew on me when he came in here! And he's wearing a mask! What's he doing riding around in a black mask, for great Caesar's sake?"

"That any business of yours? He could've taken off his mask before he brought the boy in to you. And look at *your* pants. Is that a hole in the right knee?"

The sheriff quickly crossed his legs to cover the hole.

"Are you gonna come to your senses or not?" the doctor asked, boring into the sheriff with a narrow-eyed grimace.

"All right, you win. Go home, Clem."

Clem took his gun belt from the Ranger and strapped it on.

"You gonna take out after Cavendish now?" the doctor asked, sarcasm dripping from his question.

"You go home, too, Doc," the sheriff said, impatience dripping from his reply.

The Ranger nodded to Tonto, and they left the office.

"Where're you going?" the sheriff called after him. "Where's he going, Doc? Who *is* he?"

Clem answered, "He told me he had good reason to keep his identity a secret. Didn't tell me what the reason was, though. The Indian called him the Lone Ranger."

"The Lone Ranger?" the sheriff repeated.

Through the night air came the sound of horses' hooves speeding away, followed by a cry of, "Hi-yo, Silver. Away!"

Chapter 5

Jim and the Silver Mine

The Ranger and Tonto headed toward home—the Ranger's home. They'd returned to the canyon to spend the night, then set out early next morning on the three-day trip.

"Why we go where you live?" Tonto asked. "People know you."

"I'll avoid meeting anyone, although I would like to see Linda and little Dan. That's impossible, though. We're going to drop in on an old Texas Ranger friend of my family named Jim Faraday. He's the man who brought my brother into the Rangers. A year later, he was badly wounded in a battle with rustlers. My brother brought him home, and we took care of him for months at the ranch. After he recovered, though, he had to leave the service. My father deeded over to him a stretch of ground on our property holding a small silver mine. My father discovered the mine years before and worked it long enough to buy the ranch and the ground the mine was on. Ranching was more to his liking—he called mining the most back-breaking work a man could do—and the mine sat idle until Jim needed help. He's been living in a cabin at the mine for nearly ten years. He likes the solitude and mines the silver. There's plenty for his needs."

"He know who you are."

"It can't be helped, but Jim's a tried and true Ranger, Kemo Sabe, and he deserves to know the story of

Cavendish and the Rangers… and my brother. I trust him. I've been thinking," the Ranger went on. "It will take some time to eliminate the Cavendish gang. We have to locate them first."

"That right. The law maybe not much help. Sheriff in Corbin City even think you one of them."

"The mask *will* be a problem. I need something special, a symbol, something to set me apart from the world of outlaws, despite my wearing a mask."

"What symbol, Kemo Sabe?"

"I've been thinking that over. Silver bullets."

"Silver bullets! Where you find… oh, Jim."

"Yes, Jim. He makes bullets for himself—doesn't trust store bought, he says—and he can make some from silver for me, plus provide us with enough silver for our day-to-day expenses. We won't want much. I need clothing, and we'll always need supplies. I'm hoping he'll agree to all of that. It's a lot to ask of him, I know."

"Maybe you wear uniform, too, like soldiers? Me know Indian woman who live in small camp not far from where we go. She make anything you want."

"A uniform? No, I don't think I can wear something so… official looking. Perhaps something that stands out but fits in."

Tonto looked at the Ranger a moment, then chuckled. "How you do that? It two different things."

"I don't know yet. Maybe your Indian friend will

have an idea."

"Yes, she make many things for Indians. Tonto ask, she be happy to make for you. She like it. You plenty big man, give her much work," he added with a laugh.

They could not fill up three days with conversation, so they rode on in comfortable silence, awed sometimes by the beauty of the land they passed through. Mountains in the distance; seemingly endless grasslands which, if you rode to the horizon, would reveal even more seemingly endless grasslands and a further horizon; an occasional buffalo herd to which they gave a wide berth. They gently picked their way through two prairie dog towns and crossed half a dozen streams where they often stopped to rest and refresh the horses and themselves. Tonto hunted and provided dinner.

In the afternoon of the third day, the Ranger said, "The ranch is about two miles from here. We'll skirt around it in case any of Linda's ranch hands are out riding. Jim's cabin is at the base of the bluff you can see over there." He pointed west. "We'll come to a rill past that low rise and follow it to the cabin."

They stopped momentarily when they reached the small brook and dismounted to stretch their legs and let the horses drink. Suddenly, a burst of gun fire came from the direction of the bluff!

"Tonto, let's mount! Sounds like it's coming from Jim's place."

The two men leapt into their saddles, and Silver and

Scout bolted forward. When they came in sight of the bluff, they reined up.

"There cabin," Tonto said as repeated gunshots and bursts of smoke came from one of the cabin's windows.

That outburst was answered by gunfire coming from a short distance off, where two horses stood alongside two men, lying prone and firing their rifles at the cabin.

The Ranger drew his revolver and urged Silver on, Tonto right behind.

Clods of dirt exploded from the ground a few feet in front of the men as the Ranger's bullets took effect. The attackers saw their new adversaries, and as the Ranger and Tonto disappeared momentarily behind the rise, they scrambled to their feet, made for their horses, and rode off, low in the saddle for safety.

"We follow them, Kemo Sabe?" Tonto asked.

"No, we'll check on Jim. He may be injured. They won't be back anytime soon."

"Don't forget, you wear mask," Tonto warned.

"I know. Jim!" the Ranger called. "Jim, don't shoot."

A rifle bullet whizzed by, and Tonto and the Ranger dove onto the grass.

"Jim not recognize you."

"He'll need to know who I am anyway…" In a

loud voice, the Ranger identified himself. "Don't shoot, Jim. We've driven away the two men who were shooting at you."

"He already know you. You take off mask."

"Of course," the Ranger said. He untied the mask and rose, hands in the air. "Jim, it's me."

"Reid? Is that you?" came a voice from the cabin.

"Yes. I have a friend with me. Can we approach?"

"Of course, you can, but look out for those two skunks."

"They're gone, Jim. We're coming in."

Jim opened the cabin door and, rifle in hand, welcomed his two guests. He had recently turned fifty-six years old and wore a grizzled, gray beard. His sparse hair hung over his ears and forehead. Inside the cabin, however, things were neat as a pin.

"My old eyes must be playing tricks on me," he said. "I could've swore I saw somebody wearing a mask."

The Ranger dangled the mask in his hand in front of Jim.

"What! You ain't turned outlaw, have you?"

"No, Jim. Nothing like that."

"You hurt, Jim," Tonto said. "Me see blood."

"A little nick in the shoulder. Ain't nothing."

"Let Tonto look at it," the Ranger suggested. "This is Tonto, by the way. He saved my life, Jim."

"What in tarnation happened to you? Why the mask? Where's your friend going?"

"He has medical supplies in his saddlebag."

Tonto returned and went to work on Jim's wound while the Ranger told the story of Bryant's Gap.

"Mother of mercy. So, your brother's really gone?"

"I'm afraid he is, Jim."

"Does Linda know?"

"She surely knows he's missing by now."

"Terrible. Cavendish, eh?"

"Cavendish. Now, Jim, your turn. Who were those two men firing at you?"

"Danged if I know. Clarabelle and I only go to town maybe twice month—cash in some silver and get supplies." Clarabelle was Jim's mule. "Last time I came back from town, I found two skunks poking around inside my cabin. I got the drop on them, though, and chased them off, but they took a tiny tobacco tin of silver I dug out that day. Weren't worth a whole lot, but today looks like they came back for more. Good thing I had my new rifle. You ever seen one of these? Holds fourteen shells. I slide 'em in to load here, lever the handle, it loads a bullet and cocks the hammer at the same time. No more one-shots for me."

"It's some beautiful weapon, Jim. Those two must

have thought they were fighting three of you."

"Polecats like that gonna think twice before they come after my silver again."

"It's the silver I want to talk to you about, Jim."

"So, start talking."

The Ranger laughed at Jim's astonishment over his request to make silver bullets.

"I can do it," he answered. "Of course, I can do it, but lead bullets kill just as good as silver bullets will."

"I don't want them to kill, Jim. Tonto and I will defend ourselves, naturally, but I want them to be a symbol, a symbol of justice in the West."

"You cut yourself out a real big chore there, Reid…"

The Ranger waggled a finger in front of Jim and smiled.

"…I mean Lone Ranger. I sure wish I could let poor Linda know what's happened to Dan."

The Ranger stayed silent. He knew he was placing a tremendous burden on Jim, and an even bigger one on Linda.

Jim shook his head. "Cavendish. I hope you get the dirty louse."

"We will, Jim. How long will it take you to make enough cartridges to fill my belt?"

"I'll have to dig out some more silver… go into

town for some powder… take me maybe four days. I came across a new vein last month, by the way. I'm good here for years to come."

"Great news, Jim. I'm happy for you, and four days will give Tonto and me time to find out who's been bothering you and put a stop to it."

*

The Ranger and Tonto stayed nearby in a small shack a few steps behind Jim's cabin for the next two days and nights, afraid the men who attacked him would revisit, but things stayed quiet at the mine. The morning of the third day, with Jim working hard to fulfill the Ranger's request, Tonto took the Ranger to a small Indian encampment two miles off.

"Life seems very peaceful here," the Ranger said as Tonto rode ahead of him through a spread of tepees. Women sat in front of many of the tepees, working on various chores. Children ran through the small encampment, screeching and laughing, the same as children everywhere.

"Braves off to hunt buffalo," Tonto explained. "Old woman have tepee… there." Tonto dismounted and the Ranger followed suit. "You come with me." They entered the tepee where an old, gray-haired woman in a long, gaudily decorated deerskin dress sat in a roughly made chair. She smiled when she saw Tonto, stood and extended her arms to him in greeting. Tonto talked to her and grasped her hands as they spoke together in a language the Ranger did not recognize. After a few moments, Tonto faced the Ranger.

"She say she happy to make you clothes. I tell her you want bring justice to West. She say it good thing and know what you need."

"If she knows that, Kemo Sabe, she knows more than I do."

The woman quickly peppered Tonto with questions.

"What was that about?" the Ranger asked.

"She hear you call me Kemo Sabe. It have special meaning for Indian. I tell her how we save each other life. She say you Kemo Sabe, too."

"Tell her I appreciate the honor of the title and mean to live up to it."

Tonto and the woman spoke again. When they quieted, the woman slowly walked in a circle around the Ranger, eyeing him up and down. When she finished, she addressed Tonto briefly.

"She say come back two day from now, she have what you need."

"Tell her thank you from me."

Another brief conversation followed, and a few moments later, the men remounted and headed back to Jim's.

*

That night, Tonto and the Lone Ranger, masked and wearing newly purchased black pants and a brown shirt, set out for town. Tyler's Crossing had grown from a trading post into a town of some eight hundred inhabitants whose main business was providing supplies and entertainment to ranches and ranch hands from the area. The Ranger had been sent to the town many times by his father or brother to perform a chore of some sort and knew the place well. With night fallen, his mask in place, and his knowledge of the town's layout, he felt certain he could avoid anyone who might recognize him. He and Tonto planned to look for the two men who had attacked Jim.

For the past eight years, the town had employed Kent Colson, a former ranch hand injured in a fall from his horse, as sheriff. The job didn't pay much, but generally, Colson had very little to do. Weekend nights in Tyler's Crossing often got loud, and the occasional saloon fight might get out of hand, but Colson had shown he could tamp down trouble to a tolerable level. The Ranger knew him and his abilities well and sent Tonto to him to describe the attack on Jim while he waited in the shadows behind the one-room school building on the edge of town.

"You were gone longer than I expected," the Ranger said when Tonto returned.

"Me tell you why. Sheriff ask why Jim not come himself."

"What did you tell him?"

"Me say Jim think he can protect self and not want to waste sheriff time."

"What did Kent have to say to that?"

"Me think him have some idea he no tell Tonto, Kemo Sabe. Me think him make guess about two men who attack Jim, so me wait and see what he do."

"Go on."

"He leave office, and Tonto follow to where men drink and gamble."

"That would be the Rusty Spur Saloon."

"It have heap big crowd. Tonto stay outside near door and watch. Me not know whether them want Indian inside."

The Ranger's lips pressed into a thin line and he nodded.

"Sheriff stand against wall and keep eye on table where men play cards. One man see sheriff and call his name. Others in place get quiet. Him ask sheriff if he come to welcome him and brother back to town."

"Back to town? Did you hear their names?

"Man say 'me and Clint.' Him talk more and some people laugh. Sheriff, he stay quiet and not answer. When sheriff go back to office, me come here."

"Clint. I wonder if it's Clint and Hugh Beatty. They once lived here. Their father was hanged for murder when I was, I think, fifteen years old. They left the area afterward, but I don't know what happened to them after that. I wish I could get a look at them. They certainly might know about Jim and his mine."

"You only see them if you have disguise, Kemo Sabe."

"Disguise? What do you mean, Tonto?"

"Me knows ways. Them not recognize you. Tomorrow, Tonto come to town and buy things. You visit saloon tomorrow night."

"Can you be certain I won't be recognized? This is where I grew up, remember."

"Ha, ha, ha. You not be recognized if Tonto make disguise for you."

"You seem very sure."

"Me sure."

The Ranger smiled. "Can you give me a mustache like Sheriff Colson sports?" The sheriff was noted for the bushy, white mustache he kept neatly trimmed.

"Heh, heh. You not able breathe if Tonto put one like that under nose. Me can make mustache, though."

"Okay, Kemo Sabe. That's what we'll do then."

*

Just after ten o'clock the next night, a cowboy dressed in dark pants and a brown shirt entered the Rusty Spur. His hat pulled low over his forehead, he walked with a stooped, hunch-shouldered gait, taking an inch or two off his height. Tonto had concocted a gummy substance which he put behind the Ranger's ears to extend them from his head a little further than nature intended. He also attached the mustache he'd promised under the Ranger's nose and designed two small, hollow tubes which the Ranger slipped inside his nostrils, changing the contour of his face. A brown solution Tonto made from roots and tree bark collected from the area around Jim's cabin darkened the Ranger's face and neck. When the Ranger stared into the small mirror hanging on the wall in Jim's shack, he barely recognized himself.

While the Ranger entered the saloon and moved up to the bar, Tonto took a seat on a chair across the dirt street; a chair usually occupied by any loafer needing a break from doing nothing all day. Silver and Scout stood near, lightly hitched to a post. The din inside the Rusty Spur was exactly how the Lone Ranger remembered it. Four tables of card players, small pots of money shoved to the middle of each table, attracted a lot of attention. The Ranger recognized the Beatty brothers right away, even though he hadn't seen them in ten years. They'd been around twenty years old when their father paid the ultimate price for his crimes. They dressed in black and spoke loudly as they sat at separate tables betting on their cards. Sheriff Colson was nowhere in sight.

The Ranger ordered a whiskey and let it sit. He did not drink. The progress of the evening showed both brothers losing. Their strained faces told the tale.

"You new here?" came a voice next to him.

The Ranger faced a man he recognized—Walt Lemon from the dry goods store. He'd seen him many times over the counter, his soiled long white apron never off his person. Disguising his deep voice, the way he'd practiced back at Jim's, he answered, "Passing through. Heading to Arizona to do some prospecting."

"Feeling lucky, eh?"

"Not lucky enough to gamble my poke away there." He indicated the four tables.

"Don't blame you. Those two fellas in black, they've been having night after night of bad luck. They roughed up one of the dealers two nights ago. Some fuss over a misdeal. Not good to lose to them."

"You know them?"

"Never seen them before I saw them at the tables here. Heard some stories about them since they showed up, though."

"How long have you lived in Tyler's Crossing?" The Ranger, not wanting to prolong the conversation longer than necessary, chose not to ask what stories Lemon had heard.

"'Bout eight years."

Two years after the Beatty brothers had left. The Ranger congratulated Tonto's skill. Though he knew Walt well enough to say hello in passing, if Walt didn't recognize him, his disguise was a success. Not wishing to press his luck, though, he let their conversation peter out.

Clint Beatty stood, pushed back his chair, and slammed his cards onto the table.

"You doin' any better than me, Hugh?"

Hugh, the younger and shorter of the two, also stood. "Damned cards are hexed," he complained. "I'm done."

The two brothers wended their way to the bar as two other cowpokes filled in their seats at the card tables. They settled in, one patron away from where the Ranger stood, head down, untouched drink in his hand. The man between them tossed back his drink and moved off. The Ranger slid closer. He couldn't hear every word of the brothers' hushed conversation, but he heard enough to realize they were near the end of their bankrolls. When they twice mentioned Jim Faraday, Lone Ranger decided he knew everything he needed and quietly slipped away.

The weather changed to a drizzle around midnight, so Tonto and the Ranger could not bed down under the stars, but sought shelter inside the shack behind Jim's cabin. Early next morning Jim called them in for breakfast.

"How's the wound, Jim?" the Ranger asked.

"Good as new," he answered, rotating his shoulder to demonstrate. "Your Indian pal is a darn good sawbones."

"Saw bones?" Tonto asked, turning to the Ranger with a quizzical look.

"A sawbones is a doctor, Kemo Sabe," the Ranger explained.

"Saw bones? Me not want doctor like that," Tonto said.

Both the Ranger and Jim laughed.

"It's a compliment in this case, Tonto," Jim said. "I thank you for your help."

"Me glad you feel better."

"Jim," the Ranger interrupted. "I think those two men who tried to rob you plan to pay you another visit soon, possibly even today. They're the Beatty brothers."

"Who the devil are the Beatty brothers?"

"Maybe you heard about their father." The Ranger told Jim what he knew about them. "Tonto's going back into town today to bring the sheriff out here. I'll stay with you meanwhile."

"Their pappy was hanged, eh? I do remember that. Guess the apples don't fall far from the tree, do they? More bacon and eggs, Tonto?" Jim asked.

Tonto declined and set out for town.

After eating, the Ranger ground hitched Silver out of sight behind a tall rise and stationed himself atop the rise where he could see down the road leading from town. It wasn't long after Tonto departed when two horsemen dressed in black approached. The Ranger drew his gun, newly loaded with the silver bullets Jim proudly asked him to test out that morning. The men stopped a short distance from Jim's shack, and one of the men led their horses into a small stand of trees. When he rejoined his companion, he carried a rifle. Both men ran forward, bent low, until they reached the small corral where Jim kept Clarabelle.

The Ranger lay atop the grassy knoll thirty yards to their right and above them. One of the men drew his revolver and gestured to the other, who set out to circle the shack. The Ranger could not allow them to split up.

"Stay right there," he called. "If you move, I shoot."

Startled, the two men searched for the source of the challenge. The Ranger sent a bullet into the fence post near the man who'd remained stationary.

"Don't test me," he called.

"Top of the rise," one man called and pointed, and both men sent a cascade of lead the Ranger's way.

The Ranger scuttled backward down the hill, so the bullets had no chance of finding him. Keeping low, he ran behind Jim's shack.

"Stay inside, Jim," he called, afraid his friend would walk out into an inadvertent bullet.

"Them Beatty critters?" Jim called from inside.

"Yes."

Jim's fourteen-shot rifle barrel pierced the gap in the open window of the cabin.

"If I see them, they ain't gonna be brothers to no one."

"Stay calm, Jim."

A spray of bullets struck the cabin, and Jim's rifle answered back.

One of the men circled and came up the side of the hill where the Ranger had been. He froze for a moment, searching for the hidden man who'd challenged them. The Ranger took careful aim and fired.

The man screamed and went to his knees. "He got me, Clint. My wrist. I'm bleeding."

The Ranger refrained from firing as the wounded Hugh Beatty ran back to the corral where his brother was hiding.

"Clint Beatty," the Ranger called. "It's over. Come out now and leave your gun behind. Your brother needs help."

Clint walked into the open from behind the corral fence. The Ranger noted he had his gun holstered. Clint stopped, his hand spread far out from his holster, and said, "Come out where I can see you. You're pretty good shooting from cover. Come out and meet me in the open."

"That's not something you want to happen, Clint."

"It's something I want very much to happen."

The Ranger pondered. "I warned you," he said, holstering his gun and stepping out from behind the shack.

Clint stared at the masked man. "Who the hell are you?" he asked.

"That doesn't matter. Drop your gun. We're going into town, you to jail, your brother to the doc."

Clint smirked. "I ain't afraid of no cowpoke too ugly to show his face. You here for the old man's silver, too? Ain't no need for us to fight. There's enough for all of us."

Hugh's voice interrupted. "Clint, my wrist. I'm bleeding. I'm hurt."

To the Ranger, Clint said, "Let's team up and get the old guy out of the shack and take what we can. I'll get my brother patched up, and we'll go our separate ways."

"I told you to drop your gun. You're going to jail."

Clint went for his revolver, but before he could clear leather, the Ranger's bullet slammed into it, and the shattered metal pieces flew into the air. Clint screeched in surprise and pain.

"Clint, are you hit?" Hugh cried. "I'll get him."

A far-off shot rang out, and the Ranger saw Tonto and Sheriff Colson ride up, Tonto pistol in hand.

"Other man have rifle, Kemo Sabe."

Clint walked to where he'd left his brother as Sheriff Colson rode up next to him.

Jim stepped out of the cabin. "You got 'em both!" he said excitedly. "I heard 'em, wanting to steal my silver."

"Me see two men leave town when me ride in," Tonto explained. "Find sheriff quick and ride back plenty fast."

"You got here just in time, Kemo Sabe."

Sheriff Colson was off his horse, walking a handcuffed Clint Beatty their way.

"Howdy, Jim," he said. "I'm gonna need your wagon and mule to get that wounded coyote to town. He's hit in the wrist and leg. Won't be doing any riding for a while. He was fumbling with a rifle, aiming to take a shot at you left-handed… Masked? Do I have to take you in, too?"

"You take him in over my dead body, Sheriff. Him and the Indian saved my life. Chased these two snakes off before, after they tried to rob me. You put 'em on trial. I'll testify. Send 'em to jail so they don't bother honest citizens for a good long time!"

"Settle down, Jim. They're gonna be locked up in quick order, but I need your wagon and Clarabelle."

"Take 'em. Be the best work old Clarabelle ever done. You get them buzzards outta my sight!"

Before long, the sheriff guided the wagon along the road to town, Hugh lying in the wagon moaning, his handcuffed brother alongside on the sheriff's horse, the reins tied to Clarabelle's harness.

"Looks like you saved me again, Ranger," Jim said. "I'm mighty grateful. My silver bullets worked pretty good, eh? Come and see the rest of the bullets I made for you. Load up your belt."

Jim led the Ranger inside, and after the Ranger filled his gun belt, he beamed proudly. "You really look like something. I'll keep making silver bullets and have a supply ready for you the next time you come by. You going after Cavendish now?"

"Yes, I am, Jim, but Tonto and I still have one stop to make."

An hour or so later, when Jim saw the Ranger and Tonto returning from the Indian encampment, he nearly fell off the chair where he lounged in front of his cabin.

"Well, tumblin' tumbleweeds. Would you get a look at you!"

The Ranger dismounted. The Indian woman had made him a sky-blue outfit, pants and shirt, his pants tucked into his high-heeled riding boots. With it, he wore a red bandana around his neck and tight-fitting black gloves.

"How do I look, Jim?" the Ranger said with a smile. "The Indian woman made these clothes simply from looking me over. Pretty amazing, don't you think?"

"She make them gloves, too?"

"No," the Ranger said with a laugh. "I had them already."

"Amazing don't describe it. You'll never be mistaken for anyone else. I can say that much. The blue of the sky and silver bullets."

"We're leaving now, Jim, but I'm sure we'll be back from time to time."

"Don't you go yet. You put me in mind of

something I can give you. Stay put."

Jim hurried inside his cabin and from a large chest pushed into a corner, he withdrew a bridle decorated with shining, silver-hued studs along the length of it.

"Jim, where did you get that? It's beautiful," the Ranger said when Jim stepped outside.

"Bought it when I was a Ranger, but never got to use it. Got shot too soon. I want you to have it. Think how it'll look on your white stallion."

They made the exchange of bridles, and when Silver bobbed his head approvingly, the three men laughed.

"Told you it would look good," Jim cackled.

"Thank you for everything," the Ranger said after remounting. "We'll be back before long, I'm sure."

"Like I said, I'll be ready for you."

"Let's ride, Kemo Sabe. I want Cavendish."

Silver reared high, his front legs raking the air, clearly asserting his willingness to take part in the challenges ahead.

After one final farewell to Jim, the masked man and Indian set out on their quest.

Chapter 6

Lemuel Tolliver

The Lone Ranger and Tonto stopped at Clem Hanson's place on their way back to Corbin City, the place where they hoped to find some trace of Cavendish and his gang. Mrs. Hanson was up and about, feeling much better, and she fussed endlessly over her two guests, saying, "I don't care if you wear seven masks and travel with seven Indians, you're a good man and you saved my boy." She insisted they stay for a home-cooked meal and bunk in the two spare bedrooms. The Ranger and Tonto took her up on her offer but insisted on thanking her then and there, saying they'd be gone early next morning.

"Anytime you need a good meal or a soft bed—or even a place to hide out—you come here," she said and bustled off to prepare dinner. At sunrise next morning, while Mrs. Hanson and Clem slept, the two men quietly rode off.

Clem claimed to have heard nothing new regarding Cavendish, and the Ranger had read through the latest Corbin City newspaper before dinner the night before without seeing Cavendish mentioned, so to avoid misunderstandings and gossip, they skirted the town and followed the trail south, alert for any sign of him or his gang.

They passed a few ranches, but soon the road stretched into the epic, beautiful loneliness of the West. Magnificent grasslands, majestic hills and rises, occasional buffalo, and above it all, the blistering sun composed the elements of the scene. At sundown, they camped next to a stream of cool, clear water. Silver and Scout grazed on the tall grass while the Lone Ranger and Tonto dined on the fried chicken which Mrs. Hanson insisted they take with them.

Around noon the next day, they noticed a swirl of dust ahead, and a moment later, a large, enclosed, wooden wagon painted green and white came into view, approaching along the dusty road.

"Them not look like settlers, Kemo Sabe," Tonto said.

"No, with that wagon it looks more like a medicine man's set up."

"Them not good. Sell bad drink to Indians."

The man handling the wagon pulled his horse to a halt.

"Lord-a-mercy! A masked man," he cried. At the sound of his voice, the head of a young girl, perhaps seventeen years old, popped out between the panels of a canvas curtain strung behind the driver. "Get back inside, Sadie Ann," the man snapped.

The Ranger raised a hand in peace. "Please, don't let my mask alarm you. It's on the side of law and order. I have good reason for keeping my identity a secret. Are you Lemuel Tolliver?"

"How'd you know?" the man asked. He was a short man with a stout belly, who wore black pants and a black vest atop a white shirt open at the neck. A wide brimmed hat kept the sun off his face. He dropped the reins into the footwell.

"It says so on your wagon."

"Oh, yeah. Ha, so it does. Painted it myself. That's me, Lemuel Tolliver."

"Under your name it says, 'Make Your Smile Last Forever.' How do you do that?" the Ranger asked.

"Photography. You heard of it?"

"Sure," the Ranger answered.

"Him make magic pictures, Kemo Sabe?"

"It appears so, Tonto."

"That's right, Mr. Indian, only they ain't magic. No sir. Maybe they seem like magic to the… uh, well, to those who don't understand it, but it's science. The latest invention."

"Photography's been around for some thirty years, Lemuel," the Ranger pointed out.

"You ever had your picture took?" he asked.

"No, but I've seen some photographs."

"If you ain't never had your picture took, then it's the latest invention to you, wouldn't you say?"

"You have something there," the Ranger said, laughing.

"Uh, want your picture took? Only cost you two

dollars. I take gold. Or folding money." He eyed the Ranger's gun belt. "Or silver. Them bullets silver? They look like silver."

"They are, but if I wanted my picture taken, I wouldn't be wearing a mask, would I?"

Sadie Ann's head popped out again. "Can I come out, Poppa? It's hot in here, and he sounds like a gentleman."

"Please, invite her out, Lemuel," the Ranger agreed.

"Come out and sit next to your poppa," Lemuel patted the wooden plank where he sat.

"Why *are* you wearing a mask?" she asked the Ranger. "Are you a desperado? I've always wanted to meet a desperado! You wanted by some sheriff or marshal somewhere?"

"I have my reasons for the mask, but being wanted by a sheriff isn't one of them."

"Oh. You gonna let my poppa take your photograph? I'd kinda like to have a picture of you."

Lemuel's head spun toward his daughter and he frowned.

The Ranger turned to Tonto. "Care to have your photograph taken, Kemo Sabe?"

"No. Indian no like man who takem inside spirit outside."

"I won't be taking nobody's spirit nowhere,"

Lemuel argued. "Dad-blame-it, it's science, not kidnapping, for criminy sake. You sound educated, Mister Masked Man. Sound like you been in the East. Can't you explain it to him?"

"You have a good ear, Lemuel. I did go East for school and spent four years there."

"Glad you came back. The West needs educated men like you… ahem… despite the mask. Someday, the West will have schools just as good as any's in the East."

"I'd like to go East, Poppa."

"Well, you ain't going East," Lemuel exploded. "We was born in the West, and we're gonna live in the West…"

"…and we're gonna die in the West and be buried in the West. I know, Poppa. I know," Sadie droned.

"Many people let you takem spirit?" Tonto asked.

"Mr. Indian, yes. Lots of people. For two dollars I can give you a picture lasts a lifetime. You, Mister Masked Man, you sure you don't want to pose? You look like a real western character to me."

"No, thank you."

"Mr. Indian, let me show you some science. Talk to the gentleman, Sadie Ann."

Lemuel pushed through the canvas into the wagon.

"What's your name?" Sadie asked the masked man.

"Afraid I can't say, ma'am," the Ranger answered.

"You forgot it?"

The Ranger laughed. "No, I didn't forget it."

"How about you? You have a name?"

"Me Tonto."

"Tonto. One name for two people. I'm Sadie Ann. Two names for one person. Funny world we live in, eh?" She shrugged.

Lemuel climbed back onto the wagon seat. "See this?" He held a small metal plate in his hand. "Now, this is how science happens. If I pour something called collodion onto this, I can make a picture of you, well not you, apparently, but Mr. Indian here. I dip it in developer; wash it with some water. And like magic… er, like science, your image appears. Come 'round back. I'll show you some of the photographs me and Sadie took."

Lemuel climbed behind the canvas again, and the Ranger and Tonto dismounted. The Ranger helped Sadie down and escorted her to the rear of the wagon.

"You're very gentle for a big man wearing a mask," she said.

"Gentle works for big as well as small, ma'am," the Ranger said with a smile.

"I guess so. And don't call me ma'am. I'm only seventeen, sir."

Lemuel lowered the back panel of his wagon.

"I visit lots of towns and take photographs and sell them for two dollars. These are extras nobody bought and a few Sadie had me take. Look 'em over. Sometimes, people buy photos Sadie's posed for. She's got a good eye for setting things up, arranging them, you know what I mean?"

Tonto and the Ranger casually looked through Lemuel's collection.

"Heh, you have no Indian here. Me know them no like this," Tonto pointed out.

"You could be my first, Mr. Tonto. If you let me take one of you, it might end up in the history books one day. First photograph ever taken of a real, live, Indian of the West," Lemuel argued.

"Me no think so," Tonto replied.

"Where are you heading?" the Ranger asked.

"Going to pick up supplies, mostly photography supplies, I had shipped to Corbin City. They have pretty reliable service there. Ain't far from here. You know it?"

"We do."

"After I pick up my supplies, Sadie and I'll be off again, shootin' up the West," he said, laughing.

The Ranger brought some paper money out of his pocket. "Here, take this four dollars. On the edge of Corbin City, living on a small farm, is a Hanson family—Clem Hanson and his mother. Anyone in the town can direct you. Or stop in at the livery stable. Clem works there. Tell the Hansons it's a gift from the masked man. They'll understand. Take two photographs for them. I think they'd like that."

"Well, that's mighty sporting of you, Mister. Hanson family, you say? Sadie Ann, you remember that name."

"I will," the girl replied gloomily.

The Ranger continued to leaf through Lemuel's photographs. When he came to a certain picture, he studied it closely.

"This is you, Sadie. Standing in front of a saloon?" the Ranger asked.

"She thought it was daring of her," Lemuel said, frowning in his daughter's direction.

"Who is this man? Here, see. Staring hard at Sadie."

"Dad gum, I never noticed him. You see what you bring out in people, Sadie? Such a look on his face! Man could read his intentions a mile off. You're just too darned pretty."

Sadie leaned in to study the photograph. "Ew! He's got a long scar on his cheek."

"His name is Razor Gilliam," the Ranger said. "Tonto, come and see. He belongs to the worst outlaw gang in these parts."

Tonto moved to the Ranger's side.

"You recognize him, Kemo Sabe?"

"It's Razor Gilliam for sure. Lemuel, where and when did you take this photograph?"

"Sadie, this is the town of Mustang, ain't it?"

"It's Mustang, all right. I remember the busted window. See the busted window behind the man with the scar? I made sure to get it in the picture. I thought it made a nice detail."

"Town of Mustang," Lemuel confirmed. "You want to buy it?"

"I think I do," the Ranger said, and he fished another two dollars from his pocket. "How long ago was this taken?"

"We were there the better part of yesterday."

"How far from here is it?"

"Spent the night camped not far outside the town. Been traveling since sun-up. About that far."

"How do I get to Mustang?" the Ranger asked. "I never heard of it."

"You tell 'em, Sadie. Your memory's better'n mine."

"Pa, really?" She faced the Ranger. "Straight down this road. No turns. Those horses you have, probably make it in a couple of hours."

"You goin' to Mustang?" Lemuel asked.

"We are," the Ranger said as he and Tonto mounted. "If Razor Gilliam is there, the rest of the

Cavendish gang may be nearby, and they have to be stopped."

"Shame we're heading in the opposite direction," Lemuel pointed out. "Would've liked to travel along with you two. Mighty interesting characters, both of you. Sure you don't want your pictures took?"

"No, thank you, Lemuel. Perhaps we'll meet again."

"Hope so."

They parted, Lemuel in the direction of Corbin City; the Ranger and Tonto toward the town of Mustang.

Chapter 7

Razor Gilliam

The town of Mustang hadn't been established for long, and Razor Gilliam hadn't long been in the town. Learning early in life, due to a variety of factors, that taking was a far easier and much more rewarding pastime than earning, Razor had ignored the late War Between the States, not caring one way or another about slavery, high tariffs, Abraham Lincoln, or Jefferson Davis. After hearing, through certain companions he rode with, about Cavendish's raids on Confederate arsenals and depots, he decided Cavendish knew more about the art of taking than did his current associates, so he looked him up, and they'd partnered ever since.

Razor assumed the role of the gang's assassin, and whenever a sheriff or a marshal got overly inquisitive, it became Razor's job to put an end to the lawman's curiosity. Such abrupt endings had occurred seven times since the end of the war, and it was the primary reason the job of going after the gang had fallen to the Texas Rangers and the U. S. Cavalry.

Mustang had no sheriff and didn't want one. What it did have appealed greatly to Razor. An entrepreneur named Remy Dewar had built a fifteen-room hotel he dubbed The Shady Grove, which boasted few amenities, but the ones it did offer made a night's stay there superior in comfort to sleeping under a blanket on the hard ground somewhere in the wilderness. Mattresses, door locks, bathtubs, and three fully stocked saloons nearby were the main elements which composed this unaccustomed access to high living for a certain level of society, and Razor had the means to pay for such a plush existence. The Mustang Saloon, whose sign included the encouraging words 'Dancing Allowed;' The Desperado's Paradise, whose sign promised billiards; as well as The Gamblers' Den, which made no promises, were the social hubs of the town. A dry goods/general merchandise emporium, a blacksmith's stable combined with feed store, a saddle and harness business, a gunsmith's shop, and a couple restaurants filled out the unnamed main street of Mustang, a town whose growing repute for providing everything a certain breed of hombre needed spread a bit further month by month. Razor heard about Mustang while on the trail and decided to see for himself what it had to offer, and if satisfied with its environment, he'd wait out his two months away from the gang there. And well-satisfied he was, until one day a decrepit, green and white, wooden wagon lumbered along the main street. The side of the wagon read, LEMUEL TOLLIVER: MAKE YOUR SMILE LAST FOREVER. This ignited a natural curiosity in the inhabitants of Mustang from which Razor was not immune.

"Gather, folks," called a paunchy little man in a wide hat, dressed mostly in black, as he stood atop the wagon seat to make his announcement. "Come and see the latest science has to offer. A photograph printed according to the newest methods available. Let me show you how it works. Sadie Ann."

Razor's interest blossomed when a young girl in a long, yellow dress ducked through the canvas tarp separating the wagon seat from the rear of the wagon. Razor stood only five and a half feet tall. Women larger than himself intimidated him. They always had and always would. His mother had grown into an enormous woman and treated both Razor and his father, her husband, as hired hands—when she paid any attention to them at all. Razor opted out of family life at his earliest opportunity, age sixteen, bidding his father a silent farewell with good wishes for his future.

The man had called her Sadie Ann. Sadie Ann. Razor thought it a beautiful name.

Lemuel Tolliver helped his daughter to the ground.

"Pick a spot, Sadie Ann," he ordered.

Sadie looked around, making the briefest of eye contact with Razor—immediately forgotten by her; etched into memory by him. She always modeled the first shot her father took, hoping her photogenic image would impress the gathered crowed enough to have them line up for their own photograph. She chose a spot in front of the Mustang Saloon, making certain not to block the busted window behind her. She thought it added grit to the scene.

Razor shifted over to where he could look head-on at the girl while her father set up his camera. Something about her pertness, her being in, but not of, the crowd, and most of all, her diminutive size, appealed strongly to Razor.

"Sir, may I?" Lemuel asked, tapping Razor on the arm.

Razor moved aside and found a spot on the plank sidewalk, unable to take his eyes from the magnetic Sadie Ann.

Lemuel ducked under the black cloth of his camera, and a moment later, his work done, both he and Sadie Ann disappeared into the back of the wagon with a promise to reappear in only a few minutes. When they did, Lemuel passed around the photo of Sadie, garnering murmurs of approval as well as a few good-natured laughs as people caught sight of themselves in the background of the photograph. Eighteen people petitioned him to take a photo and forked over their two dollars. Three people were unhappy with the results, and, as promised, Lemuel returned their money. The event took most of the afternoon, and finally, Lemuel packed up his gear and his daughter and trundled out of town in the direction of Corbin City. Razor Gilliam walked to the middle of the dusty street and watched the wagon bounce and sway and diminish in the distance, then, his head full of fantasy, he found himself a place at the bar in the Mustang Saloon. Much of the crowd attracted by Lemuel Tolliver's visit had already retired to the *Mustang*, some proudly showing off their two-dollar portraits. Razor ordered a whiskey and kicked himself. "I should've bought the first picture he took of Sadie," he muttered.

"Say something?" asked the tall man next to him. "That photography thing is real interesting, ain't it?"

"I should've bought one," Razor repeated in an audible voice.

"Too late now."

Razor threw back his drink and ordered another as he stood brooding. As afternoon turned into evening, he ordered a third whiskey, then a fourth, conveying to anyone who took up next to him his regret over not buying a photograph.

After moping around most of next morning, Razor, still angry with himself, walked to the livery stable and saddled his horse. He had nothing else to do with his time. That Tolliver fellow still had the photograph of Sadie. No reason not to go and get it from him. And Tolliver still had Sadie. No reason not to go and…

Razor smiled, mounted, and followed the wagon tracks out of town. When, a few hours later, he sighted two riders coming his way, he spurred his horse off the road and behind a cluster of boulders. He let the riders pass him and get far down the road before setting out again after the wagon.

*

"You wear mask into town, Kemo Sabe?"

"I'd better not. Can you disguise me again?"

"Me can do. Have things in saddlebag. Me get 'em. You change clothes."

The two men dismounted and ground hitched Silver and Scout behind a scrub-covered hill. Tonto went to work, and forty minutes later, they rode together into Mustang.

The Ranger, clad in his black pants and tan shirt,

asked directions to the sheriff's office and received the laughing reply, "We ain't got no sheriff."

"Exactly the kind of place Razor would choose to hide out," the Ranger told Tonto as they continued down the main street.

"What we do now?"

"We're going to look for the saloon with the broken window where Razor stood in the photograph. Maybe I can find out something in there."

They had little trouble locating the Mustang Saloon.

"Me wait across street, Kemo Sabe."

"I guess you'd better."

Tonto led the horses away, and the Ranger entered the saloon. Barely past three o'clock, there were few people inside. The Ranger strode to the bar and asked, "Any chance of getting coffee?"

"Sure. We serve coffee till around five o'clock. After that, not much call for it. Know what I mean?" He laughed.

The Ranger laughed along. "I do." He noted a photograph of the bartender leaning against the long mirror backing the bar. "That you? It is you."

"Yeah. We had a fellow through yesterday in a wagon. Took photographs for two dollars. I got me one."

"Yes, I passed his wagon on the road. He showed me some of the photographs he took here in Mustang.

Believe it or not, in one of them I saw someone I used to know. Short fellow with a long scar down his cheek. I bought the picture. Here, ever seen him?" The Ranger offered the bartender the photograph showing Razor Gilliam.

"This fellow? Yeah, he was in here yesterday. He kinda stands out. You missed him, though. Saw him ride out of town this morning, maybe two hours ago."

"Oh, know where he headed?"

"Heard him tell a couple people last night he wished he bought a photograph yesterday. Maybe he went looking for the wagon."

The Ranger frowned, the memory of the look on Razor's face as he stared at Sadie Ann in the photograph, fresh in his mind.

He said, "You really think he might have ridden after the wagon?"

"Could've. Why don't you check with Luther at the livery stable? Maybe your friend mentioned something to him when he got his horse."

"Good idea. I'll go look up Luther."

"Still want that coffee?"

"I'll come back for it later. Thanks." He walked out onto the plank sidewalk and beckoned to Tonto. "Razor left town this morning. I'm afraid he went out after Lemuel's wagon."

"Why him do that?"

“Sadie, I’m afraid.”

“That bad. We not pass him on road, Kemo Sabe.”

“No, we didn’t. We need to go to the livery stable to see a man named Luther.”

Luther proved to be a jovial, overweight, middle-aged man in tattered overalls busy pitching hay into the stalls.

“What’s up, gents?” he asked, leaning on his pitchfork.

“I’m looking for a friend of mine. Short man with a long scar. Here’s a photograph of him. I heard at the Mustang Saloon he got his horse this morning, though, and rode out of town. Thought maybe you could tell me where he headed.”

“He didn’t say. Did say he might not be back for a couple days, though. No problem, I told him. This place’ll be here when you do.” He ended his sentence with a chuckle.

“Did he say anything about a Lemuel Tolliver or having a photograph taken?”

“Lemuel Tolliver? He that photographer fellow was here yesterday?”

“Yes.”

Luther shook his head. “Nope.”

“Thanks,” the Ranger said, and he and Tonto walked back to Silver and Scout.

"We follow him, Kemo Sabe?" Tonto asked.

"I think we'd better. I don't have a good feeling about this, and whether he's taken out after Lemuel or not, he's someone we want badly. Once we're out of sight, I'll take off this disguise. Then we'll ride!"

Chapter 8

Sadie Tolliver

"How long we gonna stay here in Corbin City, Pa?" Sadie asked.

"We done pretty good lately, so I think we can stay awhile, rest up. Horse needs a good rest, too. Maybe we can even take a few more photographs."

"Nobody else wants their photograph took. We been here too many times."

"Never can tell, daughter. Never can tell."

Lemuel and Sadie lingered over a Sunday breakfast in the café, the kind of leisurely, late morning, conversation-filled meal they rarely enjoyed on the road.

"Where we going next?" Sadie asked, spearing the last piece of pancake with her fork. "East, I hope."

Lemuel glared as Sadie chewed and gazed at her father, a study in innocence.

"We'll head south," he said, emphatically. "Wagon's filled with enough supplies to take a whole lot of photographs. We can visit towns we never been."

Sadie began a sigh but caught her breath in the middle of it.

"Pa, that man!"

"What man?"

"Don't turn! He's looking in the window at us!"

"What man?" Lemuel repeated, annoyed.

"The one in the picture."

"What picture?"

"The picture the masked man bought from you. The man you didn't like. He had a scar, remember? I can see the scar! Oh, Pa, he's looking right at us!"

Lemuel thought back. "The man who stared at you with that look!"

"I think he's coming in." Sadie bowed her head and concentrated on her cup of coffee. "I said don't turn! Lord above, don't you ever listen to what I say?"

"How can I tell if he's the same gent if I don't see him?"

"He's the same man! Didn't I just say so? He's going to the counter. Let's leave." Sadie gestured for the waitress, and her father paid the bill. They left the café, Sadie imploring her father not to look anywhere but straight ahead. When they reached their wagon, which sat across the rutted street from the café, Sadie looked back before she climbed into the rear. She caught a glimpse of the man with the scar standing at the wide, front window of the café, staring after them.

Lemuel settled into the driver's seat and said, "We still owe the masked man a favor for his four dollars. Lucky we ran into that Clem Hanson in the livery stable. He told us to come out to his house whenever we wanted. Now's as good a time as any. Him and his mother should be home on a Sunday afternoon."

"Yes," Sadie said, remaining out of sight in the rear of the wagon. "Go anywhere you want but get us out of town."

*

Clem sat relaxing on the porch as Lemuel's wagon rumbled up to the front gate.

"Ma!" Clem shouted. "Come on out here."

Wiping her hands on her apron, Mrs. Hanson stepped onto the porch.

"I didn't tell you about these people, Ma. They brought their horse in while I was working. I didn't know if they'd really come out here, so I let it be a surprise for you." Clem performed the appropriate introductions, and Lemuel explained to Mrs. Hanson why he was there.

"That masked man is a good man and a good friend," she said. "Saved my boy's life."

"You got two photographs coming, compliments of him."

"Oh, my. I've never had a photograph taken of me in my life. I'm a real sight. Let me go inside a few moments and put myself together."

From the corner of his eye, Clem caught movement in the trees not far from his front gate, but roaming animals often passed through, and he gave it no mind. He and Lemuel chatted about life on the road until Mrs. Hanson reappeared in a flowered dress, her with hair combed and fluffed.

"Where would you like to pose?" Lemuel asked. "What do you think, Sadie? Sadie's got a real good eye."

All eyes turned to Sadie, who surveyed the front yard. "How 'bout in front of them yellow roses next to the gate?"

"Yes!" Mrs. Hanson agreed. "That will make a beautiful background."

Everyone walked toward the fence, and Lemuel detoured to get the equipment he needed from his wagon. Sadie positioned Clem and his mother, and Lemuel ducked under his black cloth. He took one photo of Mrs. Hanson and Clem, shoulder to shoulder, and another of Mrs. Hanson standing alone, making her smile last forever.

"Sadie, you do the honors," Lemuel instructed, handing the plates over to his daughter.

Sadie took the photographic plates into the rear of the wagon and set to work developing them. When both photographs were ready, she moved to the rear of the wagon and let the light fall on them. They'd come out well, clear and sharp. One detail caught her eye. Partly hidden by the trees in the distant background of the picture… was that a horse? A muzzle and one leg in one photo; surely a bushy tail in the other. She poked her head out of the wagon and stared into the small grove of trees. Nothing moved other than the leaves jostled by the warm breeze.

"Come on, Sadie," Lemuel called. "What's taking you so long?"

Sadie climbed out of the wagon and passed through the gate.

"They came out real good, Pa."

Mrs. Hanson and Clem passed the photos back and forth and admired themselves.

"I really look like that?" Mrs. Hanson said with a laugh. "It's enough to make a person's head swell up with pride or shrivel with embarrassment."

"Stop. You look very nice, Ma," Clem said, grinning. "It's me should stay indoors."

Compliments and good cheer made the rounds as Lemuel and Sadie chimed in. Mrs. Hanson invited her guests to stay for an early dinner and would not take no for an answer.

"Always eat around three o'clock on a Sunday," she explained.

The Tollivers accepted and everyone retired to the porch.

*

Later that day as dusk fell, the Ranger and Tonto reined up on the edge of Corbin City. They'd ridden hard from Mustang hoping to reach Lemuel and Sadie ahead of

Razor.

"Silver and Scout plenty tired, Kemo Sabe," Tonto said.

"We'll have time to rest them and ourselves once we find the Tollivers," the Ranger replied.

"You change into disguise?"

"There's no time. Let's look for Lemuel's wagon."

They rode slowly along the main street of Corbin City but found no trace of the wagon.

"Maybe him leave town already," Tonto said.

"Look! Next to the livery stable."

The stable was closed on a Sunday, but a lonely horse grazed nearby on the sparse grass available. Wagon reins hung from the animal. The Ranger urged Silver forward.

"That horse from wagon," Tonto said. "Me recognize white mark on back leg."

"You're right. Somehow the horse got free or was set free from the wagon and came back here to feed."

"Me look for track of horse."

Tonto dismounted and handed Scout's reins to the Lone Ranger. Head down, he walked along the road leading away from town and the stable. After a moment, he beckoned.

"Horse come from this way. See, reins drag in dirt."

"I see. Let's backtrack and try to find the wagon."

The two men rode, looking left and right, as evening deepened until a little over a mile out of town, they saw Lemuel's wagon, precariously tilted, two wheels over a small ridge at the side of the road. The two men galloped up and searched the wagon but found neither Lemuel nor Sadie.

"He has them," the Ranger muttered.

Tonto dismounted and, as darkness closed in, he studied the ground.

Suddenly, the Ranger leaped down from his horse and ran into the grass.

"Lemuel," he said, bending over the man, tied hand and foot, a gag in his mouth. Tonto rushed up, drew his knife, and cut the ropes while the Ranger removed the gag.

"What happened, Lemuel?" the Ranger asked.

After a coughing fit, Lemuel managed to say, "He took her. The man with the scar. The one you saw in the picture."

"How long ago? Can you get him some water, Tonto?"

"No more'n fifteen, twenty minutes ago."

"Do you know where they went?"

"He put her on his horse, climbed up behind her, and rode off." He pointed away from town. "We stayed to dinner with your friends after we took their photographs. When we left, he was waiting down the road. I tried to get away from him, but what with old Beulah dragging a wagon behind her… we went off the road and nearly toppled over. Sadie jumped down and ran, but he caught her and tied her hands. The man with the scar unhitched Beulah and left me like you saw. He rode off with my Sadie! You gotta find her, masked man. You gotta find her."

"We will, Lemuel. Are you hurt? Here, have some water."

"Thanks. No, I'm not hurt, but forget about me. Please, find her."

The Ranger's steely eyes met Tonto's.

"Let's go, Kemo Sabe," he said.

The two men mounted and set off.

*

Three miles further on, Razor Gilliam sat in his saddle seething. His nose dripped blood and hurt like the devil. The girl had flounced around in the saddle so much, he could barely stay balanced himself. She asked him to cut her hands loose so she could hold onto the pommel and made the request in such a sweet voice, Razor thought she'd begun getting accustomed to him. He cut the rope from her wrists, and the moment he put his knife back into his belt, the girl bent forward, then reared back and smashed the back of her head into his face. With a remarkable agility that shocked Razor nearly as much as the blow to the nose, Sadie managed to swing her left leg over the horse's neck, jump to the ground, and run into the waving grass and thick ground cover where she'd forced him to stop. By the time Razor got his wits about him, she'd vanished.

He stormed off his horse and ran after her.

"I know you can hear me," he shouted. "You better come back here. Don't think of going back to your father. If you do, I'll shoot him and maybe shoot you, too. Where are you? You've got no food or water. I'll find you."

The sun had disappeared, though, and Razor knew he had little chance of locating the girl until next morning.

"I'm telling you, you better come back here," he bellowed, but he knew it was useless. He had to choose whether to stay where he was and wait for morning, a long way off, or return to the wagon and wait for the girl to show up. But after his threat to shoot her father, he believed she'd stay away from the wagon, at least for now.

Razor chose to ride a short distance down the road toward where he'd left her father and the wagon. He left the saddle, wrapped his horse's reins loosely to some bushes so it could graze, then waded into the grass and started forward, hoping chance would lead him to the girl. He didn't want her to slip past him and make her way into town. He'd find her eventually, and when he did, he'd teach Miss Sadie Ann Tolliver a lesson she wouldn't soon forget.

*

"You hear that, Kemo Sabe?" Tonto pulled rein. He and the Ranger had sprinted their mounts down the road, hoping to overtake Razor while the day's light lasted.

"I did. Someone calling. I couldn't catch the words. Let's… there it is again. A man's voice… ordering someone to come back."

"You think maybe girl escape?"

"I don't know, Tonto. Let's leave Silver and Scout and go forward on foot."

They walked through the grass which edged the road, listening for more voices.

"Me hear nothing now," Tonto said.

"No. It's getting dark, too. Let's go back to the horses. We'll take turns staying awake in case the voice calls again. As soon as it's light, we'll search the area."

*

When dawn broke after a quiet night, the Ranger and Tonto mounted and proceeded slowly along the road. They hadn't gone far when, a short way off, they noticed a horse tethered to a bush.

Dismounting and stowing their horses out of sight, they separated and continued forward. "Let me go. Let me go!" a woman's voice cried out.

The two went to their knees, and through the waving grass they saw Razor dragging Sadie toward the horse.

"Keep your mouth shut, you little wildcat," Razor ordered. He slammed the girl against the horse's flank and slapped her across the face.

The Ranger rose from the grass.

"That's enough, Razor. Let the girl go."

Razor spun in surprise. Sadie pushed him away and ran off into the grass again. Razor drew his revolver and fired six shots in the direction of the Ranger, who dove to the ground without sending any silver bullets Razor's way, not certain Sadie wouldn't cross his line of fire. When he and Tonto rose, they saw Razor, mounted and pounding away down the road.

"Sadie!" the Ranger called. "It's me, the masked man and Tonto. Razor's ridden off. You can come out. You're safe now." He and Tonto walked out onto the road where Sadie could get a look at them.

Tonto pointed. "She come, Kemo Sabe."

"Thank God," she cried, running up to the Ranger and throwing her arms around him.

"Did he hurt you?" the Lone Ranger asked.

"No. No, I'm okay. I got away from him last night, but he found me this morning. I'm not hurt, no."

"Tonto will take you back to your father. We

found him tied in the grass near your wagon. He's not hurt, either. I'm going after Razor."

"Me catch up with you, Kemo Sabe, when girl and father together."

The Ranger whistled for Silver, who trotted up to him. He swung into the saddle and galloped down the road.

Chapter 9

Escape

The Ranger slid the cinch of the lanyard hanging from his white Stetson higher as the brim of the hat bent in the rush of breeze caused by Silver's gallant effort to overtake Razor Gilliam. Two miles ahead, clear signs of Razor leaving the road brought the Ranger to a halt before a wide-spreading ground cover of dense brush. Further off, a patch of low trees offered shelter.

The Ranger dismounted and piled three flat stones at the side of the road where he intended to enter the tangle of bushes, a sign Tonto would be sure to notice. He led Silver forward, studying the ground left and right for signs of Razor's progress. The damaged, trodden-down bushes provided a clear trail. When he reached the trees, he drew his revolver and went slowly forward, still leading Silver. He knew Razor could travel no faster than he through this maze of brush and now trees. The signs of Razor's progress were fewer there, but those few were obvious to one who could read the language. Nonetheless, the Ranger made certain to leave more clear-cut signs of passage for Tonto's benefit.

It took thirty minutes to reach the far edge of the trees where a rudimentary dirt road led up a lengthy rise. The Ranger mounted Silver and rode to the top of the rise, where a broad valley filled with rolling hills and occasional clusters of trees spread before him. A sluggish river crept along the valley floor in the distance. The road narrowed as he proceeded and eventually disappeared altogether, becoming grass and bush like the land around it. The Ranger dismounted on the nearest high ground. Below him sat a cabin and a horse he recognized as Razor's tied to a hitch rack to the left of the cabin door.

The Ranger dropped Silver's reins saying, "Wait for me here, big fellow." He circled the cabin, darting bush by bush, staying low in the waving grass. When he finished scouting, he knew the one door he'd seen was the sole means of exit. The only other break in the four walls was a small window to the right of the door. Grimly satisfied, he knew he'd trapped one of the men who'd murdered his brother.

Keeping his distance, the Ranger approached the cabin from the left side. When he reached the side wall, he pressed his back against it and peeked around the corner to where Razor's horse stood. The Ranger sidled a short way along the wall until he faced Razor's mount four feet off. Keeping a close eye on the door, he gently unhitched the horse and led it around to the side of the cabin. He smacked the beast hard on its rump, and the animal bounded away, its reins dragging on the ground. The Ranger returned to the top of the rise where he'd left Silver and studied the quiet cabin. Once Razor stepped outside, he'd have no choice but to surrender. The Lone Ranger chose the slightly longer revolver from his left holster and settled in.

After thirty minutes, the cabin door opened, and Razor stepped out to survey the quiet valley. This cabin was a hideaway he and Butch had used before when, after rousing the countryside to arms, Butch sent his men in all different directions to let things cool down, just as he did after the melee outside of Corbin City. Razor had no intention of enduring the loneliness of this valley for any longer than he had to. He wanted to get back to the pleasures of Mustang. He only paused there to hide out for a while in case whoever interfered in his capture of the girl decided to be brave and follow him. He was certain, though, the path he'd chosen to the cabin was enough to discourage anyone, and looking over the quiet valley, he smiled and decided he was right. Then, he missed his horse.

"Hey! Where'd you go, you no good nag?" he called. He closed the cabin door behind him and went looking.

The Ranger waited until Razor put some distance between himself and the door of the cabin. Then he called, "Razor! Your time is up. Drop your holster and belly on the ground."

Razor let out a roar of frustration. He drew his revolver and fired three shots in the direction of the voice. He spun and raced toward the cabin, but when four bullets, one after the other, smashed into the cabin door, he slid to a halt and raced around the side of the building. The Lone Ranger started forward, angling his approach to keep track of Razor's direction.

The panicked man ran toward the nearby muddy river, hoping to lose himself in the dense vegetation which teemed along both banks. When he reached the greenery, he looked back and fired twice more.

The Ranger saw Razor set up to shoot and already hugged the ground when the shots came. He rose quickly but Razor had vanished. Needing to stay low in case Razor lurked in ambush, the Ranger managed to reach the tangled overgrowth safely. Cocking an ear, he thought he heard the splash of someone moving in the dark water. The lazily flowing river narrowed where he stood before it disappeared around a sharp bend. It would be difficult to track Razor if he crossed the river. When the Ranger approached the bend in the river, he moved inland so he did not have to go blindly around the curve, where Razor might be waiting. He came at the river from a slant, and when he could trace the path of the river beyond its abrupt change of direction, he saw Razor halfway to the far shore, standing immobile.

As the Ranger watched, Razor looked around in confusion, then tugged at his legs seemingly held in place by tremendous weights. Suddenly, as if a crank had been turned, the trapped man abruptly slipped two inches lower into the water. Razor had gotten himself into either quicksand or mud—mud that shared quicksand's hungry appetite.

The river, slow-moving to begin with, swirled lazily around the trapped man as if taking time to inspect, then mock him before it meandered on its way.

"Razor!" the Lone Ranger called. "Toss your gun away, and I'll try to help." He wanted this murderer turned over to the law, and despite what he knew would be the man's destiny, he could not watch fate play out in this way.

Razor fired another bullet wildly in the Ranger's direction.

"If you didn't reload, that's your last bullet, and you're not reloading from where you are. Your gun belt's already under water. Toss your gun away so I know, and I'll try to help you. You don't have much time."

Razor had sunk to his waist. He twisted and turned, trying to free himself.

"The more you struggle, the quicker you'll sink. Throw your gun away. Now!"

"Who are you? Who are you?" With a profound explosion of frustration, Razor tossed his gun into the brown water.

The Ranger rose and ran back to where he hoped Silver would be able to hear him.

"Silver!" he shouted. He whistled as loud as he could. "Silver. Silver. Can you hear me, big fellow?"

An encouraging whinny came faintly to his ears.

"Here, Silver." He whistled again.

Silver appeared atop a low hill.

"Over here." He waved his arms, and Silver loped toward him. When Silver reached him, he gathered the reins and led the powerful horse through the bushes.

By then, Razor had sunk to chest level. The Ranger stepped onto the riverbank so Razor could see him.

"Help me!" Razor cried, surrendering to his panic. "Get me out of this."

The Ranger took the rope hanging from Silver's

saddle and unfurled it. He quickly widened the noose and sent the rope sailing into the stream.

"Can you reach it?" the Ranger cried.

The rope slipped past Razor, and the Ranger gathered it up for a second attempt. This toss landed almost on top of Razor, and he grabbed it desperately.

"You can't get it around your waist," the Ranger called. "Can you slip it over your head and get it under your arms?"

Razor followed the Ranger's direction as the mud crept up near his shoulders.

"Tighten it if you can and hold on," the Ranger ordered.

He tied the rope around Silver's mighty chest and neck.

"Go, big fellow. Pull." He tugged on the reins, urging Silver ahead. The great stallion staggered under the weight of Razor and the pull of the mud. Only Razor's head and arms, raised in the air, were visible.

"Hold onto the rope and try pulling yourself out," the Ranger cried. "Forward, Silver. Come on, fellow!"

Silver managed a half-dozen steps progress, and the Ranger noted the angle of Razor's body tilt toward shore.

"Good boy, Silver. Pull!"

Inch by inch, Razor's head closed in on the shore. His shoulders rose above the muck, then his back surfaced as Silver hauled the man forward. The Ranger stepped to the water's edge, and a moment later, Razor, gasping for breath, crawled on his hands and knees through the shallow mud a foot from shore.

The Ranger took him by the back of his soaking shirt collar and dragged him the rest of the way.

While Razor lay face-down on the grass gathering himself, the Ranger said, "Too bad you're such a little man, Razor. A few pounds heavier, you'd have sunk like a rock and saved the law a lot of trouble."

The small man glared at the Ranger.

"Who are you?" he asked.

"I'm the man taking you back to the sheriff in Corbin City. Your outlaw career is over."

Razor lowered his face onto the grass and said nothing.

"Up." The Ranger yanked Razor to his feet. "You're already roped. Start walking."

Leading Silver, the Ranger urged on a dispirited and filthy Razor, whose clothing dripped globs of river mud as he walked. Not a word passed between them as thoughts of his lost brother settled into the Ranger's mind. When they at last reached the main road, the Ranger saw Tonto kneeling next to the stack of three rocks he'd left behind.

"Tonto!" he called.

"Kemo Sabe," Tonto cried, rising. "You get him!"

"I did. This is Razor Gilliam. How are Sadie and

Lemuel?"

"Them fine. Me help Lemuel get wagon back on road. Then me bring their horse. Them hitch up and go back to town."

"Good. I want you to go back to town as well. Alert the sheriff that I'm bringing in one of Butch Cavendish's gang. I want a jail cell ready and waiting for him. Tie his hands in front of him first. Let me get some of this mud off my boots."

Tonto cut a clean length of rope from the Ranger's lariat and bound Razor's wrists with double knots.

"You make him walk to town?" Tonto asked.

"His horse ran off. The town's only a couple of miles or so from here. We'll be there in an hour or so."

"Me go now and tell sheriff." Tonto mounted. "Get 'em up, Scout."

"Start walking, Razor. You give me any trouble, I'll drag you to town behind me."

Their slow trip began.

*

The sheriff and a small band of men stepped off the plank sidewalk and into the street to stare when the Ranger appeared at the edge of town following a bound, roped, filthy man. Lemuel and Sadie stood across the street from the jail, leaning against their wagon. When the Ranger reached the crowd of men, Tonto slid the lariat over Razor's head.

"This man is Razor Gilliam, Sheriff," the Ranger said. "He's part of the Cavendish gang, and he's wanted in many places in Texas for robbery, murder, and in this case, kidnapping."

"Your Indian partner explained things to me. So did these two." He indicated Lemuel and Sadie, who had walked over and joined the crowd.

Lemuel said, "We're gonna stick around and testify when the judge comes through. Sheriff says he'll be here on Thursday."

"I'll take him from here, Indian," Sheriff Hosh said, and he walked off toward the jail with the prisoner, the group of onlookers moving with him. One young man with a riotous shock of blond hair and an eager manner stayed behind to address the Lone Ranger.

"My name's Hamil Peters, and I write for the *Corbin City Bugle*. I've been talking to these two people, Mr. Tolliver and Sadie, and they told me the whole story. Who are you? Why are you wearing a mask? Your Indian friend says you're called the Lone Ranger. What's your real name?"

The Ranger chuckled. "You certainly ask questions like a newspaperman, Hamil Peters. Ready, Kemo Sabe?"

"I thought your name was Tonto," the Hamil said, tossing Tonto a puzzled look.

Tonto mounted Scout. "That right. Me Tonto," he

replied.

"Wait," Hamil cried when both men turned their horses and trotted away. "No, come on. I want details for my story. Come…"

Sheriff Hosh reappeared. "Where'd the masked man go?" he asked.

Hamil pointed.

"Wanted to tell him we had that Razor fellow safe behind bars. Who is he? All I know is he calls himself the Lone Ranger."

"The Lone Ranger?" Hamil repeated.

The sheriff looked at Lemuel and Sadie. "He tell you his name?"

"Nope," Lemuel answered.

The sheriff shrugged. "I guess he'll just have to be the Lone Ranger then."

"Oh, boy! A mystery rider named the Lone Ranger! This is going to make a great story," Hamil said. "I only wish he'd stayed around so I could talk to him some more. I gotta go write it up while it's fresh in my mind." He hurried away toward the *Bugle* office, a big smile on his face.

"Sadie, let's get some lunch," Lemuel suggested, and he and his daughter headed toward the café.

Chapter 10

Clive Abramson

"Listen to this crazy story, Clive." Randy Catanga, foreman of Clive Abramson's three thousand-acre cattle spread, sat in the living room of Clive's ranch house. He waved the *Parkerburg Town Crier* toward his boss, who leaned against the mantelpiece, head downcast. "Says here a masked rider calling himself the Lone Ranger, along with an Indian partner named Tonto, captured and brought to justice Razor Gilliam, a member of the detested Cavendish gang. Razor Gilliam, wanted for murder, robbery, and kidnapping, was tried by Judge Horace Thorndyke, found guilty, and sentenced to hang on… what's today's date."

Clive glanced at Randy, frowning. Fifty-two years old and worried about his ranch's survival, he wished his thirty-three-year-old foreman would focus on the problems at hand. Fifteen years before, Clive had taken over the ranch, then a hand-to-mouth operation, from his father, but once the disruption caused by the recent war ended, he'd made it prosper, great thanks to Randy, whom he'd hired first as a common hand, then raised to foreman three years ago. The previous year's cattle drive to the railhead in Dodge City had been a disaster. Since then, Clive had lost weight from his already thin frame and saw the same thing happening to his wife Mabel. Her hair had whitened, same as his own, and the lines around her eyes had deepened, matching his. Something had to be done to pull them out of trouble.

"Today!" Randy cried. "Today. He's being… been hanged today. I heard of the Cavendish gang. Glad they don't operate around here. I guess rustling's not in their line of work."

"Randy, if you don't shut up. What do I care about a masked man and the Cavendish gang?"

"Says here he uses silver bullets, too, and rides a big, white horse."

"Who? Cavendish?"

"No! The masked man."

"Nonsense. The newspaper's making up nonsense to sell more papers. Where'd they get the story from? I'm sure nobody from our *Town Crier* wrote it. None of 'em's got that much imagination."

"Let me check… *ah*, here at the bottom. Says reprinted from the *Corbin City Bugle*."

"Corbin City's almost a day's ride from here. *Bah*, they made the whole thing up."

"I don't think they'd make up a man getting hung."

"Never mind. I said I don't care. The banker from Boston's already arrived in town. He'll be out here tomorrow morning."

"What's he want?"

"You know darn well what he wants. Money. My money. The cattle that didn't make it up to the railhead at Dodge City last year cost me plenty. The long walk around Indian country… Plus, every pound one of them cattle lost was money out of my pocket. If this Boston banker won't lend me enough to get this year's bunch to Dodge and on to Chicago, I'm out of business. To meet last year's payments and this year's payrolls, you know how I've had to sell some of the cattle down here for three dollars a head, when I could get thirty dollars, maybe forty a head in Chicago."

"That's bad, boss." What he really meant was 'that's good.' Clive missing a payroll meant Randy would miss a paycheck and that would have kept him off the faro table in Parkerburg, which no longer extended him credit and had become mighty ornery about how much he was already into them. The paychecks had to keep coming.

"Bad?" Clive scoffed. "You like to cut right to the heart of the situation, don't you?"

"Can't you get the Indian agent at Fort Davis to force the Indians to let you cross their reservation?"

Clive glared at his foreman.

"I know, I know," Randy said. "He turned you down last year."

"They settled those two tribes of Indians right above my property line and gave them the land I always drove the cattle across to the railhead. One bunch of savages would have been bad enough. Two, they take up the whole damned horizon. You know I've been using that same route every year, before and after the war. When the government settled those redskins there, they didn't give a hoot about me."

"Maybe this year'll be different."

"Well, *something* better be different, or I'm sunk."

*

Arthur Kennedy, western loan officer of the Berkeley Bank of Boston, rode up to the main house of the Lazy A ranch, where Clive Abramson and his foreman waited for him on the porch. The men knew one another and shook hands.

"Sit out here or come inside?" Clive asked, offering Kennedy a friendly smile. "My wife did some baking."

"I don't have much time. Out here would be nice," Kennedy said, and the three men arranged the porch chairs for a discussion. Clive's stomach did a jig as he watched Kennedy open his case and take out some papers.

"Let's get right to it," Kennedy began. "I'm due in Hollansburg day after tomorrow, and it's sixty miles off."

"Starting out today?" Randy asked.

"Tomorrow morning. Eight o'clock stage. Now, about this loan."

"I'll be sending more'n five thousand head of cattle to market this year," Clive explained.

"Berkeley financed last year's drive for you. You were late with the last two payments, and the final payment hasn't come in yet. *It's* a month overdue. Can you explain?"

Clive squirmed in his chair. “We had certain setbacks. The trail last year was longer than it needed to be. You know the government settled some Indians on the grasslands in my way. Strays ran off…”

“Did you hire enough hands? I know we loaned you enough money to.”

“It wasn’t that. The road we had to take went over very rough ground, and the men had trouble keeping the herd together. There was one stampede when some buffalo showed up…”

“Couldn’t you take a better route?”

Clive glared at the banker. “Didn’t I just tell you that the only good route, the shortest route, is through where they put the Indians? The Indian agent at Fort Davis won’t see fit to allow me to pass through the land, and he has the whole cavalry at hand to enforce it.”

Kennedy looked thoughtful. “So how will this year be any different?”

A painful silence fell.

Randy glanced at his boss whose lips pressed tightly together. He blurted, “This year’ll be different because we’re trying to make a deal with the two Indian encampments between us and the direct trail to the railroad in Dodge. We’ve been… been negotiating with them. When we succeed, the drive won’t take nearly as long this year, and the cattle won’t lose as much weight, maybe none since the grassland the Indians live on is so rich.”

"Ah," Kennedy said, nodding. "That would make a difference. I'll tell you what. I'll leave the details to you, but I'll stop in again on my way back to Boston, say in maybe three weeks, a month. We'll talk then, and you can fill me in on the Indian deal. Boston will want to know. Getting the cattle to market is, of course, the key consideration." He waited for a response.

"Yeah, three weeks. That'd be fine," Clive said.

The men rose and shook hands again.

Kennedy paused before he stepped off the porch. "If I'm to make a case for you, I'd like to have the final payment in hand before I go back east. It's in your own best interest."

Clive nodded, and he and Randy stood mute as they watched Kennedy mount and head back to town.

"What the hell were you talking about?" Clive exploded. "What deal with the Indians? Things are as bad this year as last, maybe worse."

"We have to find a way to go through Indian country," Randy stated.

"I know we do! I know we do! How, though?"

"Sit, boss." The men returned to their chairs. "*We* can't do anything about moving the Indians," Randy said. "Somehow, we need to give the troops at Fort Davis a reason to clear them out and stick them someplace else."

"And just how do you propose we do that?"

"I don't know, boss. We have to come up with

something."

"*Something*, right. If you can come up with *something* to get me through this... and I don't care what it is..." His voice trailed off, but their eyes met, and their consciences began to darken.

*

The Lone Ranger and Tonto headed west from Corbin City, hoping to find some trace of the Cavendish gang, but as yet they'd had no luck. As they approached Parkerburg, they reined up.

"Do you hear that?" the Lone Ranger asked. "Indian drums."

"Me hear. Drums send out message."

Both men sat quietly in the saddle, the Ranger's eyes on Tonto. When the drums stopped, he asked, "What's going on?"

"This heap bad, Kemo Sabe. Chief's son missing."

"Missing! Did they say how old the boy is?"

"Drums not say."

"Can you ride into their settlement and find out what happened?"

"We find place to camp, then me go. Stop in town on way back for supplies."

"Good idea. We're running low." The Ranger

pointed. "The only place that isn't open and flat looks to be in the distance where those rocks are. Let's take a look there."

The rocks proved suitable for a camp, and Tonto headed off on his dual mission.

When he returned, dusk had settled over the land, and the Ranger sat leaning against a boulder cleaning one of his ivory handled .44s. He got to his feet and helped Tonto unpack what they needed to make their dinner.

"Things bad in Indian village, Kemo Sabe," Tonto reported.

"How so?"

"Missing boy young. Only ten years old."

"Do they know anything about where he might have gone?"

"Him wander away to play with other boys. Him only boy not come home."

"And he's the chief's son?"

"Yes. Chief Gray Wolf son. When Indians look for him, they find coup stick."

"A coup stick? The area around here is peaceful. Why would there be a coup stick lying around?"

"Indians think maybe boys make it for their play, but boys say them no play with coup stick. Not make sense. Coup stick not from their tribe. It have marking from Chief Brave Eagle tribe. Chief Gray Wolf demand meeting with Chief Brave Eagle."

"I see. Even if the boys did make the stick, it wouldn't make sense for them to carve it with another tribe's markings. The stick may have been left to make Gray Wolf think the other tribe took his son."

"Why someone do that?"

"I don't know, Kemo Sabe, but you can see where this is heading. A confrontation, perhaps a bloody one. Have the two chiefs met yet?"

"No. Other tribe send messenger, not chief. Messenger say them know nothing of lost boy. Chief Gray Wolf angry other chief not come."

"I can see where he would be. Let's hope they can work it out peacefully."

"Me bring you newspaper from town."

The Ranger tossed the paper to the ground for the time being and set to work building a fire. After they'd eaten and cleaned up, the Ranger situated himself so the light from the waning campfire fell onto the newspaper Tonto had brought him.

"Did you read this paper yet?" he asked.

"Me no have time."

"Listen to this. There's a story about a masked man who calls himself the Lone Ranger and his Indian partner Tonto bringing Razor Gilliam to justice in Corbin City. Razor was tried and hung three days ago."

"Him bad man. You in newspaper; now people know about you."

"It seems some will. It's more important than ever to keep my identity a secret. Cavendish might see this story."

"Him not like it."

"No, to say the least."

"What we do now?"

"I'm worried about the lost Indian boy and the trouble that might come from it."

"Me worry, too. *Big* trouble come if boy not found."

"Let's get some rest," the Ranger suggested. "Tomorrow morning's soon enough to make a decision."

*

They were awakened next morning by the beating of drums. The Ranger rubbed his eyes through the holes in his mask. He kept his mask in place as much as possible so it would become second nature to him.

"What's going on, Tonto?"

"Me listen."

The Ranger got to his feet and stepped out of the covey of rocks which sheltered them. Barely half the morning sun peeked above the level, grassy plain. Two rabbits darted from behind a rock and into the high grass. He stared in the direction of the beating drums until Tonto joined him.

"Another boy missing, Kemo Sabe."

"Another one!"

"Not from same tribe. From Brave Eagle tribe."

"In retribution, you think? Is Gray Wolf getting even for his son's disappearance?"

"Brave Eagle now make demand to meet."

"It's not likely two boys from different tribes wandered off and got lost, one after the other. Something else, something very bad is happening. The Indians have had a hard enough time—being moved from their homelands, losing their hunting grounds—without putting them at war with one another over this."

"What we do?"

"We have to find those boys."

"How we do that?"

"I'm not sure, Tonto. Let's saddle up."

*

Clive Abramson sat on his porch waiting to hear from his foreman. They'd successfully executed one part of their plan to dislodge the Indians from the area, and Randy had set out to accomplish the next part. The screen door swung open, and Clive's wife Mabel, in a long, blue dress protected by with a white apron, appeared at his shoulder, holding a silver tray with slices of bread on it.

"You didn't eat your lunch, Clive," she said.

"Here. Freshly baked. Something to nibble on." She put the tray on a small, round table at Clive's elbow. "I know you're worried about this year's cattle drive, but you've had a good year, darling. Things will work out. I know they will."

He glanced at his wife and gave her a smile of gratitude, sorry again for the worry he was causing her. "I'm going to have to sell a lot more head at a cheap price in Texas to get the money to pay off the bank, so they'll give me another loan. The cowboys, at least, will wait for their money until we get to Dodge and sell the cattle."

"Listen to me. Things will work out. Who's this coming? Oh, it's Randy. I'm gonna need new glasses real soon. I'll leave you two to business." She bent and kissed her husband's cheek, then disappeared back inside the house.

Randy threw his horse's reins lightly over the fence and walked up the pathway toward the porch.

Clive's heart pounded as he waited to hear if everything had gone well. "So?" he asked.

"No problems. I stowed the second kid in the other shack. One kid in each building with food and water enough for at least a week, unless the little brats eat like horses. I boarded up the one window in each building except for a slit at the top too high for anyone passing by to look in."

"It's gonna get awful hot in those shacks. You sure no one saw anything?"

"I snatched the kids clean. Here's the mask I

wore." He showed Clive a bit of burlap sack with eyeholes, which he could slip over his head.

"You leave another one of them sticks behind?"

"No, I didn't have time to make it. I'm satisfied the one I left after I took the first kid caused enough suspicion between the two tribes."

"What happened to your hand?"

Randy unwrapped a thin swath of bloody cloth from his left hand.

"This kid was older than the first one. He carried a knife I didn't see, but I took it away from him." He tapped his belt where'd he stashed the knife.

"Looks pretty deep."

"I cleaned it. It's fine."

"What now?"

"The kids don't know who I am, never saw my face. I'm going to burn this mask as well as these clothes. After I do, there'll be nothing to connect me…"

Both men turned as two riders approached their front gate.

"What the…?" Clive muttered, rising to his feet.

One rider, mounted on a powerful white stallion, wore a black mask. His companion, an Indian, rode a paint. The new arrivals dismounted and tied their horses to the fence. Randy's horse shook itself free from the fence and started at a trot toward the barn, which sat off to the right of the house. The masked man and Indian passed through the gate and walked to the porch.

Randy laid a hand atop his gun.

The Ranger offered a friendly smile. "There's no need for any of that," he said. "My mask is on the side of the law."

"Kemo Sabe," Tonto said, pointing to a newspaper which lay next to the rocking chair Clive had vacated.

"I see you have the latest *Town Crier*," the Ranger said. "I recognize the front page. If you've read it, you may have seen me mentioned."

"I did read about a masked man and Indian. You're the two who captured one of the Cavendish gang?" Clive asked.

"Yes."

"Let me see one of your bullets."

The Ranger slipped a bullet from his belt and tossed it to Clive, who held it in front of Randy and said, "Silver." He tossed the bullet back. "What brings you here?"

"I believe there might be trouble brewing that will affect you." He went on to describe what the drums had said as well as what Tonto had learned from his visit to the Indian village.

"A chief's son!" Clive interrupted. Randy shifted his stance from one leg to the other as the Ranger completed his report.

"Are you the owner of this spread?" the Ranger asked.

"Yes, sorry. I'm Clive Abramson, and this is my foreman, Randy Catanga."

"What do you think we should do, boss? Maybe we should alert the troops at Fort Davis," Randy suggested, quietly astonished at how easily he turned the awkward moment in favor of their plan. "We can't have an Indian war going on right on our doorstep."

"Tonto and I stopped to ask whether you might have seen either of the Indian boys or noticed anything out of the ordinary. It's very unlikely boys from two different tribes could have wandered away one after the other."

"No, no," Clive said, reassuringly. "First I heard of any of this. I heard the drums, but it's only noise to me. I can't decipher them. I haven't seen anything."

"How about you?" the Ranger asked Randy. "Looked like your horse has been ridden hard lately."

"No, I was down in the south pasture checking the stock. I didn't see anything out of the way."

"You've cut your hand. Would you like Tonto to look at it? He has—"

"No, thanks. I cut it on some ragged fencing."

"Did you? If you do see the boys or anything you think might help, report it to the sheriff in Parkerburg. Things could get out of hand quickly if this blows up," the

Ranger said. "One more thing." He quickly ran through the names of the Cavendish gang still on the loose, but neither man professed to know anything about them.

"We'll be off, then," the Ranger said. "Come on, Kemo Sabe."

Clive and Randy watched in silence as the two men rode out of sight.

"What the hell, Randy?" Clive said. "A chief's son?"

"How could I know who he was? He was only a little kid to me. Let me burn these things and clean up. Oh, and you'd better write a letter with the full details of the Indian trouble. Make it good. I'll take it to Fort Davis first thing tomorrow."

"Yeah, yeah. I'll get right on it."

The Ranger and Tonto rode until they rounded a bend, where they reined to a halt.

"Did you see what I saw, Tonto?" the Ranger asked.

"Me see many things, Kemo Sabe. What you see?"

"Randy's horse. It was ridden hard and not in any leisurely ride around the south pasture."

"And horse go to barn in what Indian call 'hungry trot.'"

"Yes, I noticed it was in a hurry. Probably hadn't eaten for some time."

"Man's clothing very dirty. Not pick up that much dirt when ride horse to see cows."

"No, true. He may have made other stops, though. I'm interested in the cut on his hand."

"It look like knife cut."

"Exactly. And did you notice the knife in his belt?"

"No, me not see knife."

"You weren't standing where I was. It didn't look like a store-bought knife. The hilt appeared to be made of bone. Buffalo bone, likely."

"Indian make knife like that."

The men sat quietly for a moment.

"What we do now?" Tonto asked.

"Do you think you can track his horse, find out where's he's been?"

"Too many horses ride this road."

The Ranger studied the road beneath him. "I see what you mean. Can we both pay a visit to the Indian village? Maybe they have more information by now."

"Me go find out. Not sure what them think of white man with mask."

"I'd really like to talk to the chief. When you visit, ask if I'd be welcome. Meanwhile, I'll ride to Fort Davis and speak with the captain there."

"Where we meet?"

"In the same rocks where we camped last night."

"Me go. Get'um up, Scout."

"Let's go, big fellow."

Chapter 11

Fort Davis

The Ranger approached the wide, wooden gates of Fort Davis.

"Halt right there," came the raspy voice of a blue-clad sentry brandishing a carbine from atop the twenty-foot-high palisade.

The Ranger dismounted and waited until one of the doors swung inward. Two armed soldiers exited the fort and walked up to him.

"Who are you?" one asked. "And what's with the mask?"

"Don't let the mask concern you. It's on the side of justice. I'd like to speak to the captain."

"And who shall I say is calling?" the second soldier said, snidely.

"Let me get a newspaper from my saddlebag." The Ranger went and returned with his copy of the *Parkerburg Town Crier*. "You can tell your captain that the man described in this article wishes to speak with him. It's very important and concerns the two Indian encampments near Parkerburg."

The two soldiers huddled and looked over the article.

The first man who'd spoken said, "The captain

knows about you. I heard him mention something to Lieutenant Calender this morning. Stay here, Mitch." He returned to the fort.

"You really took down one of the Cavendish gang?" the second soldier said, this time not so snidely.

"I did. In Corbin City close to where the big shoot-out was."

"We heard about that. A lot of the Cavendish gang went down that day."

"A soldier and a Texas Ranger were killed in the fight. Cavendish, his son, and three others, now two others, escaped, though."

The soldier nodded grimly.

"Mitch!" came a cry from the gate. "Bring him in. Captain Lawrence will see him."

The two soldiers led the Ranger to a one-story building constructed against the rear wall of the fort. Mitch knocked on a door, and the Ranger entered a sparsely decorated office. An American flag as well as a photo of President Grant adorned a wall. The soldier behind the desk, Captain Lawrence, stood and gestured to a wooden chair.

"If you're really who you say you are, I'm mighty glad to see you." He walked to the window facing onto the grounds. "I see your white horse, like the article says. Let me see one of your bullets."

The Ranger handed one over.

“Looks like you’re the real thing. I’d ask about the mask, but I suppose you have a good reason for wearing one.”

“A very good reason, Captain.”

“Do you have any more news about the Cavendish gang? We’d love to wrap them up. They’ve killed quite a few soldiers.”

“And Texas Rangers.”

“True.”

“We’ve been looking for them but haven’t had any luck since we delivered Razor Gilliam over to the law.”

“We? Oh, yes. Your Indian partner. Is he here with you?”

“No, he’s on a mission to one of the Indian tribes near Parkerburg. That’s why I’m here to talk to you.”

“Start talking.”

Ten minutes later, the captain rose and paced behind his desk.

“Sounds pretty bad,” he said. “And you think someone’s behind these two disappearances?”

“I do. Do you know a fellow named Randy Catanga? He’s the foreman on Clive Abramson’s spread.”

“Funny you should mention him. You’re the second person this week who’s brought him up to me.”

“Who was the other?”

"A banker from the east, name of Arthur Kennedy. The stage to Hollansburg always stops here for fifteen minutes, and he was a passenger on it a few days ago. Seems Abramson's having trouble paying off a loan from his bank, a Boston bank. Said he'd seen this Catanga fellow heavily engaged at the faro table when he stopped in Parkerburg. Banker wondered whether the gambling fever went deeper than the foreman, and he's worried about getting the bank's money back and whether to approve another loan to finance their cattle drive this year. So he said. What makes you ask about Catanga?"

The Ranger explained about the discrepancies he and Tonto noted.

"Makes you wonder, doesn't it?" the captain said softly. "Let me send Lieutenant Calender and a detachment to Parkerburg tomorrow morning to see what's up. You're welcome to stay the night in the fort and have a meal."

"No, Silver will get me back where I need to be before dark. I want to hear what Tonto has to say after meeting with Chief Gray Wolf." The Ranger got to his feet, and the two men shook hands.

"Mind if I keep this?" the captain asked, displaying the bullet he still held.

"It's yours."

"Thanks for the warning."

"I hope the soldiers aren't needed."

"You and me both. Oh, before you go. One of

Cavendish's men—we don't have any pictures or photographs of them, but the one with the teeth—"

"Shark Lawson."

"Yes, someone fitting his description was involved in a shootout in Frederick, a small town about fifty miles from here. Settler passing through read the description of the man—we have it posted outside—and he claimed the survivor of the shootout matches up. The man called himself Billy Grayson, though, not Shark Lawson. I can't spare any men to send on a wild goose chase fifty miles off, but if you think it's worth looking into, be my guest."

"It's not surprising he'd change his name. When was this?"

"About a week ago."

"Thanks for the information, Captain. I'll be going."

"Godspeed, masked man."

*

Tonto had a fire going when the Ranger walked between the rocks, leading Silver to their campsite as twilight fell.

"You back, Kemo Sabe. Good. You see soldier captain?"

"I did. Did you see Gray Wolf?"

"Me see. Him angry."

"Go on. You first."

"Two chiefs meet. Boys not found."

"Did the chiefs accuse one another?"

"Them not do that but still angry. Them have trouble together before. Supplies sent by Fort Davis not shared fair Brave Eagle say. If boys not found, me think trouble come."

"Captain Lawrence is sending some soldiers here tomorrow to investigate."

"Me tell Gray Wolf about you. Him talk to you."

"You told him about my mask."

"Me tell."

"Good. We'll visit him again first thing tomorrow before the soldiers arrive."

"What we do when soldiers come?"

"I'm pretty sure the captain will have ordered them to speak with Abramson. If he didn't, we'll suggest it and tell them to make sure the foreman, Catanga, is included in the discussion. Afterward, we'll watch and see how Abramson and Catanga react."

At first light next day after a quick breakfast, the Ranger and Tonto set out for Gray Wolf's village.

Chief Gray Wolf, fifty years old, his face creased from many years of leadership and, most recently, having to address problems stemming from the uprooting and relocation of his tribe, stoically greeted them adorned in a regal headdress, the many feathers symbols of his bravery in battle. He indicated they should sit on the ground outside his large tepee. Four muscular, young braves stood alongside the chief, who majestically lowered himself to the ground.

"Tonto say Indians can trust you," the chief stated.

"He's right, Gray Wolf. I want to help you find your son as well as the boy from Brave Eagle's tribe. Let me assure you, I don't believe your people or his had anything to do with the boys' disappearance."

"I know my people not take boys."

"A small group of soldiers will arrive later today. They come in peace. They want to help find your son."

The chief said nothing.

"Chief," the Ranger went on, "can you tell me where your son went to play the day he disappeared? You must have spoken to the other boys when they returned."

"They play game of hiding. No one know when he disappear. They play near spring behind second hill." He gestured to his right.

"And your people have searched, no doubt."

"We search. Boy not there."

"Do you know where the other boy disappeared?"

"Chief Brave Eagle say boy walk off alone. Never come back."

"Tonto tells me you found a coup stick from Brave Eagle's tribe," the Ranger pointed out.

The chief's mouth set in a hard line. The Ranger waited.

"Me show Brave Eagle coup stick. He say his tribe never make such stick. I know son and friends not have such stick."

"I think Brave Eagle is telling the truth, Gray Wolf."

"Me not know."

"Do you mind if Tonto and I ride to where your boy was playing and take a look."

The chief dipped his head once in acquiescence.

The Ranger and Tonto rose and mounted their horses, the Ranger, deep in thought, leading the way.

"We look for place where man get much dirt on clothes?" Tonto asked.

"Exactly. Then I want to return and meet the soldiers from Fort Davis along the road."

They reached the spring which flowed through a long, shallow gully with a barren, muddy rim, surrounded by high grass.

"Let Silver and Scout drink and eat for a while," the Ranger said. "We'll take a walk." The two men released their horses and set out. Many small moccasin tracks pocked the bare earth along the perimeter of the spring, testimony to how frequently the Indian children came this way.

"Maybe we look over there where not so much grass," Tonto suggested.

They walked to a spot where they found water oozing from the ground.

"The spring must come from some underground source," the Ranger said. "Mud is everywhere."

"Man hide here get clothes plenty dirty," Tonto said.

"He would. Look there… a spread of trees thick enough to hide Catanga's horse. Let's see what we find in there."

The men entered the small stand of trees, heads down, scouring the ground as they separated and searched.

"Kemo Sabe!" Tonto called after a few minutes.

"Did you find something?" the Ranger asked, quickly joining his friend.

Tonto pointed down. "Horse with shoe stand there."

"I see. Not an Indian's horse. And the grass around the tree has been eaten down."

The eyes of the two men met.

"Catanga could have left his horse here and hid over there to watch the children play," the Ranger said.

"Then when one boy go off by self, he take him."

"It looks like it could have happened that way."

"We go find soldiers now?"

"Yes. I don't want them to pass by without speaking to them. They need to know what we know."

When they reached the road the soldiers would travel on from Fort Davis, Tonto said, "Kemo Sabe, many horse ride here not long ago."

"It must be the detachment from the fort. Let's get after them before they reach the Lazy A. Go, Silver!"

"Get'um up, Scout!"

A ten-minute gallop down the road brought the soldiers in sight. The half-dozen soldiers stopped when they heard the beat of horses' hooves behind them.

"At ease, men," the leader of the soldiers said as he moved from the front to the rear of the troop to face the approaching riders.

The Lone Ranger and Tonto reined up.

"You must be Lieutenant Calender," the Ranger said.

"I am. There's only one person you can be. Captain Lawrence told me about you."

"I wanted to speak with you before you started your investigation."

The lieutenant addressed the soldiers with him. "Dismount and take a few minutes for yourself. Let's dismount, too, masked man. I've been in the saddle since dawn."

The lieutenant, the Lone Ranger, and Tonto huddled on the side of the road.

"The captain filled me in on what you told him on your visit yesterday," the lieutenant said.

"There's more," the Ranger said, and he reported on his and Tonto's visit to Chief Gray Wolf.

"You may be right," the lieutenant agreed when the Ranger finished his story. "This isn't trouble being stirred up *by* the Indians. It's trouble directed *at* the Indians."

"Something they surely don't need," the Ranger added. "I'm sure those two boys are alive somewhere. I'd like to suggest something."

"Be my guest."

"The Lazy A Ranch is about a mile ahead. Visit the Lazy A and question Clive Abramson. Insist that his foreman, Randy Catanga, be present. If they're responsible for the missing boys, they surely have a reason. Perhaps something to do with a loan Abramson's having trouble getting from a bank in Boston. The loan depends on their being able to get their cattle to market. Tell them you're going to send a soldier back to Fort Davis and request twenty-five additional men to conduct a thorough search of the area for the two boys."

"What happens when the additional soldiers don't show up?"

"They won't have to. Tonto and I will be nearby and watch for their reaction once you leave. If they *have* hidden the children, they won't want soldiers scouring the countryside. That's my hope, anyway. You'll be visiting Chief Gray Wolf and Chief Brave Eagle?"

"Of course."

"I hope you can keep them calm."

"I'll do my best."

"Tonto tells me the two chiefs met but parted in anger."

"Let's hope we find the boys before something bad breaks out… Who's this?"

A lone figure rode toward them.

"It's the Lazy A foreman I mentioned, Randy Catanga," the Ranger said.

Randy pulled up, surprise obvious on his face. "Masked man," he said, then studied the lieutenant's uniform. "Are you from Fort Davis? You must be. I'm on my way there now."

"Maybe I can save you the trip," the lieutenant said.

"There's trouble in the Indian encampments," Randy explained. "Mr. Abramson sent me with this letter to explain the situation."

"We've been informed," the lieutenant said. "The masked man rode to the fort yesterday."

Randy cast a look of uncertainty at the Ranger.

"As a matter of fact," the lieutenant said, "we were just on our way to the Lazy A to talk to Mr. Abramson and you. I'll take your letter. Why don't you lead the way? Masked man, Tonto, thanks for your help. We'll take it from here."

"Good luck, Lieutenant," the Ranger said. "Let's go back to camp, Tonto," and they rode away. When the soldiers were out of sight, they drew to a halt.

"What we do now, Kemo Sabe?" Tonto asked.

"We find somewhere we can keep an eye on the Lazy A ranch house. It might be a long wait. They might not do anything until dark, if they do anything at all."

"That not problem. There two of us."

"Yes, we'll at least get some rest. Let's see if we can find a suitable spot."

When the Ranger and Tonto settled into a slight depression in the landscape where the horses would be cloaked, they ground hitched Silver and Scout and moved forward to the rim of the hollow.

"Soldiers still there," Tonto said.

"Let's hope Lieutenant Calender frightens them enough to make them react."

The two men settled down and waited.

*

Lieutenant Calender, along with a second soldier, sat in the Abramsons' living room along with Clive, his wife, and Randy Catanga.

"When do you think those additional soldiers will get here?" Clive asked.

"I'll send Private Saxon here back to the fort this afternoon. Soldiers should get here by tomorrow afternoon the latest. We'll find those boys if they're to be found. We have to. If an Indian war breaks out, we won't be able to guarantee your safety unless you want to relocate to Fort Davis."

"I certainly hope it doesn't get that serious," Clive said. "My cattle. What would happen to my cattle? I *must* get them to Dodge. Unless you do something about those Indians, I'll never be able to move them. Why can't they do their fighting somewhere else?"

The lieutenant fixed his gaze on Abramson.

Mrs. Abramson spoke up. "Clive, this is terrible. Those poor boys must be frightened to death. Can't you get some of your hands to help search?"

"Of course, Mabel, but perhaps the lieutenant would prefer we stay out of his way."

"Oh, he can't think that." She looked Calender's way.

"Any help we can get finding those boys, we'll happily take. The alternative is unthinkable. There will be bloodshed, and I'm afraid it won't only be Indian blood that's spilled."

"Clive, the encampments are so near us." Mabel laced her fingers together tightly in her lap.

"Randy will see that the lieutenant gets all the help

we can give," Clive promised.

Calender rose.

"We're going now to visit the two chiefs." He and Private Saxon bid farewell and returned to the soldiers waiting outside.

Clive, Randy, and Mabel followed them onto the porch and watched them go.

"This is terrible," Mable said softly as she put her hand on her husband's shoulder.

"Don't worry, honey."

Mable went inside and her husband and Randy walked toward the barn.

"What do we do now, Boss?" Randy asked.

"I don't know why I listened to you in the first place. This is spinning out of control."

"Don't start with that. You need to get the cattle through Indian land, and this will get it done."

"Maybe; if we both don't lose our scalps because of it. You gotta get those kids farther way from here. They might be found in the cabins if twenty-five soldiers are on the loose looking for them."

"I'll move them tonight. As soon as it's dark. These soldiers should be camped by then and not out roaming around, and the soldiers from the fort won't even have left yet."

"It's a hard trip to the cabins in the dark."

"No other time it can be done. I'll make it, all right."

"Okay. Move them tonight. Tomorrow, you organize some hands for a search and lead them anywhere but where you took the boys. We have to look like we're cooperating."

"Don't worry."

"Not much, I won't."

They separated and Clive returned to the house.

Chapter 12

Randy Catanga

Clive sat across from his wife at the table, their dinners steaming in front of them.

“Excellent stew,” he said, smiling in hopes of keeping his wife in the dark about the jagged nerves sending flashes of fear, dread, and morbid anticipation through him. “My favorite.”

“Do you want to invite Randy in for some when we finish? Is he gathering some of your hands to help search for the Indian boys?”

“He told me he’d go to the bunkhouse and explain what needs to be done. Let’s you and me have a quiet night and let them be.”

“Are you going with them, honey?”

“No. I don’t want to leave you alone with those Indians beating drums and being so unsettled. I’m sure when the additional troops get here, they’ll handle all of this. Now, let’s enjoy our dinner and no more talk of Indians.”

*

Randy settled onto a stack of hay in the barn to await darkness. He pictured a valley he knew of some five miles off, well away from the Indian encampments. It would be the perfect place to take those two accursed

Indian kids. He'd chosen two horses, smaller mounts, to bring along with him. He couldn't very well walk the kids five miles in the dead of night, nor could he ride triple with them, especially the bigger one who'd displayed a temper… and a knife. Suddenly, he sat upright. The Indian drums were starting up again. Their constant thumping along with his own impatient need to wait until dark soon had him pacing the barn. He planned to wait until one hour after full darkness fell before setting out. He'd made himself another mask and dressed in his oldest, rattiest clothing, which he'd burn the first moment he could after he got back. If either of the kids tried something, he wouldn't try it for long. He'd already loaded his saddlebags with water and food. When he reached the distant valley, he counted on finding a deserted hunter's shack, any kind of hovel would do, even a cave—where he could leave the two kids and hope the turmoil would ultimately force the displacement of the Indians so Abramson's cattle drive could proceed along the shortest, most profitable route. He expected Abramson to offer him a handsome bonus, cash he badly needed, for having enabled this success. Paying off his faro debt would give him a new start and, he hoped, a change of luck. He continued to pace, nervously awaiting the night, the ominous Indian drums pounding in the distance.

Not far off in a small clump of trees, both the Lone Ranger and Tonto snapped to attention.

"War drums, Kemo Sabe," the Ranger said.

"Come from direction of Brave Eagle tribe."

“I wonder what happened to set them off.”

“Me think drums give warning to Gray Wolf. Soon Gray Wolf answer back.”

“Fighting could break out tomorrow then.”

“If drums come again in morning, there be big trouble.”

Silently, the Ranger and Tonto ate a cold dinner. About two hours later, the Ranger touched Tonto’s arm. He said, “I see light.”

“It come from barn.”

Both men stood and stepped out where, shielded by darkness, they could get a better view.

“Many shadows move,” Tonto said.

The men waited for a clearer perspective. The road lay forty yards from the edge of the trees where they hid, the barn well beyond that. Minutes later a rider passed, leading two rider-less horses.

“Two children; two horses,” the Ranger said. “He’s going to them. We must have those children back to their tribes by morning. Lieutenant Calender knows what those drums mean as well as we do. He’ll send back to the fort for reinforcements at first light.”

“There plenty of moonlight, Kemo Sabe,” Tonto pointed out. “We not lose trail.”

“The moonlight also means we’ll have to give him plenty of room. This may be our only chance, and we don’t want to spook him.”

They allowed Catanga a five-minute start before setting out after their prey.

*

Over an hour later, angry at himself for taking a wrong turn at a cluster of rocks he mistook for a different landmark, Randy came in sight of the two rundown shacks where he'd hidden the children. The landscape appeared serene and brightly lit. He rode up to the shack housing the younger of the two boys and dismounted. He donned his mask, lit a torch he'd brought along, unlocked the door, and entered. The boy lay in one corner and opened his eyes sleepily.

"Don't make a move. Stay still." Randy planted the torch in the dirt of the cabin floor, tied the boy's hands behind him, and pulled him to his feet by the scruff of the neck. Marching him outside, he boosted the boy onto the smaller of the two horses and secured his ankles by means of a stout rope running beneath the horse. He tied the horse's reins to his own horse to keep the boy from bolting.

He opened the door of the second cabin with a higher level of trepidation. The older boy, awake, squatted in a corner. Randy studied the boy's hands in the light from his flickering torch. Empty. He gestured for the boy to lie on his stomach, and the boy complied. After planting the torch in the floor, he knelt beside the boy. When he grabbed the boy's right wrist to bring it behind his back, a fistful of dirt flew into Randy's face. He wiped frantically at his eyes, inadvertently twisting his mask out of alignment. When he felt the boy getting to his feet, he lifted the mask off his head and, blinking madly to clear his vision, dove at the boy's ankles as the boy rushed for the cabin door. The boy fell, and Randy knelt on the small of the boy's back and delivered a lusty smack alongside the ear. He cleared his vision, grabbed his mask, shook the dirt out of it, and pulled it over his head. Then he wrenched the boy's hands behind him, causing the boy to screech in pain. He circled the thin wrists with a length of rope pulled from his belt and yanked the knots brutally tight before dragging the boy outside.

"Up, you stinking redskin." Randy got the young Indian mounted and bound the boy's ankles under the horse. "You'll be lucky if I don't push you off a cliff along the way." He got astride his own horse and, holding the reins of the Indians' horses, led the way, seething with anger.

*

"This must be where Catanga hid the children," the Ranger said, dismounting and rushing to inspect the two empty shacks. He called back, "Yes, I see discarded food and water buckets."

"Three horses go up this way, Kemo Sabe."

"They can't be far ahead. He has the children with him now. It's time to bring him in."

The Ranger remounted and he and Tonto rode briskly along the only pathway leading from the shacks.

"Where you think him go?" Tonto asked.

"Somewhere he thinks the soldiers would never look for the children."

Twenty minutes later, Tonto leapt down from Scout and knelt to study the ground. They'd come to a spot where a change of direction was possible. Tonto rose and faced the Ranger.

"What is it, Tonto?"

"Them start this way but come back and go other way. Me see tracks on top of tracks."

Suddenly, a shot, then another, rang out.

The Ranger, hearing the whistle of a bullet not far from him, jumped to the ground, drew his gun, and sent six silver bullets in the direction the sound of the shot came from. He and Tonto swatted their horses and sent them off to safety before hustling for what cover they could find.

"I shot high, Kemo Sabe," the Ranger explained. "He might be using the children as cover. He'll make a stand here. He knows he can't elude us now with two children in tow."

"Maybe him let them go and get away himself."

"I'd settle for that," the Ranger said softly. "But even if he escaped, it would end his life in this part of the country. No, I don't think he's willing to go that far. We may have to wait for daylight to do anything. Do you hear that?"

The sound of horses galloping in the distance reached them.

"Him try get away, Kemo Sabe!" Tonto said.

"Wait. Listen. I don't hear the horses any longer."

"Them not run far."

"Even in this moonlight, no one would gallop at breakneck speed down a dark road, especially tending to two captives. He's trying to lure us into the open. There's enough moonlight for what he wants to do."

*

Randy first noticed the two men trailing him when he looked back to check on his captives and caught their silhouettes in the moonlight. His heart nearly burst when he realized how close they were to him—not close enough to identify, but clearly, they weren't soldiers. It had to be the masked man and the Indian. Now, everything depended on his getting rid of them.

After quickly running through his limited options, he decided to make a stand where he was. Dismounting, he found a suitable sniper's nest and settled into it. Then, leveling his rifle, he waited for his pursuers to come within range. Before he could squeeze the trigger as the first figure appeared, the older Indian boy kicked at his horse, and the movement distracted Randy and sent his first shot wildly off target. He quickly reloaded and fired again but realized he hadn't hit anything. He yanked the two boys from their horses and gave the larger boy a second clout on the side of the head, this time with his rifle butt. A bloody gash opened where the metal of the butt scraped along his scalp. The younger boy stared wide-eyed at the spectacle but remained quiet as Randy pushed them between two nearby boulders and tied their legs together.

"You see what happens if you act up," Randy said. He didn't know whether either boy understood a thing he uttered, since neither boy had said a single word to him the whole time he'd been with them, but he felt better barking at them. A sudden inspiration suggested a possible way out. He set the boys' horses running through the night, hoping the masked man would think he and the boys were escaping. He tilted his head toward where he thought his pursuers were, hoping to hear them mount up and see them ride out after him. They would be inviting targets if they did, but he heard nothing. The Indian boys lay motionless where he'd tied them together, so he moved to a bare space of ground which had trees to the rear and a sprinkling of boulders in a semi-circle around him. He knew he'd get no sleep tonight. The Ranger and the Indian could creep up on him from any direction. Let them try, he told himself.

*

The night passed with excruciating slowness. As the moonlight waned and dawn crept forward, neither the Lone Ranger nor Tonto thought of taking a break and letting the other do the night's work. They knew the Indian drums might recommence with the new day, and the reinforcements from Fort Davis would be on the move at daybreak. If they didn't get the children back before those two realities met, a bloody battle might be the result.

The first glint of the fresh day's sun brought with it confirmation of Randy's location.

"There horses," Tonto said. "Me see near trees."

"I see them. Stay low, Kemo Sabe. I'm going to try and reason with him. You know what to do."

Tonto lay on his stomach behind a hillock whose elevation barely shielded him. The Ranger slid a few yards to his left to the steeper slope of a grassy knoll. He looked toward Tonto and nodded.

"Catanga!" he called.

A rifle bullet sailed over his head.

"It's no good, Catanga. I'll make a deal with you. Give me the two boys and go your way. I doubt you'll manage to stay free for long, but it's your only chance. Tonto is already on his way back toward the fort. Soldiers will be here later today. All I need to do is keep you in place. You can't think they'll be eager to reason with you. It's your fault the Indians are beating war drums. I know you heard them before you left the ranch last night." The Ranger gestured to Tonto, who began to move.

Three vain shots sent bullets above the Ranger's position as Catanga desperately searched for an escape plan. He could leave the children behind, but what good would it do? By the time he reached his horse, the masked man would have sent any number of bullets into him. Besides, where could he go? And it certainly made no sense to sit and wait for a troop of cavalry to show up. If the masked man was alone out there, his best chance of escape would be to deal with him now, one on one.

"Here's my offer," Catanga called. "You mount up and ride away, or I shoot the boys, then come after you."

"You'd be signing your death warrant if you did that, Catanga."

"I don't think so. Once I plug you, I ride out of here. You decide if their lives are worth what you're doing."

"Even if you succeed, you might ride out but not back toward Abramson's ranch. Tonto will identify you to the soldiers, who already suspect you. You'd have killed a chief's son. When the soldiers catch up with you, they might simply turn you over to Gray Wolf for tribal justice."

The Ranger's prediction brought sweat to Randy's brow and terror to his heart.

"I'm leaving," Randy called, "and I'm taking the kids with me. You shoot and you might hit them." He stood, cut the ropes on the boys' legs, and pulled them to their feet. Walking backward he dragged them toward their three horses. When he reached the horses, he gathered the reins and led them out of sight behind the rocks.

The Lone Ranger moved forward, gun ready, when

he heard a voice he recognized as Tonto's shout words he did not understand. Then came shots. Suddenly, from around the rocks ran Catanga, his left arm pressed tightly to his side.

"Stop!" the Ranger cried.

Catanga faced him and went for his gun.

The Ranger fired and a silver bullet sent Randy's gun sailing into the air as if by magic. Randy stood as if hypnotized, staring at his empty hand. Then he tried to shake away the sting of the Ranger's bullet.

"Kemo Sabe," came Tonto's voice. "Indian boys safe."

"Go," the Ranger said to Catanga, gesturing with his gun toward Tonto and the children.

"I'm shot," Randy said meekly. "The Indian shot me."

"Go!"

They circled the rocks and came upon Tonto cutting the two boys free.

"One boy have bloody head. Not serious. Me fix quick," Tonto said.

The Ranger took the ropes Tonto had unwound from the boys. "On your stomach, Catanga," he ordered.

Randy obeyed and the Ranger tied his wrists behind his back and bound his ankles.

"What was that you called out, Kemo Sabe?" the

Ranger asked.

"Heh, heh. Me tell boys fall on ground. Them do and me shoot."

"How is the young boy?"

Tonto spoke to the boy for a moment.

"He say him good. Want go home."

"Tell him that's exactly where he's going, Kemo Sabe. I'm going to take… what's his name?"

Tonto and the boy spoke.

"Him Little Wolf."

"Tell Little Wolf I'm going to take him back to his father as fast as we can go. We must stop this battle. You stay here with Catanga and the bigger boy. I need to travel fast. Do what you can for their wounds. I'll be back as soon as possible."

Tonto explained to the boys.

"This boy name Running Buffalo. Say him not scared."

"Tell him he will be a great brave one day. He's one right now."

The Ranger took Little Wolf by the hand and, carrying a length of rope, went to find Silver.

Chapter 13

Peace

The Ranger lifted Little Wolf into the saddle and climbed up behind him. He wrapped the rope securely around their mid-sections, looping the pommel as well.

The boy looked back and said, "I like big white horse."

"Oh, you do speak some English. Well, then, hold on tight." He kicked the white stallion gently in its flanks and cried, "Hi-yo, Silver. Away!"

Silver seemed to sense the urgency of the mission and raced ahead. The boy flew back against the Ranger's chest. The Ranger made much better time in daylight than he and Tonto had made the night before, and Silver ran tirelessly, his mane sailing out behind him.

They passed the two deserted shacks and soon reached the main road. A few miles along the road, the Ranger pulled Silver to a halt to be certain of what he heard.

"The drums again," he said.

"War drums," Little Wolf said, craning his neck to look back at the Ranger.

"We *must* hurry. Go on, Silver. Go, big fellow."

Soon it became clear two sets of drums beat out tattoos of war, one seemingly answering the other, matching threat for threat, anger with anger.

"Faster, Silver, faster!" the Ranger cried, holding tightly to Little Wolf. Around a slight curve in the road, two dozen soldiers came in view. The Ranger slowed enough to safely pass by them and rein to a halt.

"Lieutenant Calender! I'm glad to see you," the Ranger cried. "This is one of the missing boys, Gray Wolf's son, Little Wolf. We've also recovered Running Buffalo, the lost child from Brave Eagle's tribe. I must get this boy to Gray Wolf before the Indians go to war against one another and against you for trying to stop them."

"Ride on, then," the lieutenant said. "We'll follow as quickly as we can."

Silver danced uneasily, agitated by the moment. The Ranger pulled the reins tightly, setting direction for the mighty horse.

"Go, Silver!"

"My lord," Lieutenant Calender muttered. "Look at that horse run. Forward, men, double time."

The scene at the Indian encampment, far different from his previous visit, sent a chill through the Ranger. Braves in battle attire, faces streaked with color, danced madly about an enormous bonfire, their singsong voices lifted to the sky in passion, drums thumping relentlessly, goading them further into war fever. The Ranger recognized Gray Wolf's tepee and walked Silver forward. There sat Gray Wolf, sternly looking on at the manic war preparation playing out before him. The Ranger loosened the ropes around Little Wolf, and they dismounted.

Without warning, the drums stopped. Like a strange, paralyzing wave sweeping slowly over them, the Indians halted their fearsome dance of war.

Gray Wolf turned his head to follow the gazes of the braves and squaws who noticed the Ranger's arrival.

Gray Wolf rose to his feet, and Little Wolf broke away from the Lone Ranger and ran to his father. They locked in an embrace. The Ranger came near, and Gray Wolf put his son to the side.

"You have brought my son back to me."

"He is safe, Gray Wolf. So is the boy taken from Brave Eagle's tribe. Have your drums say so. Do not let there be war between you and Brave Eagle."

"The drums will beat your message."

"I will return to Running Buffalo and deliver him to Brave Eagle's tribe. Let their chief know. Tonto and I will deliver the white man responsible for this trouble to the soldiers for justice."

Gray Wolf gave a curt nod, and the Ranger rode away. He met the approaching soldiers, now only a few moments away.

"Lieutenant, go to Brave Eagle's tribe," the Ranger advised. "Gray Wolf has stopped his war drums. Say you've seen the return of Gray Wolf's son. Tell Brave Eagle the boy from his tribe will be returned to them in a few hours. I'm on my way to get him now, and I'll have the man responsible for this trouble when I return. I'll turn him over to you. For now, go to Brave Eagle's tribe and keep the peace."

*

None of Clive Abramson's ranch hands had gone in search of the two missing Indian boys. They were positioned, instead, before his house behind wagons which they'd overturned to provide a makeshift, miniature palisade. Boxes of ammunition lay next to each man, armed with a six-gun and a rifle.

Mabel Abramson clung to her husband's arm as they stood on the porch, while he oversaw preparations. Clive presumed Randy had those two Indian boys miles away by then. The soldiers would *have* to clear out the war-mongering Indians blocking his way, and soon, he could get his cattle drive organized and head his livestock off to Dodge City.

"Don't worry, Mabel. The soldiers will be here before any trouble starts, and you see how we're protected."

"I've read about Indian attacks, Indians on the warpath," she said, her face a welter of concern. "I'm so frightened, Clive."

"Go inside. You'll be safe."

Mabel looked up at her husband and, more in frustration than relief, obeyed. It puzzled Clive when one set of Indian drums ceased to beat. When the second set ceased also, he feared an attack was imminent. Randy had certainly stirred up a hornet's nest with his scheme, but if things turned out as they hoped, it would have been worth it. Moments later a brief burst of drumming unnerved him even more.

The morning passed into afternoon. Clive walked among his men, telling them to stay alert for the appearance of any hostiles, but rather than Indians appearing along the road, a troop of cavalry approached. The soldiers spread out along the road fronting his property and dismounted. A man he recognized as Lieutenant Calender rode up to his gate.

"Abramson!" the lieutenant called. "I'm ordering you to disarm your men. The two Indian boys who were missing have been found and returned to their tribes."

The hairs on the back of Clive's neck rose.

"Tell them to leave their weapons where they are and return to the bunk house," Calender continued. "There will be no Indian war today. Do it now."

Many men behind the wagons looked back at their boss.

What could he do? Clive asked himself, panic rising as the seconds passed.

"Men!" he cried. "Leave your guns and head back to the bunk house like the lieutenant says."

After the men dispersed, Clive saw the masked man, Indian, and his foreman ride up and join Lieutenant Calender at his gate. He turned and went into the house.

"Here is one of the two men you want. They're responsible for stirring up this trouble," the Ranger said.

"Two?"

"The other just went into his house."

"Abramson was in on it, too, eh? I don't guess I'm surprised."

"Kemo Sabe," Tonto cried. "There!" Abramson had found a horse and was sprinting away across the grassland behind the house.

"I'll get him, Lieutenant," the Ranger said. "Wait here. Get up, Silver. Go, big fellow."

The Ranger bent low in the saddle as Silver closed the distance quickly. Abramson, looking back, fumbled for the pistol at his waist, and the Ranger drew his own gun. When Abramson's weapon dropped clumsily to the ground, the Ranger holstered his. Silver neared the fleeing man, and the Ranger guided him alongside.

"Pull up, Abramson!" the Ranger shouted, but the man simply kicked maniacally at his horse's sides.

The Ranger gathered himself and flew out of his saddle, tackling Abramson and driving him off his horse onto the ground. A moan escaped from Abramson as the Ranger scuffled to his feet and drew his gun.

Abramson crawled onto his knees and rose slowly. "You won't shoot me," he said and dashed away into the knee-high grass.

The Ranger smiled wanly and deposited his gun back into his holster. He ran after Abramson, caught him quickly, spun him around, and leveled a crashing blow with his gloved right fist to the man's jaw. Abramson crumbled like a liberated marionette. The Ranger retrieved the man's horse and hoisted him onto his stomach across the saddle, tying his wrists to his ankles beneath the horse. He whistled for Silver, mounted the white stallion, and led Clive Abramson back to his ranch, his dignity and freedom left behind in the waving grass of the Lazy A.

Lieutenant Calender set Abramson to rights once he regained consciousness and, with him and Randy Catanga surrounded by soldiers, prepared to start back to Fort Davis.

"Masked man," the lieutenant said, "thanks for what you've done. You saved a lot of bloodshed today, for sure."

"Good-bye, Lieutenant," the Ranger replied.

"What we do now, Kemo Sabe?" Tonto asked.

"I told you what the captain said about a man resembling Shark Lawson. The town of Frederick is a two-day ride from here."

"We go there now?"

"Yes. If it really was Lawson, we might be able to pick up his trail."

"Maybe him still there."

"That would surely be a great piece of good luck, Kemo Sabe."

"Lady on porch."

Mabel Abramson sat on the porch, her hands to her

face. A young cowhand stood next to her, his hand on her shoulder. The Ranger nodded to Tonto, and they mounted and rode slowly up to the house.

"I regret how things worked out, Mrs. Abramson," the Ranger said softly. "I'm sure your husband isn't the man this makes him seem."

"Oh, it was Randy," she moaned. "I know it was Randy who led him into this. What am I going to do now?"

The cowhand spoke up. "Don't worry, ma'am. We'll get your cattle to the railhead. Charley and I will run things for you, if you approve. You have good men working for you at the Lazy A." He glanced at the Ranger. "We'll be sure she's taken care of, mister."

"I hope so. I wish you good fortune, Mrs. Abramson. Let's ride, Kemo Sabe." The white horse and the paint, side by side, set out in the direction of the small town of Frederick, Texas.

"That man," Mrs. Abramson said, "who is he, Harry?"

"I heard the soldiers refer to him as the Lone Ranger, ma'am. That's all I can tell you."

"The Lone Ranger. Oh, if only he'd shown up earlier and kept my Clive from…"

"Don't cry, Mrs. Abramson. He's returned peace to the area. We'll get your work done for you."

They kept their eyes on the departing men until they were lost around a bend in the road.

Chapter 14

Shark Lawson

Two very happy people climbed down from the stagecoach when it stopped in Frederick, Texas, a small town like any other frontier town. One and two-story buildings lined the main street, the central hub composed of the stores and entertainment spots essential for those who chose to live in the wide-open spaces of the largest state in the union. Belinda Hathaway and Reggie Burbage had married four months earlier in Boston and spent their honeymoon on the Union Pacific, heading west. They continued their honeymoon in a wagon train heading across the dusty trails and grassy plains to Texas and, finally boarded a stagecoach to Frederick. Their happiness stemmed from several things beside their lifelong commitment to one another. She, an actress, and he, a director, had scored a great triumph in Philadelphia with his production of *Macbeth.* Her portrayal of Lady Macbeth had received wide praise in the City of Brotherly Love before the production moved to New York and then on to Boston, where the plaudits continued. Belinda and Burbage had known one another by reputation only before the play, but after one audition reading, Burbage knew he'd found his leading lady. After the six-week run in Philadelphia and the two-month run in New York, they headed to Boston, where Burbage proposed, and Belinda accepted. When the Boston run ended, they married and came West.

Burbage, a writer along with being a director, had a

great play inside him, he told his new bride. She happily professed her belief in him. He vowed to work on the play as they traveled to San Francisco, where they would open their production at the Metropolitan Theatre and make their name and fortune. At least, that was his plan. She would again be his leading lady, and he would tailor her part specifically to her strengths. When he had the first three scenes written, he let Belinda read them. They entranced her, and she promised to help him in any way possible to allow him to finish his work and get them to San Francisco.

Their savings took them as far as Frederick, Texas, where they rented a small room atop the sundries and gun repair store. Burbage worked on his play, and Belinda, gifted with a lovely singing voice along with her acting talent, took a job she didn't much like—saloon girl in the Alhambra. Her singing, however, allowed her to remain a cut above the common run of saloon girls, who hustled to have men buy them watered down drinks at elevated prices—on commission. Farley Harigold, the owner of the Alhambra, expected Belinda to participate in drumming up business, but he allowed her to keep that part of her responsibilities to a minimum. Harigold knew when he had a good thing and slipped her an extra twelve dollars a week for her singing, which, on its own, he knew, drummed up plenty of business. She and Burbage calculated that three months of work in Frederick, her in the saloon, him working on their play every morning, would put them in good shape to continue their journey to San Francisco and their ultimate goal: to get Burbage's new play into production.

Belinda had been working six nights a week for two weeks when Billy Grayson showed up at the bar for the first time. She noticed him right away as she sang "The Alabama Blossoms" to a rapt audience of farmers, ranchers, miners, and other assorted males. He was hard to miss. When he smiled at her from the bar, right off she noticed his teeth, oddly large with a pronounced gap in the upper middle. The teeth were so large, in fact, that Grayson's mouth could never really close up tight, and no matter what kind of look he had on his face, his teeth played a prominent role. Belinda knew she had gazed at the man too long, but the bizarre spectacle of him was hard to turn away from. Once she managed to glance away, though, she made certain not to look back.

When she finished her set of songs, the final set of the night, Grayson walked over to introduce himself.

"My name's Billy Grayson," he said, without bothering to doff his Stetson. "What's yours?"

"I'm the singer here."

Grayson laughed. "I think I know that much. But you have a name, don't you? What is it?"

She glanced at the batwing doors to the saloon before answering. Reggie would be along any time now. He knew what her job entailed, but he wasn't crazy about her having to chat with strange men. She consoled him, though, with the understanding that three months would put an end to it, and they'd be on a string of trains and stagecoaches to the West Coast. He always worked through the morning and afternoon on his play, and when

Belinda left for work, he took a long nap so he could come and get her when the saloon began its closing ceremonies around one o'clock.

"Belinda."

"Pretty name. Belinda what?"

"Belinda Burbage. Oh, sorry, I have to go. My husband's here." She walked off.

Grayson spun slowly as she passed by him and took note of the man she kissed and then departed with so he would recognize him the next time he saw him.

Grayson didn't come in every night at first. The week after that, he came in twice. The following week, three times. From then on, Belinda lost count. He never failed to engage with her on his visits to the Alhambra, and for the sake of her job and knowing that in a matter of weeks she'd be gone, she spoke with him when she had to. By then, Burbage had seen Grayson enough times to know he expected Belinda's attention whenever he showed up, and it made him uneasy. Despite Belinda's trying to persuade her husband not to, he decided to speak to Sheriff Elmer Hosgood about it.

Hosgood, a thin man with twenty years of sheriff's experience behind him, stared at Burbage perplexed. He said, "You don't like his looks? What's that to me? Ain't your wife a saloon gal? Ain't it part of her job to talk to the men? What do you want me to do?"

"Why don't you ever show up in the Alhambra? You should stop by once in a while, at least, so the ruffians who show up there know about you."

"Ruffians. Heh. Don't you worry. They know about me plenty good enough."

Burbage argued on, but the sheriff said he had work to do, and if Burbage didn't like the work his wife did, she should get another job.

Burbage left the sheriff's office wishing she *could* get another job, but he knew she wouldn't get hired for the short space of time they planned to remain in Frederick, and even if she did, she'd never earn what she did at the Alhambra, and that would mean sticking around even longer in this hellhole of a town. He promised himself he'd never miss a night picking her up, and from then on, he'd show up even earlier to keep her safe.

Two nights later, Burbage nursed a beer as he stood at the bar listening to Belinda finish up for the night. Someone on his right jostled him. He turned and stared into the toothy face of Billy Grayson.

"How are you, husband?" Grayson asked smugly.

Reggie responded with a nod and turned back to watch his wife sing.

"Asked you a question," Grayson said.

"Look," Burbage said, tilting his head toward Grayson, "I don't know what you want, but I'd appreciate it if you'd direct your attentions elsewhere."

"*Ohhh.* You'd appreciate it, would you? Direct my attentions elsewhere, eh? You got yourself a pretty wife…"

Burbage moved to the far end of the bar. He gave

the audience a once-over, hoping to spot Sheriff Hosgood among the crowd, but he didn't see him. As soon as Belinda left the stage, Burbage took her by the arm and marched her out of the Alhambra, straight home. The next morning, he passed up working on his play and went out to buy a gun.

"Where did you get that?" Belinda asked when he returned home.

"Where do you think I got it?" he responded.

"*Why* did you get it?"

"I don't like the way that fellow, the one with the teeth, haunts you every night. I don't like the way he taunts me."

"And the gun will do what, exactly?"

"It may give him pause. Lots of men in Frederick carry one."

"Reggie, darling, I don't want you to wear that. You don't know anything about using it. You're from the East, remember, not Dodge City or Abilene."

"I'm thinking we might move on from here—right now, I mean."

"Move on where? We don't have enough money saved."

"Move on to another town—anywhere. This place gives me the creeps."

They discussed their future and decided to hold on for one more week and see how things went before making a final decision.

*

Shark Lawson rode a winding trail for days after the Cavendish gang had separated from one another looking for suitable refuge. When the trail got too tedious to endure, he simply stopped at the next small town he came to, which happened to be Frederick, Texas. He saw a deserted cabin on the edge of town and investigated. The unlocked door swung open to show a low, wooden bedstead in one corner with a thin, dusty mattress crumpled in a corner of the bed. A wooden table and two chairs were pushed against a wall. A wood stove, vented through the roof, allowed some cooking. Four windows let in the light. Lawson deemed it suitable for his purposes, but not wanting to call undue attention to himself by simply moving in unannounced, he asked around to see who owned it. A helpful citizen directed him to Bronson Alcott, the town's lawyer, who told him the widow March owned the cabin. Lawson met her and rented the place for two months. Money changed hands, and he moved in. He gave the name Billy Grayson to the lawyer and the widow March. Cavendish hadn't worked the area around Frederick, one reason Lawson traveled in this direction, but Lawson couldn't be certain his name wouldn't set off alarms and bring a horde of Texas Rangers down on the town. He'd lay low in Frederick, entertain himself as best he could, and pass the days.

Frederick had two night spots. The Golden Goose, which featured a bar and gambling tables, and the

Alhambra, which featured a bar and a singer. Lawson spent most of his time gambling in the Golden Goose and dropped into the Alhambra occasionally, but when a new singer showed up at the Alhambra, he began spending more of his time there. It turned out this new singer came from the East and had some sappy Eastern husband, whom Larson disliked at first sight. He found it enjoyable to make the thin, prissy, nose-in-the-air husband nervous. Besides, the wife was pretty to look at and pleasant to hear. He also found it enjoyable to make her squirm. He could have a lot of fun watching those two Easterners react to his every move. Even a hello on the street from him sent the little singer marching past him, her face a frozen mask of discomfort. If he passed the husband on the street, a cold stare sent beads of sweat down the man's back, or so Lawson laughingly imagined. Gambling, drinking, playing with these two babes in the woods would allow the time away from the gang to tick harmlessly by.

Lawson was surprised the night the husband showed up in the Alhambra wearing a revolver on his hip. Surprise followed by quiet laughter. What did that pale-faced swamp weed think he was going to do with a six-shooter?

"Nice looking piece you got there," Lawson said, sidling up to Burbage at the bar.

Burbage immediately thought the man had chosen his words as an insult to his wife, but then realized the reference was to his newly purchased sidearm.

"When in Rome," he answered.

"When in Rome? When in Rome what? What's Rome got to do with it?"

"It's a saying. When in Rome, do as the Romans do." Burbage did not want this man to think he'd bought a gun because of him. "Seems like everybody wears one. Almost everybody."

"You know how to use it?"

Burbage didn't answer.

"Do you?"

"I'd like to listen to the singer, if you don't mind."

"Maybe I do mind."

Burbage felt the man's shoulder nudge him, so he moved away. This was too much, he thought. Putting up with even another night of this was untenable. He and Belinda had enough money to go somewhere else—not as far as San Francisco—but somewhere else. The next town they settled in, *he* would get a job. If necessary, work on the play could wait until they reached the coast. He wanted quiet days and nights to think and create more than anything else at the moment. Maybe he could do his writing at night in the next place…

Lawson interrupted his thoughts. "I like listening to the singer, too," he said, leaning close to Burbage's ear.

Burbage jumped. "What do you want?"

"I want to listen to the singer. Like you. I want to be just like you."

"Can you please not bother me? And stop bumping

me."

Lawson slid closer to Burbage.

"I said stop it. I have a gun, you know."

Lawson's eyebrows rose and he said, "Ohhh, baby boy from back East has a gun, does he?"

"Yes," Burbage said, drawing the gun from his holster merely to show it off.

When the gun left Burbage's holster, Lawson drew his revolver and fired.

Chapter 15

Billy Grayson

Nearly two weeks later, the Lone Ranger and Tonto pulled Silver and Scout to a halt.

"There it is, Tonto. Frederick, Texas."

"It not very big."

"A perfect spot for Shark Lawson to lay low until Butch Cavendish calls the gang back together, if he ever does."

"Why sheriff not arrest Lawson after him shoot man, Kemo Sabe? Sheriff not know him bad outlaw?"

"The captain at Fort Davis said Lawson used a false name—Billy Grayson. If it is Lawson at all. I'll need to get a look at him, then I'll be sure."

"Sheriff not recognize him? You say him plenty strange looking fellow. Even if him not arrest Lawson for shooting man in Frederick, Lawson wanted for many other crime."

"I don't know what the sheriff was thinking, Kemo Sabe. I want to talk to him, too."

Tonto glanced toward the sinking sun.

"It be dark in two hours."

"Let's find a place to camp. Then help me get into disguise. I want to see if Lawson is somewhere in the town."

*

A tall, mustached Ranger, well-tanned from the application of herbs and roots Tonto had brewed into a thin paste, and dressed in a tan shirt and black pants, walked through the batwing doors of the Alhambra. He surveyed the men sitting at two dozen round tables and crowding the bar. No Shark Lawson. He found himself an opening at the bar and ordering a whiskey. When many customers erupted in applause, the Ranger followed their gaze to the stage, where a young woman, dressed no differently from the saloon girls circulating among the male customers, smiled and nodded her appreciation for their reaction. Many of the seated men rose to their feet as they applauded. The piano player waited until the welcome subsided, then he started to play. The men quieted and the woman sang.

"What was that all about?" the Ranger asked the bartender.

"You're new here, I guess."

"Just got into town this afternoon."

"That's Belinda Burbage. A real songbird, isn't she?" he reported, a smile creeping over his face. "Someone gunned down her husband 'most two weeks ago. Right here at the bar. Fellow named Billy Grayson. Hasn't been in since."

"He wasn't arrested?"

"Nope. Poor fool of a husband drew first. Lots of

people saw it happen. Sheriff couldn't do nothing about it."

"This Billy Grayson still in town?"

"I seen him a couple times out walking. He's still around. Goes to the Golden Goose most nights to gamble. Belinda hasn't sung since it happened. Tonight's her first night back."

"Oh, I see." The Ranger listened to the young woman perform. He'd walked the main street of town before entering the Alhambra and knew the Golden Goose sat directly across the wide, dirt street. Leaving his untouched whiskey on the bar, he headed for the door.

The Ranger entered the Golden Goose and approached the bar. He ordered another whiskey and laid down his money. A steady hum of voices came from this crowd along with the occasional shriek of ecstasy at winning a large pot or of agony at losing one. Shark Lawson sat at a table with four other men, an angry look on his face. He tossed his cards face down and glared at the man sitting across from him who, smiling brightly, circled his hands around the pile of money sitting in the middle of the table and swept it his way.

Lawson pushed his chair back and stood.

"Going off to see your favorite singer?" one man asked, laughing. "I hear she's back at work tonight."

"Yeah, and she's single now," Lawson answered.

A few men laughed; most frowned. The Ranger stepped back as Lawson walked past him and out the door. He waited a few minutes before following him.

When he arrived back at the Alhambra bar, the bartender apologized to him.

"Gosh, mister, I didn't know you were coming back. I dumped your whiskey. Here, let me get you another."

"That's very kind of you, my friend. Not your fault, though. I'll pay. Is that Billy Grayson?"

"It is. Kinda thought he might show up tonight, what with Belinda being back."

As the Ranger watched both Belinda and Lawson, he saw their gazes meet. Belinda faltered in her song for a moment but managed to carry on, directing her talents anywhere but in Lawson's direction.

When Belinda's series of songs ended, she moved to the far end of the room away from the bar. Some men approached her, a few offering to shake her hand, all of them removing their hats as they said a word to her. Lawson stayed put, his eyes tracing her every move. When her break ended and she started back toward the stage for her second set, Lawson approached her. Belinda's eyes widened when she noticed him, and she halted. Lawson removed his hat and said something. Belinda's mouth tightened, and she stepped around the man to reach the stairs and climb back onto the stage. Lawson, wearing a sly grin, walked casually back to the bar. The Ranger took his whiskey and walked to a side wall where he watched Belinda's second performance. When it ended, the piano player joined her on stage.

"Folks, Belinda is back with us. I know she usually makes three appearances each night, but we don't want to overburden the little lady right off. Show her how much you appreciate her return, and we'll let her get on home for the night."

The men applauded, and Belinda bowed shyly before disappearing backstage. The Ranger shifted his attention to Lawson. If Lawson left the bar, he would follow the man. But Lawson didn't leave the bar. He ordered another whiskey and drank alone, keeping his thoughts to himself.

*

The next morning, Tonto and the Lone Ranger, masked and dressed in blue, rode into Frederick. They hitched Scout and Silver in front of the Sheriff Hosgood's small jail. The Alhambra and the Golden Goose were a block further down the dirt street. The Ranger knocked at the jail's wooden door, waited a moment, then opened it and entered. Sheriff Hosgood lay, fully dressed, his hat covering his face, on a cot in one corner of the office. A large desk covered with papers, a soiled food tray, and a set of handcuffs dominated the room. A few plain, wooden chairs stood against one wall. Two cells fully open to view lined the back of the room. There were no prisoners.

Sheriff Hosgood yanked his hat away and spun into a sitting position. His eyes went to his holster, hanging on a coat rack in the corner.

"Don't let my mask worry you, Sheriff," the Ranger explained, offering a warm smile. "It stands for justice, the same as the badge you wear."

"Who are you? Why don't you show your face?" the sheriff barked.

"I have my reasons. My friend Tonto knows them. No one else needs to. I'm here about Shark Lawson."

"Who?"

"You know him better as Billy Grayson."

"Oh."

"He's part of the Butch Cavendish gang, and he's wanted in many places in Texas. I understand he killed a man here a few weeks ago."

"Now, hold on." The sheriff got to his feet and walked past the masked man to take a seat behind his desk. "What's this about Shark Lawson and Billy Grayson?"

"They are one and the same person."

The sheriff rubbed his chin thoughtfully with his left hand. "How do I know that?" he asked.

"You know it because I'm telling you it's true, Sheriff. I've seen the man before. His deformed teeth are unmistakable. I turned over one of his partners from the Cavendish gang, Razor Gilliam, to the sheriff in Corbin City, where he was hanged recently for his crimes."

The sheriff shifted nervously in his chair.

"*He* says he's Billy Grayson. I never heard of no Shark Lawson."

"You've heard of Butch Cavendish, haven't you?"

The sheriff paused before answering.

"I heard of him."

"Tonto, would you get the newspapers out of my saddlebag?"

Tonto left the room.

Clearly aggravated, the sheriff said, "He says he's one person; you say he's another. Why should I believe you any more'n I believe him?"

"Sheriff, I'm hoping to show you why… Tonto, let the sheriff read the articles."

The articles the Ranger referred came from the *Corbin City Bugle* and the *Parkerburg Town Crier*. The *Bugle* article named the five members of the Cavendish gang who'd escaped the shootout with the Texas Rangers and the cavalry outside of Corbin City, and the *Town Crier* article detailed the capture of Razor Gilliam by the Lone Ranger and his subsequent execution.

The sheriff found his glasses in the top drawer of his desk and read. When he finished, the Ranger said, "I'll need those back." The sheriff handed the newspapers to Tonto.

"You're the masked man in the article; the Lone Ranger?"

"I am." The Ranger withdrew a silver bullet from

his belt and put it on the desk in front of Sheriff Hosgood.

The sheriff studied the bullet for a moment.

"I can't arrest a man because you say I should," he said softly. "I tried that once before. Never again."

"What do you mean?" the Ranger asked.

"Pull up a couple of chairs."

The Ranger and Tonto moved two chairs from the wall and settled down before the sheriff's desk.

"Seven years past, Webster Johnson got knifed—killed—at the Golden Goose. That's a gambling den down the way."

"I know of it."

"Two men swore they saw Corey Billups do the knifing in the middle of a big brawl. Demanded I arrest him right away. I did. Billups said he had nothing to do with the knifing. Said he only picked up the bloody knife from the floor when the melee was over. I locked him up and the case went to trial. Town jury convicted him and hung him a week later. I had to supervise the hanging. I don't ever want to supervise another one."

"If the man was guilty…" the Ranger began.

The sheriff interrupted him abruptly and in a loud voice said, "He *weren't* guilty. He was innocent! Those two witnesses were close friends of Johnson, the murdered man. They must've wanted to be sure somebody paid the price. Problem was, Billups didn't do it. He died for it, but he didn't do it."

"How do you know that?"

"Four years after, that'd be three years ago, Randy Kitters passed. The day after he got buried, his wife came into this very office all teary-eyed and repentant. She couldn't live with it, she said. Said she had to when her husband was alive but couldn't do it anymore. Told me her husband did the killing. He admitted it to her. Told her he grabbed a knife from somewhere and jabbed it into Webster Johnson's stomach for no particular reason, just the excitement of the brawl. Drunk, I reckon. Corey Billups was unlucky enough to pick the knife up from the floor at the moment people noticed Johnson got stabbed. I ended up sending him to the gallows. My two witnesses left town when the truth got out, but I'm still here, and you better believe me, mister. I ain't about to go hanging nobody on somebody else's say so."

"I'm very sorry to hear that tale, Sheriff. Justice is often an elusive goal, but it's still a worthy goal worth aiming for."

"Fancy words don't help my conscience none."

"No, I don't guess they do."

The three men stood silent for a time. Then the Ranger said, "Sheriff, if I can satisfy you Billy Grayson is really Shark Lawson, would you take action?"

"I'm the sheriff here, and a good one, by my lights. Your words do have truth to them, fancy or not. If he's a member of the Cavendish gang, I'll throw him into one of these cells, all right."

"You do that, and I promise I'll get a troop of

soldiers here to take him back to Corbin City for trial."

"How you gonna convince me? I promise you; it won't be simple."

The Ranger smiled.

"Sheriff Hosgood, you're an open-minded man. I'll get you that proof. I'd like to speak to the widow of the man who was shot."

"That'd be Belinda Burbage, the Alhambra singer."

"Yes, I know."

"Let me arrange it for you. She's been through a lot. Being approached by a masked man probably won't do much to settle her nerves. Come back around three o'clock. I'll do my best to have her here."

"Let's return to camp, Tonto," the Lone Ranger said.

A moment later, the sheriff sat alone in his office.

*

"Belinda, this is the masked man and his Indian friend I asked you to come and meet," Sheriff Hosgood said.

It was a few moments after three o'clock. The Lone Ranger and Tonto had spent the time since their morning meeting with the sheriff in camp, talking over ways to prove to the sheriff that Billy Grayson was, indeed, Shark Lawson. They'd come up with a plan—a very difficult plan to see through, start to finish—but one that would do the job, if everything went right. The Ranger and Tonto agreed they'd have to meet Belinda Burbage, though, and convince her to take part in the plan since its success depended largely on her.

The Ranger removed his hat. "I happened to hear you sing last night, ma'am," he said. "You have a fine voice."

"You were there? I don't remember seeing a man with a mask in the audience." She looked coldly at the sheriff. "I did see Billy Grayson, though."

"I was in disguise. It's because of Billy Grayson that I'm here to talk to you," the Ranger said. "Sheriff, may Tonto and I speak with Mrs. Burbage alone for a moment?"

"I'll be in a chair outside the door," the sheriff replied, seemingly relieved at being dismissed.

"Let's sit," the Ranger said when the door closed behind the sheriff.

"So, what's this all about?" Belinda asked.

"To state it simply; we believe—no, we know—that Billy Grayson is actually Shark Lawson, a wanted killer and thief and a member of Butch Cavendish's outlaw band."

"What! Why hasn't Sheriff Hosgood arrested him then?"

The Ranger repeated the sheriff's rationale for not taking Lawson into custody.

Belinda stood. "Why can't *you* take Grayson back to be tried?"

"Tonto and I have no official authority. It might cause legal problems that would benefit Lawson rather than subject him to justice. What we need to do is convince the sheriff about the real identity of the man who killed your husband. If we do, the sheriff has promised to lock him up while Tonto and I go for the U. S. Cavalry. The cavalry will come for him, and justice will be served. I can promise you that."

Belinda's chin dropped onto her chest, and she sobbed. The Ranger and Tonto exchanged glances and gave her a moment. She composed herself and said, "My husband was a wonderful man."

"I have no doubt he was," the Ranger said quietly.

"He was writing a play." Belinda went through her history with Reggie Burbage for the Ranger and Tonto. She concluded, "When we reached San Francisco… I'm certain the play would have been produced and been a success. We would have been happy. He loved to write."

"And you love to act."

Belinda offered an accepting smile.

"Tonto and I have a plan to convince the sheriff, but we'll need your help. In fact, the plan cannot work without you. Your being an accomplished actress will be a decided benefit."

Belinda's chin lifted. "Tell me what I need to do."

"Let me get the sheriff back in here." The Ranger

went to the door and beckoned him.

"You two have a good palaver?" the sheriff asked, settling behind his desk.

"Sheriff," the Ranger began, "Mrs. Burbage—"

"Please, Belinda will do," she interrupted.

The Ranger placed his hat on the sheriff's desk.

"Belinda has agreed to help prove that Billy Grayson is Shark Lawson."

The sheriff stared at Belinda.

"I have," she said.

The sheriff nodded slowly. "I'm listening," he said.

"You refuse to arrest Lawson," the Ranger began, "because you cannot make a positive identification of him. We need to make Lawson think that a positive identification is on its way to you."

"And how do you figure to do that?" the sheriff asked, frowning.

The Ranger returned his attention to Belinda. "It will require you to act a very difficult role."

"Go on," Belinda responded grimly.

"Somehow you must get near enough to Lawson to demonstrate a cold, quiet anger toward him."

"Ha! No acting there. I can surely accomplish that much."

"You tell him you know who he is—Shark Lawson—and you've contacted the law. You need be no more specific than that. Tell him the law is sending someone to Frederick from Corbin City who can positively identify him, and you have Sheriff Hosgood's promise to arrest him when the identification's been made. Tell him the man who can identify him will arrive—today is Friday. If you can get to him tonight, tell him the man is due in town Monday before noon. If for some reason you can't speak to him tonight, add a day at a time to the arrival of the witness."

The sheriff interrupted.

"What if she tells Grayson—Lawson this and he runs? What if he simply leaves town?"

"Tonto and I will be watching him. If he does try to run, Sheriff, will it be enough to convince you to hold him until I can get the cavalry here to positively identify him for you?"

"Why don't you go get the cavalry now?" the sheriff asked gruffly. "Forget about this play-acting."

"Because it's possible Lawson may leave town on his own. He can't be certain news of his murder here and a description of him hasn't already reached the cavalry or the Texas Rangers. Tonto and I need to stay here and keep an eye on him."

"Why don't one of you go and one of you stay?" the sheriff asked.

"He could possibly avoid notice if only one of us were watching him. Tonto and I will take shifts. He won't escape the two of us. I want this done right. We've found him, and I don't want to lose him and have to start over again."

"Well… I guess you're right," the sheriff muttered. "So, finish this plan."

"Belinda will threaten him as I described. If he runs, Tonto and I will be there and bring him back. He may react in a different manner, though."

"And that would be…?" the sheriff asked.

"He very well might wait on the road, the one obvious road, into Frederick from Corbin City and ambush the man coming to identify him."

"There ain't no man coming to identify him!" the sheriff burst out.

"I will be that man. I'll change into a disguise and be riding alone."

The sheriff jumped to his feet.

"You're gonna let that sidewinder take a shot at you? Shoot you down even?"

The Ranger looked at Tonto, and they both smiled.

"No. Tonto will be watching him, following him. He'll fire three warning shots when the time comes for me to be on guard against Lawson. Lawson won't get a shot off with Tonto trailing him. When I hear those three shots, when Lawson hears those shots… He won't make it back to town. We'll get him."

"You're walking a mighty fine line, mister," the

sheriff said, a glimmer of admiration in his eye.

Belinda said, "I don't want you getting hurt or killed over me."

"Heh, heh, heh," Tonto chuckled. "Him no get hurt. Me see to that."

The Ranger added, "I will be in the Alhambra each night until you're able stage your scene with Lawson. I promise you, you'll be safe if I'm there. Sheriff, you should be there each night, too. Make Lawson think he's under observation. It will increase the pressure on him. Deputize a couple men to guard Belinda's residence. Can you do that? Belinda, are you all right with this? This plan isn't without some danger for you."

Belinda stared at the sheriff.

"Yes, yes. Charley and Wally will help. I've deputized them before."

"Tell them Belinda needs protection, nothing more. Say nothing of the plan," the Ranger advised. The four people sat silent for a few moments, each mulling over their role in the Lone Ranger's scheme. Finally, the Ranger reached for his hat. He put it on and tightened the lanyard.

He said, "I'll be in the Alhambra tonight. You won't recognize me, but I'll be there, and Tonto will be nearby. Sheriff?"

"Yes, yes. I'll be there, too," he said. "I hope this works. I'm starting to think you might know what you're talking about, masked man."

The Lone Ranger opened the door, Tonto stepped through, and they returned to their camp until nightfall.

Chapter 16

The Plan

Wearing his disguise, using Tonto's holster and gun as part of it, the Lone Ranger stood against the wall in the Golden Goose, untouched glass of whiskey in hand. Shark Lawson had forgone the poker game this evening for the faro table and was doing well, his grotesque teeth on full display with every victorious smile.

"That's it for me tonight," Lawson said, rising and stuffing his pockets with his winnings. He threw some coins on the table. "Drinks on me. This table's been mighty good to me tonight." The other men at the faro table offered wan smiles of gratitude for the drinks. Lawson slipped the dealer a silver coin and wended his way toward the door. The Ranger waited a moment before placing his drink on a window ledge and passing through the swinging doors in time to see Lawson enter the Alhambra. Tonto sat on a bench in the dark two storefronts away, Silver and Scout hitched nearby. He and the Ranger nodded at one another, and the Ranger crossed the street. Midway to the batwing doors of the Alhambra, the Ranger heard the lovely voice of Belinda coming from inside.

Belinda, already on stage for half an hour, had scoured the crowd looking both for Lawson and the man whose plan she was part of. Neither one was apparent—not until Lawson pushed opened the doors and made his way to the end of the bar nearest the stage. She had one song left in her first set and as she sang it, she cast frequent glances toward Lawson, never noticing the big man who followed him into the Alhambra. When she completed her performance, she stepped down to the floor and walked to a nearly deserted spot next to the kitchen. She was in the midst of a desultory conversation with two cowboys who passed by, when she felt a presence behind her. The cowboys gazed over her shoulder and moved off. She turned and looked into the smiling, repulsive face of Shark Lawson.

"Oh, it's you," she spat.

"It's me. Please, wait. Give me minute. I want you know I never intended what happened to your husband. I've already apologized to you once. I consider what happened an accident."

"I imagine your conscience helps you to do that often."

"What do you mean?"

Summoning up her considerable acting skill, she slowly looked over the nearby scene, intimating she needed absolute privacy for what she intended to say next. She leaned in close to Lawson, and in a slow, precise voice said, "I know who you are."

"I told you who I am. Billy Grayson."

She locked eyes with the smug killer. "You are Shark Lawson, and I'm going to prove it."

Lawson's gaze dropped below the freezing point.

"Cat got your tongue?" Belinda asked, offering the killer an evil curl of her lips.

"Who told you such rot? I never heard of Shark Lawson."

"Your, uh…" She tapped her front teeth. "They give you away, don't you think?" She saw the muscles in Lawson's face do a dance. "I'm going to have you arrested."

Lawson's face relaxed.

"By this sheriff? I don't think so. If he wanted to arrest anyone, including me, he'd have done it already."

"When the person I sent for from Corbin City arrives Monday morning, someone who can positively identify you, we'll see who gets arrested and who doesn't. He'll be here by noon, so have a good breakfast that day. You'll need it."

Lawson's eyes froze over again as Belinda pushed by him and ducked backstage.

The Ranger had moved himself into a spot where he could watch Lawson's face but not hear his confrontation with Belinda. The rapid changes to Lawson's expression indicated she'd done her job warning Lawson. The Ranger took a silver bullet from his pocket and palmed it.

Sheriff Hosgood sat at a table off to the side of the gambling action talking with two men. The Ranger walked to the table.

"Sheriff, I think you dropped this," he said and placed the silver bullet into the sheriff's hand before moving over to the bar.

The sheriff glanced at the bullet, and his gaze followed the Ranger.

"Be right back," he told the two men he sat with. He shoved in next to the Ranger and whispered, "That you?"

"Belinda has bearded the lion in his den," the Ranger replied.

"I suppose you mean she told him about the witness. I saw them talking."

"You and your men keep a close watch on her now. She needs protection. Tonto and I will handle Lawson."

Both men's eyes went to the bar, where Lawson had just thrown back a healthy glass of whiskey.

"Looks like your plan's started off just right," the sheriff said.

"More importantly, it ends just right. I'm going to tell Tonto what happened, then I'll be back. Either he or I will be tracking Lawson until he makes his move. You and I shouldn't be seen together again. If I need to tell you anything, Tonto or I will come to your office."

"Back door?"

"Yes."

"I'll leave it unlatched."

The men parted.

*

The Lone Ranger spent Saturday evening in the Alhambra, along with Sheriff Hosgood and his two deputies. Shark Lawson failed to appear. Sunday, the town shut down and remained quiet, Tonto assuring the Ranger that Lawson hadn't left his shack on the edge of town. Both men spent until Monday morning within view of Lawson's shack and his horse, one of them always alert to any move Lawson might make.

"You go now, Kemo Sabe?" Tonto asked. He'd helped the Ranger into his disguise at sun-up after they'd eaten a quick meal.

"If Lawson were going to run away, he wouldn't have waited until now," the Ranger replied grimly. "He wants the messenger. You'll have to keep a close eye on him."

"Me follow. Him not see me. Why you not have sheriff follow Lawson too?"

"I have confidence in you, my friend. Besides, the more people on Lawson's trail, the greater the chance he'll detect them. No, I trust your skills. Lawson won't know you're anywhere near him." He mounted Silver. "Here's hoping luck is with us. Let's get moving, big fellow."

Silver galloped off into the brightening day.

The Ranger rode Silver hard until they were three miles out of town. He wanted Silver to have a good rest and the opportunity to graze. Timing concerned the Ranger. Lawson would not want to miss the arrival of the man who would send him to the gallows. He'd had

Belinda tell him that the man coming to identify him would be in town before noon. The obvious place for anyone planning an ambush was two miles outside of town, where the landscape changed into a smattering of low mesas and shallow, winding arroyos—a wealth of hiding places. The Ranger assumed Lawson would want to eliminate the witness as far from town as practicable. The sound of gunshots carried in the warm air of south Texas. And Lawson would doubtless want to get back to town to appear in public as close to the time of the witness's murder as possible. All things considered, the Ranger decided the time for him to move would be a little before the sun reached its noon-day summit. Silver nibbled the grass, and the Ranger waited for the sun to rise in the sky.

*

The Ranger, scanning the landscape for any sign of danger, kept Silver to an easy pace as he guided him toward Frederick. The mesas and arroyos where he assumed danger would begin were moments ahead, but nothing out of the ordinary met his eye at the moment.

"Be ready to run, Silver, big fellow. We'll hope the first shots we hear come from Tonto's gun."

Silver neighed at the sound of the masked man's voice, and they moved forward.

When the first shot cut through the air, the Ranger tensed, listening for the whiz of a bullet, but when a second, then third shot followed in quick succession, he knew Tonto had done his job.

"Go, Silver!" he shouted, and the white stallion sprang forward. The shots came from the right, so the Ranger guided Silver to the left and down into the nearest arroyo. He followed the arroyo a short distance and waited for Tonto's next signal. When three more shots sounded, he urged Silver up the slanting arroyo wall and saw a horseman racing away toward the mesas and arroyos further ahead. A moment later, Tonto astride Scout came into view, hard on the trail of the fleeing assassin. The Ranger joined the chase.

Lawson dashed across a mesa and down into an arroyo. He emerged to the left of where he'd entered and surged ahead, Tonto and the Lone Ranger converging and closing on their prey. When Scout and Silver drew abreast, Tonto pointed. Lawson seemed headed for a waving field of what appeared to be tall reeds whose height declined as the ground in which they grew fell away into a stream bed. When the Ranger and Tonto reached the edge of the arroyo, they reined up.

"Him hide plenty good down there, Kemo Sabe," Tonto said.

"We'd better dismount. We're too easy a target in the saddle. You take this side of the water. I'll cross over."

They left the horses where they stood and descended the arroyo wall. The stream was no more than a few inches deep and a yard wide. The Ranger leaped the distance and crouched in the reeds as he and Tonto, one on each side of the water, stalked Lawson, listening for the sound of his horse should he decide to flee again.

A moment later, Tonto called, “Me find horse.”

“Lawson’s?”

“Yes. Rifle missing.”

“Keep low, Kemo Sabe.”

They continued forward.

Moments later, loud whinnying came from behind them.

“We miss him!” Tonto cried.

Both men hurried back the way they’d come. They paused for a moment, surprised at finding Lawson’s horse still where he’d left it.

The Ranger leaped the stream, and he and Tonto scaled the slanting, overgrown eight-foot wall of the stream bed. When they reached level ground, they saw, fifty yards off, Lawson tugging on Silver’s reins as the horse pranced in revolt. While struggling to mount the rebellious white stallion, he spotted the Lone Ranger and Tonto rushing toward him and sent two wild pistol shots their way. He gave Silver a frustrated smack on the rump and grabbed onto the saddle horn, desperately trying to get the stallion to be still.

“Silver,” the Ranger called. “Come here, big fellow.”

Silver bucked and Lawson had to release him. He bent into the tall grass, and when he rose, he held a rifle.

Silver, excited by the summons of his master, whirled toward the Ranger's voice, knocking Lawson down the dirt wall on that side of the stream. Tonto and the Ranger rushed down to the bank of the trickling water and saw Lawson on his back, his rifle in the water. They raced ahead and by the time Lawson got to his hands and knees, the Lone Ranger had him by the shirt collar. He spun him over on his back and knelt on his chest.

"His guns, Tonto. The rifle too."

Tonto disarmed Lawson.

"Now, get up," the Ranger ordered.

"Me get his horse," Tonto said.

"You're riding back to Sheriff Hosgood's jail, Lawson, while I ride for the soldiers at Fort Davis. Or perhaps you'd prefer to ride Silver?"

Lawson rose on wobbly legs. At the Lone Ranger's jibe, he swung a limp fist. The Ranger easily knocked it aside and, with a greater pleasure than he would ever admit, swung his fist at Lawson's jaw, knocking him onto his back into the shallow stream again. Lawson floundered, clumsily splashing his groggy way onto his knees. He spat blood, and when he glared hatefully at his captor, the Ranger allowed himself an icy smile. He'd chipped two of Lawson's prominent front teeth. The Ranger drew his gun, and Lawson submitted.

*

Back in Sheriff Hosgood's office, Belinda Burbage

glared at the captive through the bars of his cell. Lawson refused to react, simply lying on his cot, face to the wall, his back to the world. The Ranger, Tonto, and the sheriff stood with her.

The sheriff said, “Don’t you worry, Miss Belinda. Me or one of my deputies will be in this office every minute till the soldiers come to pick him up. We ain’t gonna take no chances of him escaping.”

Lawson could hear the conversation but remained stock still.

“Let’s step outside,” the Ranger said to Belinda. They and Tonto moved out onto the wooden sidewalk. “What will you do now, Belinda?” the Ranger asked.

“What can I do?” Belinda replied. “I’ll have to keep singing if I want to keep eating.”

“Are you still planning to head to San Francisco? I’m sure they need actresses of your capabilities there.”

“Probably. As soon as I get enough money together, though I doubt my skills are what you imagine. Reggie and I were hoping to make our marks there… together.”

“How far along was he with his play?” the Ranger asked. “Did he tell you how it would end? Perhaps you could finish it.”

Belinda frowned. “You seem to have a great deal of confidence in me.”

“‘We know what we are, but know not what we may be,’” the Ranger quoted with a smile.

Belinda's eyes widened. "You know *Hamlet*," she said, then laughed. "I really don't want to spend the rest of my life in Frederick."

"If Tonto and I ever get to San Francisco, the first thing on our agenda will be to check the theatre listings."

Belinda laughed again. "You do that."

"Ready, Kemo Sabe?" He and Tonto had volunteered to ride to Fort Davis and bring back a troop of soldiers to escort Shark Lawson to his fate.

"Me ready."

"I'll see you when we get back," the Ranger said to Belinda.

He and Tonto mounted up and rode away.

Belinda returned to Sheriff Hosgood's office.

"They left?" he asked.

"Yes, they're on their way to bring the soldiers back. Sheriff, I just realized… I have no idea who that man is, the masked man. Do you know his name?"

"He don't go by any name, Miss Belinda. I heard him called the Lone Ranger."

"The Lone Ranger? Strange."

A faint shout reached the ears of Belinda and the sheriff.

"Hi-yo, Silver. Away!"

The sheriff gave a shrug and settled behind his

desk. Belinda went back to her room to rest up for the night's performances.

*

A week later, Shark Lawson sat on a government-issued horse, his hands tied to the pommel, his ankles tied together beneath the horse's belly. Lieutenant Calender along with two soldiers rode in front of Lawson, one soldier rode on each side of him, and three more rode behind. The Lone Ranger and Tonto rode at the forefront with the lieutenant. They were ten minutes outside of Frederick on their way to Fort Davis.

"You've brought in two of Cavendish's gang," the lieutenant was saying. "That's quite extraordinary. This one, the captain says, we're going to try in a military tribunal for the murder of U. S. Army personnel. He won't get off."

"Cavendish is still out there," the Ranger said.

"You're going after him, I suppose?"

"Him and his son, as well as Montana Jenkins. They're the final three members of the gang. Lawson wouldn't tell us anything about Cavendish's plans, so Tonto and I will simply keep at it."

"I hope you find…"

The men pulled to a halt, a gruesome spectacle before their eyes. A dead man dangled from a stout tree branch. The Ranger and Tonto exchanged glances.

"Good lord," the lieutenant muttered. He, the Ranger, and Tonto rode to the body. "A Negro. And look at that!" A Confederate army cap hung impaled by a knife in the dead man's chest. "The war ended five years ago."

"Lieutenant, Tonto and I will take the body back to Sheriff Hosgood. I planned to see Lawson back to Fort Davis with you, but—"

"Would you like me to leave you a couple soldiers?"

"No, we'll look into this on our own."

"Let's get this man down," the lieutenant ordered,

"Hold on, Lieutenant. Let Tonto take a look first. Keep your soldiers back."

Tonto dismounted and walked carefully around the scene. He knelt on one knee in places and once got onto his stomach, his face inches from the ground.

"Kemo Sabe, you come see this."

The Ranger knelt alongside as Tonto pointed.

"In horseshoe print. It look like nail missing. See strange mark next to missing nail?"

"I see it. You think it's from the horse of one of the men who hung this poor soul?"

"Must be. See where dead man horse run off. This horse… It turn and go back toward town with two other horse."

"Yes. Yes. Good job, Kemo Sabe." The men rose, and the Ranger addressed the lieutenant.

"You can proceed," he said.

Lieutenant Calender signaled for two soldiers to cut the body down and wrap it in a blanket the Lone Ranger provided. Two others constructed a simple pallet, which they attached behind Silver and on which they secured the body.

Their tasks done, the soldiers re-formed, and bid farewell. Then, in grim silence, the Lone Ranger and Tonto turned themselves back toward Frederick.

Chapter 17

Hertie Horsy

Tonto had ridden ahead when he and the Lone Ranger neared Frederick. The sheriff, along with a small crowd of people, alerted to the situation by Tonto, waited outside Sheriff Hosgood's office and watched the Ranger tow the body into town. The Ranger dismounted as the sheriff and others went to see who he'd brought in.

The sheriff removed his hat as did most of the other men.

"It's Hertie Horsy," Hosgood announced.

"What name?" Tonto asked, uncertain he'd heard correctly.

"Always told us his name was Hertie. Said his old master used to call him Horsy."

"Him slave?" Tonto asked as the Ranger detached the pallet from Silver.

"Used to be. Showed up around here after the war. Did okay, all things considered. Kept pretty much to himself. Even married a woman named Abby who worked for the Davenport family. They live outside of town. Him and Abby got one daughter and another baby on the way. This ain't good."

"We found him hanging from a tree," the Ranger said. "The soldiers continued on with Shark Lawson. Tonto and I dropped out to bring—what was the name again?"

"Hertie Horsy.

"To bring Hertie back to town. What do you know about him?"

"I was just telling your pard, here. Good man. Married. Hard worker. Lives outta town. Baby on the way."

"Who would do this?" the Ranger asked.

"All right, everybody. Show's over," the sheriff said, as he shooed people back about their business. "Wally, can you get the body over to Doc's? Can't have it lying here in the street."

"I'll borrow a wagon," Wally replied and hurried off.

"You asked me who could do such a thing?" the sheriff said. "First off, who knows? Second off, for some people around here, the war never ended; the South never lost. More 'n one person 'round here fits that description."

"You sound a bit too accepting of this, Sheriff. You're going to investigate, aren't you?" the Ranger asked in a stern voice.

"Oh, yes. I'll investigate."

"Is the war over to you?"

Hosgood and the Lone Ranger locked eyes.

"Yes. Yes, it is. Those days are gone, and they

ain't coming back."

"Do you mind if Tonto and I stay and look into this?"

"Be my guest. Glad for the help."

Wally pulled up in a wagon, and Tonto and the Ranger lifted the body, still covered by the Lone Ranger's saddle blanket, into the back. The Ranger addressed Wally.

"Can you ask the doctor to examine the body closely? Perhaps he can find something that might be helpful. Tell the doctor I'll stop in to see him later."

"Will do," Wally answered as he gave the reins a shake. "Hiya! Git up!"

The wagon rolled away, and to the sheriff the Ranger said, "You said this man was married? Someone has to let this man's wife know what's happened."

No one spoke for a moment. Then the sheriff said, "I guess that's my job. Wouldn't want to come along, would you?"

"Yes, Tonto and I will join you. Perhaps the woman will have some idea of who did this to her husband."

"Let me lock up the office, and we'll head out."

*

After the war, Abby Withers had stayed on at the

Davenports' farm, which lay a mile and a half outside of Frederick. Rather than continue to live in one of the slave shacks behind the barn, Abby moved into a rear bedroom in the Davenport house and received a salary of three dollars a week, plus meals. Her new situation satisfied Abby. Though only twenty-five years old at war's end, she had no desire to uproot herself and follow the other slaves once bound to the farm on their trek into the unknown. A year after the war ended, the Davenports hired a jack-of-all-trades handyman named Hertie Horsy, who happily stayed on his own in Abby's deserted shack, the best kept up of the bunch. He and Abby met and grew fond of one another. Their relationship had the Davenports' blessing, and when they married, Millie Davenport, whose husband had died the year before, gave them a small patch of verdant ground as a wedding present. Assisted by some neighbors who, at the recommendation of the Davenports, previously hired Hertie for odd jobs, Hertie put up a solid cabin next to a small stream. He and Abby raised their own food, selling any excess. Hertie earned money doing carpentry, repairing wagons, anything within his considerable range of skills. Their first child came along nearly two years into the marriage, and Abby expected their second child at any time.

As the three men rode toward the cabin, they saw Abby tossing grain to a dozen chickens who happily pecked their lunch from the ground.

"Sheriff," she said with a welcoming smile, "you capture somebody?"

"No, Abby. This man is a friend. Abby, we have

bad news for you."

The change which came over Abby's face touched the heart of the Lone Ranger, relieved the sheriff had taken on the responsibility of informing her of the catastrophe.

"What?" Abby asked, her expression frozen in fearful anticipation.

"Hertie's been killed."

The bucket of grain in her hands fell to the ground. The chickens nearby fluttered away at the woman's scream then clustered back to deal with the feast she'd left for them.

The Ranger dismounted and went to the distraught woman.

"No, no, no," she wailed. She balled her fists and struck the Ranger's shoulders.

"We found him along the road," the Ranger said, wrapping his arms around the woman.

There was nothing the men could do but let the woman's grief pour out until it spent itself. The Ranger released the woman.

"It was them, wasn't it?" she cried.

The Ranger and Tonto exchanged glances.

"Who do you mean, ma'am?" the Ranger asked softly.

"The sheriff knows. Oh, my man. My Hertie."

She sank to her knees and covered her face with her hands.

"What did she mean, Sheriff?"

Sheriff Hosgood took in a deep breath.

"There's a bunch…" He shook his head. "They came home after Appomattox angry, and they stayed angry. I told you. Some don't accept the war's over and lost. They still dress up in their grays on special occasions. You might guess their attitude…" He nodded toward Abby.

"They pass comments," Abby said, tearfully. "Every time I go to town, if one is there, he say something. Something nasty. Hertie didn't let me go to town anymore. 'Specially not now. Oh, Hertie never gonna see his baby." She began crying again. The Ranger bent, took her by the elbow, and lifted her.

"For your baby's sake," he said, "you have to get through this, Abby."

Hearing her name, she made eye contact with the masked man.

"Who you?"

"I told you he's a friend, Abby. He's gonna help me find out who took Hertie away from you."

"You're a good man, you do that," she said. "What I do now, Sheriff?"

"I'll take you into town, and we'll bring Hertie home."

"I'll have to bring Liza with me, Sheriff. She asleep inside. I got nobody to watch her."

"Tonto and I will stay here, Abby. We'll watch her and prepare a grave for your husband."

Hearing the word "grave" brought another burst of tears from the overwrought woman.

"Is there somewhere special you would like him to rest?" the Ranger asked.

Abby gathered herself. After a moment she pointed. "You see that tree?"

"I do."

"He always liked to smoke a pipe under that tree."

"Then that will be his resting place," the Ranger promised.

"Do you need to do anything before we go, Abby?" the sheriff asked.

"Let me check on Liza. Then I wipe my face. I don't want none of them men see I cried." She walked toward the cabin, and the sheriff accompanied her.

"She seem like good woman, Kemo Sabe," Tonto said. "Me not like see her cry."

"Me either, Tonto. We won't leave Frederick until someone pays for this crime."

"Me get shovels?"

"Yes, but let's not start digging until they're out of sight."

*

Hertie Horsy had awakened that morning looking forward to a fine day. Abby had her eye on a cute, lace cap for a newborn, a cap she'd seen in Wagner's Dry Goods store that cost a dollar. He had the dollar, having done some wagon repair for a farmer on the other side of Frederick, and he looked forward to seeing his wife's face when he presented her with the cap. He glanced at Abby asleep next to him and Liza, in a small bed he'd made with his own hands, on the floor nearby. He'd been on his own now for nearly five years, the twenty-five years before those five merely a dark and awful nightmare. He rose and put on the coffee.

Abby, awakened by his jostling the bed, rolled over and saw him leave the cabin. She struggled out of bed—she'd be so relieved when the baby arrived—and put herself quickly to rights. Hertie returned with half a dozen eggs in hand.

"Morning, precious," he said. "Breakfast on the way."

"You a small man with a big heart, Hertie Horsy," Abby said. Hertie stood five-foot-six.

"You a beautiful woman with a big belly," he replied. She waved her hand dismissively at him.

"Weren't my doing," she chided.

Hertie chuckled and said, "Come and eat. I need to go into town today. Gotta get a couple things for wagon-fixing."

"You be careful," Abby warned. Both had had bad experiences at times when they left their small farm.

"I'll be in and out. Don't you do no work, remember. You just rest yourself and get ready for what you gotta go through. I'll stop in to see the doctor. Tell him to be ready."

They ate and chatted about their plans for caring for the new baby, and when Abby shooed him away, insisting she was quite able to clean up after breakfast, Hertie left for town.

After a quick visit to the doctor's office, he made a beeline to purchase the baby cap, a white, frilly thing with tiny holes for airing the baby's head. At least, that's what Hertie took to be the holes' purpose. It was a nice piece of work, no matter.

Three men stood alongside his horse when he came out of Wagner's.

"It's Horsy-man," one of the men crowed. "And here be Horsy's horsey." He and his friends laughed.

"'Scuse me," Hertie said. "I gotta get back. Baby on the way." He moved toward his horse, but one of the men put a hand against his chest.

"About that. What makes you think we want more of your kind here in Frederick?"

"We don't bother nobody," Hertie said, his stomach knotting at the budding confrontation.

"Just your being here, walking around free, bothers me."

"Me too."

"Me too."

Hertie eyed the three men. "Sorry," he said.

"Sorry. He says he's sorry."

"We heard him," one of the men said. "Don't help me none. Help you?"

The third man replied, "Don't help me none, neither."

The first man said, "Ride on out. We'll see you soon."

Hertie maneuvered his way through the men and mounted. He gave his horse a kick and trotted away.

As Hertie passed along the road out of town, he imagined the smile he was about to bring to Abby's face when she saw the cap he carried in his pocket. He was so deep in his daydream, he didn't notice the hoofbeats until the men were nearly upon him.

"Told you we'd see you later," said the man in the lead. The three riders blocked his way.

"I don't want no trouble," Hertie said nervously. "Just wanna get back home."

"So's you can make more babies?" one of the men said. "Uh-uh. Not gonna happen."

"What you mean?" Hertie asked as one of the men

reached back for the lariat hanging behind his saddle. "What you gonna do?"

Two men rode close to Hertie and grabbed the reins from his hand.

"Don't ask questions," one of them said. They led his horse under a tall tree.

"What you gonna do?" Hertie cried, panic-stricken. He'd seen things like this happen back in South Carolina. How could it happen to him here in Texas? He was a free man.

The man fussed with the rope a moment, then threw a loop over Hertie's head and drew it tight. Hertie grabbed at the rope to get it off. The second man drew his gun and struck Hertie alongside his temple. Hertie's hands dropped to his side.

"Hurry up. Somebody might come along," the leader of the three men said as he watched one of his friends toss the rest of the rope over a tree limb high enough off the ground to accomplish their purpose.

Hertie, stunned by the blow of the gun, shook his head and blinked repeatedly. He felt the rope tighten around his neck and realized he was no longer in the sun, but in the shade of a tree.

"What you doing?" he cried. "This ain't right."

"He set?" asked the leader.

"Rope's tied."

The leader rode up to Hertie.

"You and your kind gotta go," he said softly. "We did this before the war; ain't no need to stop now." He struck Hertie's horse sharply on its rear, and the horse ran.

The three mounted men sat, quietly watching.

Finally, one of them said, "That boy could dance." The others laughed and the leader rode up to the dangling body. He drew a confederate cap from his belt. One of the other men handed him a knife.

Chapter 18

Cal Ramsey

The sheriff arrived back at Abby's cabin driving a wagon, in the back of which lay Hertie Horsy's body, still wrapped in the Lone Ranger's saddle blanket. Abby sat up front. Next to them on horseback rode the town doctor, Percy Mikkels, a slim man in his sixties, who decided ten years earlier to settle in the quietest town he could find. Frederick fit the bill, at least until lately. The Lone Ranger walked forward to greet the sheriff.

"The doc's gonna stay here with Abby for a while," the sheriff explained as the Ranger helped the woman down from the wagon seat.

"This excitement," the doctor said. "Abby will need some help real soon. I'll stay with her long as I can. The sheriff knows where to find me in case anyone falls off a horse."

"May I speak to you?" Abby asked, addressing the Lone Ranger. They stepped aside and Abby said, "I feel my baby coming. My Liza gonna have a bad time of it, just her and me and a baby. I'll keep her inside the cabin now. Will you put my husband in the ground? I don't want Liza to see."

"Certainly, Abby."

"Say something nice over him."

"I'll do that."

Liza sat atop Silver, stroking his gleaming neck. When the Ranger and Abby finished their talk, the Ranger lifted the little girl out of the saddle. The sheriff helped Abby into the cabin, Liza following behind.

"She's got to rest," the doctor said. "You can guess how hard this is for her."

"I'm glad you came back with them, Doctor," the Ranger said. "I wanted to ask you, did you have a chance to examine the body? Did you find anything that might lead us to who did this?"

"He died from hanging, but I guess you don't need me to tell you that. That knife in the chest came after he was dead."

"The knife and Confederate cap," the Ranger said, "do you have them with you?"

"No, they're back in my office on my desk. I was looking them over when Sheriff Hosgood brought Abby in. She took it real bad."

"Anything about the knife or cap that might be helpful?"

"Hard to say. Quite a few men around here have those caps. Came home from the war in their uniform. Only clothes they had."

"And the knife?"

"Common, cheap knife. Wagner's stocks them."

"Was the knife new or old?"

The doctor gave a shrug. "Nothing about it

indicated it was old. No nicks; not worn down. Still quite shiny, in fact."

"Would you mind if I went to your office and got them? They might help Tonto and me."

"Sheriff told me about you. Sure, take them. Door's unlocked. They're right on the desk. Can't miss them. Oh, this one other thing was in his pocket."

Doctor Mikkels pulled out a small, white, baby's cap from his black bag and handed it to the Ranger, who examined it and nodded.

"May I keep this? I'll see that Abby gets it."

"Okay with me."

Sheriff Hosgood approached. "Abby's calling for you, Doc," he said. "Getting pains, she says."

"I thought this might set off the birth of her child."

"She's worried about Liza," the sheriff went on, "and I gotta get back to town."

"Tonto and I will stay. The child and I are already good friends, and she's especially taken to Silver. Sheriff, Abby's alone and she's going to need help out here. She needs to recover and care for two children."

"Don't look at me," Sheriff Hosgood said. "I don't know nothing about taking care of no babies."

Tonto leaned in and whispered something to the Lone Ranger.

"Just what I was thinking, Kemo Sabe. Sheriff,

will you ask Belinda to ride out this way. I think she'd be willing to help out."

"Me go with sheriff," Tonto said. "Make sure her get here safely."

"Sure, sure. I can do that," the sheriff promised.

"Tonto, when you go back into town with the sheriff, stop in Doctor Mikkels' office and bring the knife and cap when you return."

"Me savvy."

"Come with me, masked man," the doctor said. "I'll send the little girl out to you."

"Not yet, doctor. You go and look after Abby and keep Liza inside until I come and get her. Sheriff, will you drive the wagon over where Tonto and I dug a grave? We have a short service to perform."

*

"We'll have to pay another visit soon to Jim Faraday at the silver mine," the Lone Ranger told Tonto. "Our cash is running low."

They camped in a shallow arroyo near Frederick. Abby's baby had arrived two days before, described by Doctor Mikkels as, "A healthy, caterwauling bundle of life." After the Ranger promised to make up for any lost salary, Belinda successfully petitioned Farley Harigold, the Alhambra owner, for two weeks off to stay and help Abby.

Earlier in the day, the Ranger and Tonto had accompanied the sheriff to Wagner's dry goods store to ask whether anyone had bought a new lariat or a new knife in the past few days. Benny Wagner said no to the lariat but recalled Cal Ramsey buying a knife some four or five days before. When the sheriff produced the knife used in the hanging, Wagner said it was the type he'd sold Ramsey but pointed out how he sold, on average, five or six such knives every month.

"That strange about knife, Kemo Sabe," Tonto said, as he leaned back against the bank of the arroyo. "Me think much about that."

"It is strange, Tonto. If this Cal Ramsey bought the knife *after* Horsy was killed, it would make more sense and point to him as the one who left the knife in Horsy's chest and so needed to buy another one."

"Sheriff say Ramsey one of men who like to sometimes wear gray uniform."

"Yes, that's something else pointing his way but not nearly enough to arrest him."

"When sheriff say them have march?"

Sheriff Hosgood related how the lingering remnants of the Confederate army who lived in and around Frederick, those who refused to acknowledge the war's rightful end, marched in full gray uniform on the Fourth of July under the banner of the Confederacy. The parade, maybe two-dozen men, did not turn out much of a crowd, but the rest of the inhabitants made no complaints about their behavior, too busy with their own red, white, and blue celebrations.

"The sheriff says they'll march in two days, on the country's ninety-four birthday, Tonto. Your mentioning the knife again has given me an idea," the Ranger said, tossing the remnants of his coffee cup into the dirt. "I want to ride in and talk to the Sheriff Hosgood again while it's still light."

"Me go with you?"

"Yes, thanks, Kemo Sabe. Let me tell you what I have in mind."

*

The Lone Ranger and Tonto hitched Silver and Scout behind the sheriff's office and knocked lightly on the back door of the jail.

Hosgood opened the door to them.

"I thought it might be you. Come on in." He turned up the oil lamp and the men found chairs.

"I have an idea of how to get on the track of the men who killed Hertie," the Ranger said.

"Spill it," the sheriff said. The Ranger had spoken in a low voice so Hosgood moved his chair nearer the masked man and leaned in.

"Wagner reported that no one had bought a lariat from the dry goods store in over a week. Tonto checked at the stable on our way here. No lariat sales there, either."

"So?"

"So, it would appear someone is doing without a lariat for the time being. I recall seeing just about every horse hitched on the street carrying a lariat."

"Of course. It's what you might call an essential tool in these parts."

"I'm glad to hear it. Tonight, when the Alhambra and the Golden Goose are full, let's check along the hitch racks and see which horses aren't carrying lariats."

"That's your scheme?" the sheriff asked, wide-eyed.

"If the horse of one of those bitter-enders you told us about lacks a lariat…"

"Maybe, maybe," the sheriff said dubiously. "Seems a stretch, though."

"About Cal Ramsey buying that knife from Wagner's—would you be willing to go and ask to see it?" the Ranger asked.

The atmosphere in the room changed as the sheriff stared hard at the Ranger.

"You want me to confront Cal Ramsey over him buying a knife?"

"No, no confrontation. You could say you're thinking of buying a knife and heard he'd recently bought one. You want to take a look at it and see if it's suitable."

"Him not having it won't make me arrest him," the sheriff said, a challenge in his tone.

"I'm aware of your thoughts on that, Sheriff, but if he has the knife, then he'll be less of a suspect."

"That sounds true enough, I guess." The sheriff removed his hat and scratched his head. "You two ate your dinner yet?"

"No, I thought we'd go back to camp and return to town after nightfall."

"No need for you to make two trips. Stay here. I'll have Gertie at the restaurant send over three trays. Meatloaf special today. Real good. Always get it when it's the special. Okay with you?"

Tonto gave the Ranger a nod.

"Sure thing," the Ranger said.

The sheriff stepped out, and the Ranger and Tonto settled down to await both dinner and darkness.

*

The voice of Belinda's replacement drifted into the street. Sheriff Hosgood, accompanied by the Lone Ranger and Tonto, walked slowly along one side of the street, then the other, examining the horses clustered mainly outside of the Alhambra and the Golden Goose. Of the forty-two horses they counted, eight saddles lacked a lariat. The sheriff was able to link three of those horses with their owners, two brothers who ran a small ranch nearby and who, he said knowingly, came from Chicago.

"They don't do any marching in gray," the sheriff

assured the masked man.

Doctor Mikkels' horse was the third.

"We'll have to stay up a while until the two saloons empty," the Ranger said, adding a weary smile, "to see who the other five horses go home with. Sheriff, did you make up your mind about talking to Cal Ramsey?"

"About the knife?"

"Yes."

"I guess I oughta."

"Tonto and I will be right over there." The Ranger pointed to a dark alley three buildings down from the Golden Goose. The sheriff walked off, and the Ranger and Tonto retreated into their lair.

"We go see Abby tomorrow, Kemo Sabe?" Tonto asked as they nestled into the gloom.

"As soon as we can. She's really going to have a rough time. She'll never be able to manage the farm by herself."

"Maybe she hire somebody."

"That will have to work itself out the best it can. I hope, Tonto, that one day this new country of ours will learn to treat all men—and women—equally. One profound thing that President Lincoln said, among many profound things, really sticks in my mind. He said that a house divided against itself cannot stand."

"That heap easy to understand."

"But very difficult to protect against."

The two men settled into thoughtful silence as they waited for Sheriff Hosgood to return.

"Here he comes," the Ranger said.

"Him walk plenty fast."

"He may have learned something. Sheriff, what did you find out?"

"I really don't know what to think about this town these last few weeks." The sheriff removed his hat and ran his palm across his forehead. "It scares me."

"What does?" the Ranger asked.

"Okay, listen. See if you end up thinking like I do. Cal admits he bought a knife. How could he deny it? I did what you suggested and asked to see it. He said he lost it, but you should have seen the blade he pulled from behind his back. I never noticed it before, with his shirt hanging out all the time. It was longer and wider than the knife we found in Hertie, and it had a big red ruby, or more likely a big piece of fancy red glass, in the middle of the handle. He said as long as he didn't lose that knife—claimed his father gave it to him—he didn't care about the other knife. He'd just go buy one if he needed. I wanted to ask why he bought the one knife if he already had a better one, but I didn't want his suspicions set off. I only told him I didn't want anything as fancy as his knife, complimented him on it, and left soon as I could."

"And what do you make of that, Sheriff?"

"I wanna know what *you* make of it."

Tonto spoke. "Him not want to leave knife with red stone behind in body, so him buy other knife before hanging."

"Yes, Tonto," the Ranger agreed grimly. "It would indicate they planned their attack on Hertie well ahead of time."

"Just my idea!" the sheriff said. "Means they're a mighty evil bunch to do what they did in cold blood. A drunken binge would be bad enough, but to plan it out and buy a knife only for the purpose of leaving it… I'll spend the whole night here to find out who owns those five horses. If it's one of Ramsey's crowd, I'll recognize him. All damn night, I swear."

"We'll be right here with you, Sheriff," the Ranger promised.

Chapter 19

The Parade

Early next morning, having very little rest, the Lone Ranger and Tonto returned to the sheriff's office. The sheriff had coffee on the stove and offered the two men some.

"Marv Johnson's the man we want," the sheriff said after distributing the steaming cups.

"You're certain?" the Ranger asked. He put his coffee cup down on the desk to cool.

"Gotta be. No lariat. Close friend of Cal Ramsey. The other men without lariats I already checked on. Nothing there. Not one of them is part of this Confederate bunch. I was out early this morning to check on Johnson's horse. It's like you described—a nail missing from the shoe on the right rear leg as well as some damage to the shoe near the missing nail."

"Tonto is certain there were four horses involved in Hertie's hanging."

"That right," Tonto agreed. "Me sure. One horse belong to dead man. Three men hang him."

The sheriff said, "About twenty-five or so of them Confederacy lovers will dress up and march tomorrow, and I'm sure Ramsey is one of the men we want—'cause of the knife, and Johnson is another—'cause of the lariat and the damaged horseshoe. There ain't but two, maybe three others they're close enough with to partner up for something like this. Len Carper is usually the one they bow down to, but there are other men who might… but like I say, no more 'n two or three." The sheriff paused. "If I had to guess, Len Carper would be the one."

"And they'll be marching tomorrow?"

"Do every year."

"In full uniform, you said?"

"You bet."

"What if one of them marches lacking a cap?"

The sheriff's eyes widened. "Without a cap," he repeated softly. "Might make him the third one. *Will* make him the third one."

"Very possibly," the Ranger said. "Unless it's either Cal Ramsey or Marv Johnson who lacks a cap."

"Heh. Either of them got no cap, cinches it against them."

"How we make them admit they kill man?" Tonto asked.

"You've hit upon the real problem, Kemo Sabe," the Ranger responded. "There were no witnesses. Sheriff, Tonto and I will ride out to check on Abby today. Tomorrow, I'll be here in disguise to watch our friends in gray parade down the street, and we'll see what we see."

"You'll be that mustached fellow again?" the sheriff asked.

"Yes."

"I'll be on the lookout for you."

*

The sound of gunshots a half-mile or so out from Abby's cabin sent Silver and Scout into a sprint. They covered the ground quickly, and when the Lone Ranger and Tonto pulled up before Abby's door, Belinda rushed out to them carrying a rifle.

"Three… three men were here. They tried to get in," she sputtered.

"And did they?" the Ranger asked, gun drawn. Tonto scanned the countryside for riders. "No. I saw them coming and locked the door. They banged on it, but I wouldn't open up. They called out horrible things to us…to Abby. They shot off their guns, and I sent a bullet through the door."

The Ranger glanced at the door and saw the damage.

"After I shot, they rode off. Maybe they saw you coming. Did you see them? Who were they?"

"No, we were on our way here and heard the shots. How is Abby? Are she and the baby safe?"

"Abby's scared but everyone's fine."

"Kemo Sabe!" Tonto called. "Come see."

"Go on back inside and see to Abby," the Ranger said. He joined Tonto.

"Here track. See shoe?"

The Ranger squatted down and studied the hoof prints.

"I see. One shoe has a nail missing, and there's the same, strange mark near the missing nail, too. Abby and Belinda can't stay here any longer."

"Where else them go?"

"I don't know yet. Let's go inside."

When the Ranger and Tonto entered the cabin, Abby lay in bed, her baby, its legs kicking, its hands balled into dancing fists, cuddled next to her.

"How are you feeling, Abby?" the Ranger asked softly.

"What them men want?" Abby asked, fear rich in her eyes. "They the men kill my Hertie?"

"They may have been," the Ranger said.

"We can't stay here," Belinda added.

"You're right. It isn't safe. Abby, do you think Mrs. Davenport would take you in? I'll go speak with her if you think it's worthwhile."

"She been so nice to me…" Abby began, but Belinda interrupted.

"Abby's told me about the things Mrs. Davenport's helped her with. How she gave her and Hertie this land. How she took care of her after the war. Go, please. Talk to her. No one would dare to bother her there."

"Tonto, stay here in case those men return," the Ranger said.

"Me do."

"I'll be back as soon as I can, Abby. Oh, and you have a very beautiful baby."

"He my son."

"Did you name him?"

"Not yet. Too much goin' on. There be time."

"I'll hurry back."

*

The Ranger, accompanied by two riders, returned an hour later, driving a wagon with Silver hitched behind, bringing word that Mrs. Davenport insisted Abby and her child be brought to her immediately. She promised that her crew of four workers, hired since the war, would keep away any band of marauders.

"Any trouble, Tonto?" the Ranger asked, leaping down from the wagon seat.

"It quiet, Kemo Sabe. Baby sleep."

Belinda noticed the Ranger's return and stepped outside the cabin. The Ranger reported on Mrs. Davenport's graciousness while Mrs. Davenport's pair of workers, who'd made the return ride to Abby's place, spread out the bedding they'd brought with them in the back of the wagon.

"She's happy to have you too, Belinda," the Ranger said. "I explained you'd likely be coming along but were going back to work at the end of two weeks."

"Belinda," came Abby's voice from inside.

"Let me tell her the good news," Belinda said.

"What you think, Kemo Sabe?"

"Riding back in the wagon I thought of a plan. I'll tell you about it as soon as we get Abby and her baby to safety."

*

The Fourth of July dawned sunny with the promise of blue skies and a hot day ahead. The Lone Ranger and Tonto rode into town separately and hitched Scout and Silver not far from the sheriff's office. They'd returned to camp the day before after alerting the sheriff about the attack at Abby's place and informing him of her relocation.

After being apprised of the telltale hoof print, the sheriff once again repeated his position that he would not arrest anyone without absolute proof of guilt, especially if a hanging might result. The sheriff and his two occasional deputies, Charley and Wally, accepted the Ranger's invitation to accompany him to Abby's house and see for themselves the hoof prints left behind by the men who'd harassed her. Unknown yet to the sheriff, the plan The Ranger laid out earlier for Tonto depended on the sheriff making at least one arrest.

Red, white, and blue bunting decorated the storefronts in Frederick on this very special holiday. Flags hung from posts high enough to let the colors unfurl. President Grant's picture hung in many store windows; Jefferson Davis's hung in a few others. The two saloons opened early, and the streets filled with celebrants. There were both foot races and horse races, outdoor food stands, shooting contests, and, planned for later, dancing in the streets. At noon, the streets emptied, and people vied for spots along the plank sidewalk. A fife and drum duo began the parade, and anyone who wanted to march in it was welcome. People waved flags and cheered. When the last of the parade passed by and people began to disperse, a second procession of men came into view, this group dressed in their Confederate army grays. Leading the line of some twenty-five men, a man carried a Confederate stars and bars.

The sheriff and his two deputies stood outside his office waiting for the second procession to pass by. The disguised Lone Ranger and Tonto stood on opposite sides of the street; Tonto outside the Golden Goose, the Ranger outside the Alhambra. The Ranger trained his eyes on the approaching array of men strutting down the center of the main street and saw it at once. A steady field of gray topped the group of marchers except for one small island of exposed blond hair. The Ranger studied the face of the man without a cap as he passed by, then slowly made his way through the milling crowd toward the sheriff's office.

When he reached the sheriff, he bent near and said, "Who is he?"

The sheriff understood the question.

"He's Len Carper, the biggest big mouth of the bunch. I'd've bet the ranch on it being him. I told you it would be."

"Are the other two there?"

"Yep, marching right along next to him."

Tonto joined the group. "You see, Kemo Sabe?"

"We saw. Sheriff, where do these men go now?"

"Ha! No doubt back to the Goose or the Alhambra."

"If you don't think you can arrest anyone, Sheriff, do you think you have enough evidence to take Marv Johnson in for questioning? The hoof print…?

"Those three'll probably be together all day. How can I…?"

"Take him in right in front of the others. Ask him if he's been out to Abby's place recently. Ask Carper what happened to his cap. Ask Cal Ramsey whether he found his knife. Then bring Johnson to the jail. The other two will surely wonder what he's telling you. Put me in a cell so I hear what you two talk about."

"You get some mighty peculiar ideas, but come on," the sheriff said, leading everyone inside. The sheriff indicated the two cells and said, "Pick one."

The Ranger chose the left cell, which allowed a better view of the area in front of the sheriff's desk. When the sheriff picked up his keys, the Ranger said, "Be sure to sit Johnson right in front of your desk so I can watch him. And simply close the cell door. There's no need to lock it."

"Ha! Yeah, I guess you're right about that. Put your guns under the mattress. Tonto, where'll you be?"

"Me be right outside."

"Charley, you stay here. Wally, let's go get 'im."

The Ranger lounged on the cell's cot when the door to the office opened and the sheriff, accompanied by Wally and Marv Johnson, walked in.

"Sheriff, what reason would I have to go out there? I tell you I ain't been nowhere *near* her place," Johnson argued. "What are you bothering me for on a day like this?"

"Sit down," the sheriff demanded.

"Who's he?" Johnson asked, falling into a wooden chair positioned before the sheriff's desk.

"What's he look like? He's a prisoner just like you're gonna be if you don't answer me with the truth." The sheriff leaned back against his desk and crossed his arms. "I know you rode out to Abby's farm yesterday, Marv. I got proof. You better tell me why you went there, and I mean right now."

Johnson's body stiffened.

"You got no proof of nothing. I tell you I wasn't there."

"And I say you were! Let me ask you something. Len Carper wasn't wearing his army cap today. Always wore one before. Why didn't he wear it today?"

At Sheriff Hosgood's question, the Ranger noticed Johnson's chest rise and fall in a way it hadn't a moment before.

"You already asked him, and we both heard what he said. He misplaced it."

"That cap in *your* hand; is it yours or did you lose yours and borrow Carper's?"

"Sheriff, you ain't making any sense. Of course, it's my cap."

"You lend anybody your horse yesterday?"

"No."

"Your horse run away yesterday?"

"No."

"Horse stayed put in town all day?"

"Yes. Hitched up. What kind of questions are these?"

"Had your horse shod lately?"

"What?"

"Your horse; your horse. When you had its shoes looked at?"

"I don't know. What's going on here?"

"Your right rear shoe's missing a nail, Marv, plus it's got a funny looking, worn-down part near the missing nail. Leaves a pretty sharp mark behind. I know 'cause I seen it."

"What do you mean you've seen it?"

"Saw it out at Abby Horsy's place yesterday. It's how I know you were there."

The Ranger inched back a bit on his cot to better study Johnson's face.

"What's wrong, Marv?" the sheriff asked. "You look a bit peaked."

"I may've passed by her place yesterday."

"Passed by? You just said you weren't there at all. Let me tell you it weren't on the road I saw the hoof print. I saw it right up close to the house, like you went visiting. Who else went out there with you?"

"Sheriff..." A look of distinct pain crossed Johnson's face.

"Who were the other men who rode out with you? Tracks I looked at say there were two more of you. Answer me quick. I still got one empty cell here; you can see that, can't you?"

"Sheriff, I..."

The sheriff pounded ahead. "There was a lynching nearby not so long ago. You heard about it?"

"I heard." Johnson's eyes could no longer meet the sheriff's gaze.

"Seems like three men did the hanging."

For a moment Johnson raised his head and glared at

the sheriff, but he dropped his gaze quickly.

"One of those men rode your horse. That's murder, Marv. Now, you want to help me or not? Maybe we'll only need to hang two murderers 'stead of three. That is, if you help."

Johnson appeared on the verge of a decision when Tonto opened the office door.

"What?" the sheriff barked.

"Other two men in gray, one with no cap, get on horses and ride out of town in big hurry," Tonto reported.

The Ranger rose from his cot.

"Me get horses," Tonto said.

"They've figured out we know about them, Sheriff," the Ranger said, opening the cell door and slipping his .44s back into their holsters.

"What the…?" Johnson cried, eyes wide in confusion.

"Get in the cell," the sheriff ordered.

Johnson rose, staring first at the mustached Ranger, then back at the sheriff. With some rough help from the sheriff, he ended up inside the cell vacated by the Lone Ranger. The sheriff closed the cell door, and this time he locked it.

"Leave one deputy here," the Ranger said, "in case they double back and try to get to their friend out."

A moment later the Lone Ranger, Tonto, Sheriff

Hosgood, and Wally rode out of town in pursuit of Cal Ramsey and Len Carper.

Chapter 20

The Chase

"It look like men ride to Abby cabin," Tonto shouted over the sound of sixteen beating hooves.

"Good thing no one's there any longer," the Lone Ranger shouted back.

When the cabin came into view, they saw Len Carper stalking toward the door holding a flaming torch and Cal Ramsey on one knee, aiming a rifle at the cabin door.

The Ranger urged Silver on. "Faster, big fellow. Faster!" He longed for his pearl-handled revolvers, but they were in his saddlebags along with his standard clothing. Nonetheless, he drew his gun and fired twice, hoping to keep Carper from setting Abby's house on fire. Carper and Ramsey spun to see where the shots came from. Ramsey threw his rifle up to his shoulder and began pumping lead toward the four charging horsemen, who immediately scattered. Carper dropped the torch, and he and Ramsey ran to their horses, mounted, and spurred them hard.

The Ranger, Tonto, Sheriff Hosgood, and Wally regrouped.

"I'll check the cabin to be sure," the Ranger called. He brought Silver to a stop alongside the door, leaped to the ground, and looked inside the cabin. "Empty," he called. "Let's get after them."

The road twisted through hills and clusters of trees, making it impossible to keep visual track of the men they followed. When they arrived at a fork in the road they halted.

"Tonto," the Ranger urged.

Tonto dismounted and studied the ground. One narrow path led into a field of rocks and boulders offering places of concealment but difficult to gallop through. The second trail was a continuation of the original road.

"Me see tracks go both way, Kemo Sabe."

"Did they split up?" the Ranger asked.

"No. Two horses go this way, two horses that way. Four horse."

"Strange," the Ranger muttered. "Then we'll have to split up. Sheriff, take your deputy and head up through the rocks. I think it more likely they kept straight along the road, though. If so, they won't outrun Silver and Scout."

"Your horses can fly," Sheriff Hosgood agreed. "No question 'bout that. Come on, Wally. Let's see what we find." He and his deputy started through the rocky maze.

"Get up, Silver," the Ranger cried, and he and Tonto raced ahead.

Ten minutes later, the Ranger saw two horses racing toward them, neither horseman dressed in gray. When they converged, the four riders pulled up, and the Ranger asked, "Did you see two men dressed in

Confederate army uniforms riding hard along this road?"

"What? Confederate uniforms? No, no one's been on this road, mister. Whitey and I been having races along here. We're breaking in these new horses. They're pretty fast, too," he ended, excitement in his tone.

"You've been riding up and down this road?" the Ranger asked. "For how long?"

"We've been up and down it four times now, and we haven't seen any Confederate soldiers. War's been over a long time," the boy said, joining in his friend's laughter.

"Thanks," the Ranger cried, pulling on the reins and putting Silver into a gallop back toward the rocky road the sheriff had taken.

Suddenly, they heard gunfire.

"Ambush!" the Ranger cried. "Go, Silver! Get up!"

When he and Tonto reached the rocky turn off, by necessity they slowed. Each held the reins in one hand and his revolver in the other. When they rounded an enormous boulder, there lay Sheriff Hosgood and Wally. Hosgood offered a weak wave.

"They rode off," he said weakly. "See what you can do for Wally. I think they got him bad."

Tonto bent over the deputy, but after a moment's inspection, he rose to his feet.

"Him dead. Two bullet in chest."

"Where are you hit, Sheriff?" the Ranger asked.

"My hip. I don't think it's much. Help me up."

The Ranger took the sheriff by the armpits and hoisted him. The sheriff moaned when he put weight on his right leg.

"They're going back to the jail to break Marv Johnson out," the sheriff said. "Heard 'em say so. They figured I couldn't go after them."

"Here your gun, Sheriff," Tonto said.

"Thanks. I emptied it at them twice. They knew they hit me but didn't want to hang around in case you two showed up, I guess. Good thing. Otherwise, I'd be lying there with Wally."

"We'll come back for Wally later. Tonto, help get the sheriff to Doctor Mikkels. I'm going after those two. We'll meet at the sheriff's office if need be."

"Get me on my horse," the sheriff insisted. "I can ride."

"Help him, Tonto. Come on, big fellow. Hi-yo, Silver. Away!"

*

The Ranger saw only the deputy's horse hitched in front of the jail. When he threw the door open, he found Charley's body sprawled lifeless on the floor. The jail cell was empty, its door swung open. Carper and Ramsey had made good on breaking Marv Johnson out of jail.

The Ranger considered. He needed Tonto whose tracking skills were exceeded by no one; plus, three against two were better odds than three against one. He went outside and took his holster and clothing from his saddlebags. It wouldn't take Tonto long to get there.

As the Ranger tied his mask on, he suddenly realized Doctor Mikkels would not likely be in his office, today being a holiday. He mounted Silver and rode to the Alhambra. He entered the building, and ignoring the stares occasioned by his mask, he searched the crowded room. Not seeing the doctor, he climbed onto the seat of a wooden chair.

"I need your help," he called loudly. "Everyone." His deep voice commanded the room, and heads turned his way. "Sheriff Hosgood has been shot, and my partner is bringing him back to Frederick. They'll arrive soon, and I need Doctor Mikkels. Does anyone know where he is?"

A buzz of chatter filled the room, and the Ranger waited. Finally, a voice called, "Who shot the sheriff? Wasn't you, was it?"

"No. Three men are responsible. Len Carper, Cal Ramsey, and Marv Johnson. The sheriff arrested Marv Johnson earlier today for the lynching of Hertie Horsy. The other two have just broken him out of jail. They also killed the sheriff's two deputies, Charley and Wally. Listen to me. Where is Doctor Mikkels?"

A voice called above the murmur of the crowd, "I saw him playing cards at the Goose ten minutes ago."

"Can you go get him and bring him here?" the Ranger asked.

"I'll go," called a bearded man standing nearer the door.

"Can any of you tell me where those killers might go to hide? They're responsible for the deaths of three men and the wounding of your sheriff." From his elevated perch, the Ranger saw men's eyes dart around the room, many toward the dozen or so men still wearing their Confederate uniforms. No one offered a suggestion. The Ranger understood. Fear had silenced the men's tongues.

"No one?" he asked again. The doctor entered the Alhambra. The Ranger waited another moment to see whether anyone would come forward to offer help. When no one did, he stepped down from the chair, took the doctor by the elbow, and led him outside.

"What happened?" the doctor asked, and the Ranger told him all he could. "How bad is he?"

"I don't think it's serious. He was able to get onto his horse… there! I see them."

Tonto rode into town on Scout, leading a second horse by the reins. Sheriff Hosgood held tightly to the horn of his saddle.

"Have your Indian friend bring him to my office." The doctor hurried away.

"Sheriff weak," Tonto said by way of greeting.

"I found the doctor. He's waiting in his office. I'll

meet you outside the jail. The deputy's been killed, and all three men have escaped."

"Me come quick."

The Ranger mounted Silver and rode slowly toward the jail. When he noticed a young boy running along the sidewalk trying to keep up with him, he pulled Silver to a halt. "Keep going, mister," said the boy, who looked to be fourteen or so. "I don't want them to see me."

The Ranger rode on until he reached the jail.

"Around back," the boy ordered, and the Ranger complied.

"What can I do for you?" he asked, dismounting.

"You wanted to know where Len Carper would go to hide."

"How do you know that?"

"I was outside the Alhambra, listening. I heard what you said."

"Do you know where he might go?"

"I think so. Maybe."

The Ranger offered a soft smile. "Can you tell me?"

"He gave me a dollar couple weeks ago to go with him and help clean up a broken-down old shack. He even borrowed me a horse to ride on the trip."

"Where is this shack?"

"It's built right up against a cave. It doesn't have a back wall, well, not much of one. The back wall's just the opening to the cave."

"Where?"

"You know where the mesas and arroyos are?"

"I do."

"Well, it ain't that way out of town. It's the other way."

"Toward the Davenport farm?"

"Right, but a ways out of town you gotta find a small road nearby where there's a tree." The boy looked down, embarrassed.

"What's wrong?"

"It's the tree where people found that man hanging."

"I understand."

"You have to go around some rocks and hills right across from the tree before you can see where the road starts. You can't see it easy from the main road. You follow that maybe two miles, and you'll come across the shack he took me to."

Tonto rode up.

"Come and listen to this, Kemo Sabe," the Ranger said. He turned back to the boy. "Were you inside the cabin?"

"Of course, I was. Didn't I say he took me there to

clean it up?"

"Yes, you did. Tell me about the cave. Does it have another entrance, or can you only get to it through the cabin?"

"I didn't see no other way out. The shack has a couple windows, but it's really dark inside the cave. If there was another way out, there'd be some light, wouldn't there?"

"I think you're right," the Ranger agreed. "How big is the cave?"

"It ain't a big cave, but for an extra room in a cabin, it's a pretty big room. It ain't so deep but it's pretty high." The boy glanced around, nervously.

"You've been a big help…?"

"You don't need my name. I gotta go. If one of those grays see me talking to you, it won't be so good for me."

"You go then. And thank you."

The boy ran along behind the buildings lining the main street and disappeared from sight.

"Boy tell you where men hide?"

"He offered a very good suggestion. Let's hope he's right. I'll fill you in as we ride."

*

When the three fugitives reined up in front of a

tumbledown shack built against a low-rise wall of rock, Len Carper ordered Cal Ramsey and Marv Johnson to dismount.

"Where the devil are we, Len?" Cal Ramsey spat bitterly.

"Settle down, Cal," Marv Johnson said.

"Yeah, settle down," Carper repeated.

"Settle down? How can I settle down after you botched things up so bad? I knew lynching that no account farmer would get us into trouble not to mention knocking off the sheriff and his two deputies. And you," he said, directing his anger toward Johnson. "What'd you tell the sheriff when he pulled you in? How'd he know to come after us? We left the Alhambra, and they were on us pronto."

"I didn't tell them anything, Cal," Johnson said, raising his voice. "You're the one who bought the knife and left it behind."

"Bah," Ramsey growled. "Wasn't me who left my cap stuck in the guy's chest for the whole world to see. I *told* you two; things are different now. Abraham Lincoln, General Grant, abolition. The world's upside down, in a total mess, and now we're in a mess, too."

"Will you both shut up," Carper ordered. He opened the door to the shack. "Get your horses inside."

"Inside there?" Ramsey cried.

"Move. The shack opens onto cave where there's plenty of room for our horses. We hide out here for a few days, then move on. We can't go back to Frederick."

"Why not?" Ramsey argued. "We plugged the sheriff…"

"Did you plug the masked man and his Indian pard too? I don't know who they are, but they seem to be everywhere. We gotta hope they move on. If they don't…"

Ramsey and Johnson exchanged glances.

"More killing," Ramsey muttered.

"Now, get your horses inside. I planned for something like this. There's a half a wagonload of hay in the cave and food and water enough for two days. Nobody will find this place. We can cool down and think this through."

*

The Lone Ranger and Tonto followed the boy's directions and found the hidden road. They followed the uneven path, and when the shack came into view, they dismounted and left Silver and Scout behind. They found a safe niche amidst some large rocks and studied the layout.

"Nobody there, Kemo Sabe. Tracks lead to shack but disappear."

"I'm not so sure they disappear. I think they simply went inside the shack. Remember, the boy said the shack concealed a large cave."

"That right. How long you think they plan hide out here?"

The Lone Ranger chuckled.

"How long would you like to live in a confined space along with three horses?"

"Heh, heh, heh. Them not stay too long. What we do now?"

"Let's move nearer. Perhaps we can get them to leave sooner."

The shack had two square windows, one on each side of the door, each window having space for four panes of glass. The window to the left of the door had one unbroken pane; the window to the right, two unbroken panes.

The Ranger drew the Colt .44 from his left holster.

"Do you see those three unbroken panes of glass?" he asked Tonto.

"Me see 'em."

Bam! Bam! Bam!

"And now you don't. Stay low, Kemo Sabe. They know they have company."

*

"What the devil?" Cal Ramsey squawked as glass exploded into the one-room shack.

"Down! Down!" Carper cried.

"You said they'd never find us," Ramsey exploded. "We're here half-an-hour and already they're shooting at us."

"Who you think's out there?" Johnson asked.

"Why don't you go look?" Carper responded.

"No thanks. What do we do now? They may have a whole posse out there, a dozen guns maybe. We gotta know." He crawled to the window left of the door and gently raised an eye to it. "I don't see anything."

"They're not gonna stand around in the open! They know we're armed, and they know we'd shoot them as soon as look at them," Carper said. "What would we have to lose?"

"I'm not staying in this shack. I know that much," Ramsey said. "It'd be suicide."

"You care to tell us your plan?" Carper asked snidely.

"Don't take that tone with me, Len. We stay here, we're cooked. Two days food. Hell, they could easy set fire to the shack and pick us off as we left. Not for me. I'm leaving right now, when they don't expect it." He rose and disappeared inside the cave.

"What do you think he's gonna do?" Johnson asked softly.

"How do I know? Keep an eye to the window. Make sure they're not creeping up on us," Carper ordered.

"I'll go see."

Johnson heard Carper and Ramsey's voices arguing, but the cave echoes obscured the words. When Carper exited the cave, he said, "Marv, go saddle your horse. We're opening the door and riding out blasting. Cal's right. We say here, we have no chance."

"Ride out into their gunfire? I'd rather surrender."

"Surrender and be hanged?"

Johnson exhaled, defeated. "Why did I ever hook up with you?"

"Too late for that now. Go saddle."

The Ranger and Tonto were unprepared when the door of the shack flew open, and three riders awkwardly navigated the entrance, then rode hard off to the right, firing blindly at the rocks in line with the shack door.

"Tonto!" the Ranger cried.

Tonto, who'd been moving to a spot with a better vantage point, said, "Me see!" He and the Ranger returned fire.

The random bullets coming at them posed little threat, so they took time to aim. First, Cal Ramsey fell from his horse, a bullet from Tonto entering his ribcage. The Ranger took careful bead, and before Marv Johnson could reach shelter behind some rocks, two bullets lanced into his left shoulder. The hellfire of pain he felt knocked him to the ground. Carper rode on.

"Let's see how badly they're hurt," the Ranger said.

He and Tonto moved forward, both fallen men visible as they advanced. Neither injured man attempted any retaliation. Tonto picked up Ramsey's gun and checked him for other weapons.

"I'm hit," he moaned. "You gut-shot me. I need help."

"Help may be a while coming," the Ranger said, and he moved off to check on Johnson, who had slowly gotten his legs under him. "Johnson, drop your gun or feel another slug."

His back to the Ranger, Johnson froze, contemplating a decision. He spun and leveled his revolver, but before he could fire, a silver bullet ripped into his shooting shoulder and he went down, his gun sailing ten feet away. Johnson lay writhing in anguish as a sudden cascade of gunfire came from above, and the Ranger and Tonto dove into the shelter of the rocks.

"It third man. Why him not ride away?" Tonto asked.

"Maybe he knows his horse is no match for Silver. Or maybe he's trying to save his friends."

"Him not that kind of man," Tonto said softly.

"I agree. Can you see him? Let me try to make him show himself."

The Ranger emptied his guns with a spray of bullets aimed at the rocks above him. As he reloaded, he asked, "Any movement?"

"Me see him. There. Him move under big rocks."

"Tonto, can you get up behind him. One good push and those rocks above him will come tumbling down."

"There one open space me have to pass. You see?"

"I do. When you get there, signal. I'll fire and keep his attention away from you. When you get to the top, let those rocks go."

"Me do."

The Ranger kept a close watch on Carper. At any sign of movement from him, he'd blast away to keep Carper in place. When Tonto reached the short, open area, he gave a wave to the Ranger, and immediately the Ranger let loose with a fusillade of bullets from both guns. By the time his chambers were empty, Tonto had safely crossed the divide, and the Ranger reloaded.

A moment later an assortment of bouncing, careening rocks and small boulders rumbled down toward Carper. He heard the noise, turned, and dove aside as the crush of the avalanche struck where he'd been hiding. The Ranger sent three shots toward Carper, now exposed and running for new cover. The third bullet took him high on the arm. From above, Tonto sent a second bullet into the rear of his right thigh, and he fell. The Ranger and Tonto converged on him.

"Not one move, Carper," the Ranger's voice rang out. "Both of us have you in our sights."

Carper struggled to rise, but his legs went out from under him and he lay still, all hope gone.

"Let's get them into the shack, Kemo Sabe," the

Ranger said. "We'll tie them, if need be, and you do what you can for them. Take no chances, though. Once we get them squared away, I'll ride into town, report to the sheriff, and bring back a posse. Get his gun."

*

Hours later, the Lone Ranger spoke to Sheriff Hosgood. "I'd rather you didn't know how Tonto and I trailed them to the shack, Sheriff," he said.

Sheriff Hosgood lay on the cot in his office, lit now by the oil lamp on his desk. Night had fallen and the sounds of the Independence Day celebrations still going on in the Alhambra and the Golden Goose filtered into the room. Len Carper and Marv Johnson, patched up by Doctor Mikkels, sat quietly in the two jail cells. Cal Ramsey, the most seriously wounded of the three, remained handcuffed to a bed in the doctor's office, watched over by two volunteers the sheriff had recruited. The bodies of Charley and Wally had been collected and their burial scheduled for next morning.

"I don't care how you found those snakes. I'm just glad you did," the sheriff said. "Judge Lemon will be through here about the twentieth, and that'll put an end to these three buzzards. Doc says I shouldn't move around for a few days, let my hip heal up, but I'll be at the cemetery tomorrow. We lost two good men." His gaze went to the men he'd locked up. "You gonna stick around for that?"

"We are. Tonto and I will spend the night in camp,

attend the services tomorrow morning, and pay a visit to Belinda and Abby at the Davenport house. After that, we'll be off. Our job here is finished."

"You done a lot to help this town, mister. Wish I knew more about you."

"That's not important. Adios."

*

When the Lone Ranger and Tonto rode up to the Davenport house late the next morning, Abby and Belinda sat on the front porch, the new baby in Abby's lap. Liza played nearby, feeding flowers to a raggedy doll she held. Belinda rose and descended the two steps to the ground to welcome the Ranger and Tonto.

"I have some news," the Ranger said, "which I think Abby will want to hear." He and Tonto took chairs and told Abby of the previous day's capture of the men who'd murdered her husband.

After she'd dried her tears, Abby said, "You a fine man. I hope my little boy grow up to be half like his daddy and half like you."

"I thank you for the compliment," the Ranger replied. "Have you named the young fellow yet?"

"He be named after his daddy. But folks gets two names sometimes, don't they?" Abby asked.

"They do," the Ranger confirmed.

"Belinda, would you take the baby for me?" Abby

asked. She handed the baby over and to the Ranger said, "Would you walk a little with me?"

"Certainly."

The Ranger followed Abby from the porch a short distance until she turned to him and said, "I want his second name to be your name."

"Abby…" the Ranger began.

"He be named after two good men, he turn out to be a good man hisself," Abby said, her mind made up.

The Ranger leaned near Abby and whispered in her ear. She grinned and led the Ranger back to the porch.

"There's one more thing, Abby," the Ranger said. "I nearly forgot. Silver! Here, Silver."

The great white stallion whinnied and trotted up to the Ranger, who went into one of his saddlebags and withdrew a small, white, lacy infant's cap.

"Hertie had this in his pocket that day. He was bringing it home for you and the baby."

Abby's eyes misted up again, but she maintained her composure as she took the gift in her hand.

"This is my Hertie telling me things is gonna be all right."

"Tonto and I will be going now," the Ranger said. "We wish you well."

They mounted up, turned their backs on Frederick, and set out for Jim Faraday's silver mine.

"Belinda," Abby said, "where would I be without that masked man's help?"

"He's quite a fellow. We *both* owe him a lot."

"Give me little Hertie back. I decided on a second name for him."

"What name?"

"He be known as Hertie John Horsy."

They kept their eyes on the departing figures of the Lone Ranger and Tonto, and when they could no longer see them, they returned to their chairs on the Davenport porch.

Chapter 21

Garth Cavendish

One hundred and fifteen miles southeast of Frederick, Garth Cavendish pulled his mount to a rough stop before a three-story wooden hotel in the town of Stony Creek. He and his father had taken rooms there and lived a quiet life, drinking and gambling and sleeping away their two-month hiatus until they would reunite with what was left of the Cavendish gang. Garth snatched a pair of newspapers from his saddlebags and took the stairs two at a time to the third floor, where he banged on his father's door.

"What? Who is it?" Butch Cavendish, unshaven and shirtless, opened the door, pistol in hand. "What the devil's the matter with you? You crazy or something? We're here to live quiet, and there you are banging on the door to wake the dead."

"You're not gonna like this, Pop."

Butch tossed his gun onto the bed.

"What do you got?"

"Newspapers. Here, read. I can't bring myself to tell you."

Butch read the first article quietly before dropping the newspaper on the floor. He looked at his son.

"Read the other one, Pa. It's bad."

When Butch finished the second article, he

crumpled the paper and angrily tossed it away.

"Where'd you get these?" Cavendish growled.

"Some peddler passing through had them. I looked them over, saw the news, and bought the papers from him. Did you see? Did you read? Both of them, Pa. Razor's been hung, and Shark's being held in Fort Davis till they execute him." He watched for his father's reaction to the news, but he sat in utter silence, his lips drawn into a thin, tense line. "Pa?"

"They were caught by a masked man and an Indian? Who the devil are they, and why are they butting in?"

"The masked man is called the Lone Ranger, Pa."

"I can read," Butch snapped.

"What are we gonna do? You think Montana knows about this?"

"How should I know?"

"What are we gonna do?"

Butch's eyes turned icily to his son. "What do *you* think we should do?"

"Come on, Pa. Don't talk that way. Don't make fun of me. Want me to go after him? I'll go after him."

"Go after who?"

"The masked man, of course. I'll get him before he can get Montana or us."

"What makes you think he won't get you first?"

"Come on, Pa. Have some confidence in me."

"I do, I do, son," Butch replied, catching himself. Butch loved his son more than he loved anything in the world. His pride blossomed, as any father's would, when his son chose to follow him into the family business, in this case murder and robbery. He knew of Garth's hungry yearning for his approval, but he also knew he was often too busy or preoccupied or unimpressed with his son, to give it. Garth always obeyed his orders to the letter—he had to give him credit for that much, at least—but his son had shown no signs of being an initiator. Now, the boy stood before him, asking for permission to go after this Lone Ranger. Perhaps one such triumph was all Garth might need to boost him up and prepare him to *really* follow in his father's footsteps. This Lone Ranger had reduced his gang to only three members. Practically the whole outfit would have to be reformed. With Razor and Shark both gone, Garth would *have* to step up. Perhaps allowing him to go after the Lone Ranger would be the act that transformed him. Anything was possible.

"Pa?" Garth prodded.

"You think you could do it?"

"Of course, I think so. He ain't never seen me, I don't think. And for cripes sakes, he walks around in a mask with an Indian at his side! How hard could it be to find him? He'd sorta stand out anyplace he went, wouldn't he, Pa?" Garth gave an encouraging chuckle.

"How would you know where to start looking for him? It's less than a month till we meet up with Montana at Cold Stream."

"I'll start at Corbin City and pick up his trail from there. I can be there in a couple days."

"You might be recognized."

"I don't think so. How 'bout if I disguise myself? I'll cut my hair and wear glasses. I'll dress like a dude."

Butch knew he could not reconstitute his outlaw band if this masked troublemaker kept picking off his men one by one.

Butch decided. "Okay, boy. I'm gonna trust you with this."

"I won't let you down, Pa."

"Eliminate this masked man and his Indian friend. You may have to hide out after you deal with them. If you do, don't come back here. Meet me in Cold Stream. Me and Montana will wait there till you come. Don't come if it's not safe. Do you hear me? We'll wait for you as long as it takes."

"Don't worry. I'll get the masked man and Indian or die trying." Garth laughed, drew his gun, and spun it around on his trigger finger. "Or die trying, Pa."

Garth immediately went to get his hair cut and buy some clothes. Then, he bought a pair of weak glasses from the Stony Creek General Store. Unable to see much through them, he figured he could wear them low on his nose or pushed up onto this forehead whenever he needed them as part of his disguise. He spent the night mulling over ways he could somehow get close to the Lone Ranger—close enough to plug him. He didn't think too hard about it, though, knowing he had a days-long ride on the trail to come up with an idea, but something he saw in the general store when he bought the glasses caused a plan to fall right into his lap.

On his way out of town next day, he stopped into the store. A metal stand filled with small magazines sat on a shelf, a sign above them reading BEADLES DIME NOVELS. The title of one book caught his eye. He took it from the rack and leafed through it. THE MASKED MESSENGER, or, *The Maid of Gresham Greene*. His eye fell upon a second flimsy pamphlet: THE MASKED GUIDE, or, *The Road Agents of the Plains.*

He paid for the two short novels and, once outside the store, he tucked them into his saddlebags and started riding. He realized he had too little education to pass himself off as a writer of these tales, but there was no reason he couldn't be someone sent by the company to be on the lookout for a good story. A person didn't need any education to do that. He could claim that fanciful stories of Western masked heroes were popular back East and as evidence, display the two masked rider books he'd brought with him. He could claim that Beadles Publishing had heard of such a character in the area calling himself the Lone Ranger, and they'd sent him. He realized he needed a name other than his own, which anyone might see on a wanted poster. He laughed aloud as a name sprang into his mind. Clarence Witty. The publisher had sent him, Clarence Witty, to find this masked man and interview him.

He wished he could let his Pa know about his genius inspiration! The plan couldn't fail. When he asked around about the masked man, it wouldn't arouse any suspicion. If the masked man heard of someone looking for him and learned why, he had no reason to suspect that Clarence Witty had come to kill him. Garth set his sights on carrying out his plan without a hitch. When he met his father a few weeks hence, he would greet him with the story of how he'd killed the Lone Ranger and Tonto. His Pa would never doubt him again.

*

The Ranger and Tonto approached Jim's cabin in the late afternoon. Jim sat outside smoking a cigarette and snapped to attention when he noticed the men approaching. He recognized them, jumped to his feet, tossed his cigarette on the ground, and waved his right arm lustily above his head. The Ranger and Tonto waved back.

"Well, ain't you two a sight for sore eyes," Jim crowed. "Get down off them horses and come inside."

"Jim," the Ranger said, "did you hear the news? Tonto and I helped bring Razor Gilliam and Shark Lawson to justice."

"What! Already! That's fantastic. How'd you do it? How'd you get 'em?"

They went inside Jim's cabin, and the Ranger went through the story.

"So, Razor's done for, eh?"

"He is, and Shark's locked up at Fort Davis."

"I don't guess he's long for this world, either."

"You're probably right, Jim. But I'm surprised you didn't know. Tonto and I read the news in different newspapers we came across in our travels."

"I don't get to read no newspapers. Tyler's Crossing is a nice little town but too one-horse to have a newspaper. You know that."

The Ranger laughed. "Yes, I do."

"Anyway, I'm glad to hear it," Jim said. "You two are some pair. Who ya goin' after now?"

"We still need to find Cavendish, his son, and Montana Jenkins."

"They're the last of 'em, eh?"

"They are. We need to find them before Cavendish recruits a new gang of killers and robbers."

"I got some news for *you*, Ranger, but it ain't as good as what you told me."

"Go on, Jim. What is it?"

"Linda and little Dan are planning to head back East."

"Oh," the Ranger said softly. "I'm... I'm sorry hear that. Do you know why they're going?"

"I talked to her some. She said something about memories being painful and wanting the best for little Dan."

"I see. When are they leaving?"

"September first the latest. She sold her place... your brother's place... your place, I guess. Anyway, the place is sold."

"What happens to you, Jim?" the Ranger asked.

"Nothing. She rode out here special to tell me this piece of ground and even a little more she added to it are mine. It's gonna be deeded to me and wasn't sold to the new people. Andrews is the name of the new outfit. Nice people, too. Husband, wife and a passel of young'uns."

"I'm sure Linda will have plenty of money to keep her and Dan well provided for back East."

"She said she hoped they might come back out West one day."

"I'd really like to see them..." The Ranger hung his head and went outside the cabin.

"Him miss family heap much," Tonto said to Jim.

"I guess he does. A good family it is, too."

The Ranger stepped back inside.

"Seeing them is impossible. It might change their mind about staying, and not knowing how things with Cavendish will turn out, they'll be safer far away from here. Jim, make sure you tell Linda to keep in touch with you. If she knows an address where she can be reached, get it. You never know."

"I'll ride over tomorrow, Ranger."

"Mind if Tonto and I stay in the shack out back?"

"Course not. I got a good supply of bullets for you—I see your belt needs refilling—and plenty of silver to take to the bank for spending money."

"Jim, I can't thank you enough. Tonto and I will let the horses rest up a few days, then we'll be out after Cavendish again," the Ranger said, extending his hand.

Jim shook it, then went inside to prepare some dinner.

*

Garth's search for the Lone Ranger and Tonto began in Corbin City, the town in which one of the articles he'd read placed the hanging of Razor Gilliam. Not wanting to waste an opportunity, however, in the one small town he passed through along the way, he stopped in at the sheriff's office and the newspaper office. He chatted up the sheriff in as friendly a manner as possible, showed off his two Beadles dime novels, and explained what he was looking for. The sheriff told him he'd heard of the masked man but had never seen him. He bought an advertisement in the town's newspaper, condensing the reason for his search for the Lone Ranger into as interesting blurb as he could come up with.

Now, though, he'd reached his destination. Dressed in his new clothes and looking like he'd come from the East, wearing a derby in which he felt foolish, but which surely distanced him from any connection with an outlaw band, and with his useless glasses pushed up on his forehead, he pranced his horse into Corbin City. He couldn't be sure when he might encounter the two men he was after, so he wore his gun as always and kept his Sharps rifle loaded and in its scabbard on his horse. His initial stop would be the first saloon he came across, and Corbin City had two, the Lucky Deal and the Silver Nugget. He tied his horse to the hitching post outside the Lucky Deal, not busy at this time of day, and walked inside.

"Afternoon," he said to the bartender, a rough-looking, bulky man.

The bartender eyed him with amusement. "Afternoon, yourself, stranger. How can I help you?"

"You can gimme a beer."

The bartender complied and, having no one else to serve at the moment, opted for some conversation.

"Where you from?" he asked.

"Back East, New York City."

"You don't sound like you're from the East."

"Born in Texas, went East, and now I'm back. I'm looking for a fellow. Maybe you seen him. People call him the Lone Ranger. I work for a publishing company. We write books."

"I kinda figured that's what they did," the bartender said, frowning.

"Yeah, well, I been sent out here to find out if this masked man is real or not. You see…" He produced his two dime novels. "…masked riders are big business in the East. Excitement, adventure. That kinda thing."

"He's real, all right. Been a help to people in this town. Brought in a criminal we hung not so long ago. Member of the Cavendish gang. Heard of them?"

"Cavendish? No, they famous around here?"

"I don't know if famous is the word. Anyway, the masked man passed through recently."

Garth's stomach fluttered. "Really? When? You know where he headed?"

"Not long ago, four, five days. Can't say where he was going. Sheriff Hosh might know. Jail's down the street. What's your name, friend?"

"Clarence. Clarence Witty."

The bartender strained to keep a smile from his face and said, "Drink up, Clarence. Knock if you want another." He moved away.

On his own, Garth would have happily chosen to spend the rest of the day drinking at the bar, but he knew his father was depending on him, so he finished his beer, paid his bill, and went in search of the jail.

Sheriff Hosh glanced up from his paperwork when an odd-looking fellow walked in after knocking.

"Help you?" the sheriff asked.

Garth went through his recital.

The sheriff paged through THE MASKED GUIDE, *or, The Road Agents of the Plains*.

He handed it back to Garth and said, "*Road Agents of the Plains,* eh? You say they go for this silly stuff where you come from?"

"They do. Can you tell me where I can find this Lone Ranger? I'd love to talk to him. He plays his cards right, I can make him famous back East."

"He headed out north from here, but I can't say where to."

"What towns are out that way?"

"First one you come to is Tyler's Crossing."

"Think maybe he stopped there for some reason?"

"No particular reason I know of, but I guess he could've."

"How far is it?"

"Two, maybe three days."

Garth's hopes fell. He needed to act before his father and Montana Jenkins met up in Cold Stream. Three days was a good chunk of the time he had left to work with. He rose.

"You been a help, Sheriff. I'm gonna stop in the newspaper office."

"The *Bugle*? What for?"

"Put in an ad. Let people know I'm looking for the masked man. Maybe someone'll tell him, or he might read it himself. I'll find him one way or the other. Thanks again, Sheriff."

Garth placed his ad then, after a few moments' consideration, decided to sell his horse if he could find a better one to buy. He needed to make up time, plus he wanted a fresh mount under him in case the Lone Ranger gave him any trouble.

Chapter 22

Clarence Witty

Jim had returned from a trip into Tyler's Crossing to exchange some of his mined silver for spending money for the Lone Ranger and Tonto.

"I still have some more silver to swap if you think you need it," he said.

"No, Jim. This will keep us a good, long time. I can't thank you enough. Besides, we don't want it getting around you're cashing in too much silver. You know what happened with those Beatty brothers."

"No need to thank me, Ranger. You know how much I appreciate what your family's done for me. You're doing God's work, and you got a lot more to accomplish yet. Here, I brought back these boxes for the silver bullets that won't fit on your belt. You can keep 'em in your saddlebag for when you run out."

"Thanks, Jim."

"I stopped in at your sister-in-law's place on the way back."

"How are Linda and little Dan?"

"Heh heh. Little guy's starting to walk, Linda tells me. He's gonna be a real rip-snorter, he is."

The Ranger laughed. "That's good to hear."

"Something else," Jim said hesitantly.

"Well?"

"There's some new fellow in town. Arrived yesterday, I hear. He's asking around for you."

"Me?"

"You, the 'Lone Ranger'," Jim explained.

"What him look like?" Tonto asked.

"I only got a passing gander at him, and I can tell you he don't look like no cowboy. Got one of them fancy, round hats, wears glasses, and he goes around asking questions about you."

"What kind of questions?"

"Like, does anybody know you? What's your name? Where you from? What've you done? Where can he find you?"

"Did he say who he is?"

"I talked to Briscoe, down at the blacksmith's, and he said he's from a book publishing company back East, and he's interested in writing a book about you. Name's Clarence Witty, according to Briscoe."

"Lone Ranger name travel fast," Tonto said.

"He mentioned you, too, Tonto," Jim said.

"I don't see how we could've become known a thousand miles away in the short time since Bryant's Gap," the Ranger said.

"How him know you come here?" Tonto wondered.

"Another good question, Kemo Sabe."

"You want me to do anything about him?" Jim asked. "Or just leave him be?"

"Jim, go back into Tyler's Crossing. Try to find out what publishing company he works for. I'd like to check into him."

"I already know," Jim said. "Them books of his is sold at Walt Lemon's store. Beadles dime novels. You seen 'em. I read one once. Pretty silly stuff. This Clarence Witty was showing them all around town, and both titles he showed off had do to with masked men. So says Briscoe, anyway."

"This gets even stranger," the Ranger said. "Tonto, will you ride over to San Felipe and telegraph Beadles Publishing House and ask about this Clarence Witty? I think I'll go into town and try to get a look at this fellow."

"San Felipe long ride," Tonto said.

"It's the nearest place with a telegraph office. I think Scout can make it in four or five hours."

"That right. How long you want me wait for answer?"

The Ranger spread his hands. "Let's hope it's no later than tomorrow, Kemo Sabe. I'd go myself, but I'd really like to get a look at this fellow."

"Me not mind. Leave right away."

"Help me into my disguise first. Before you go, I'll write out a message for you to send."

*

Two hours later, Tonto was on his way to San Felipe, and the Ranger, in disguise, rode into Tyler's Crossing. The dirt street, dry and dusty from the summer heat, had its usual assortment of people shopping, working, riding in and out of town on various errands. The Ranger hitched Silver outside the Rusty Spur and went inside. Three men stood at one end of the bar, sipping beers and talking. The Ranger took a spot apart from them.

"Help you, mister?" asked the bartender, a man new to the Ranger.

"Sure, I'll have one of what they're having."

"Beer is it."

The Ranger looked over the nine people spread at tables and saw no one matching Jim's description of Clarence Witty. Where could he find him? he wondered.

Toward the edge of town, Garth Cavendish grew tired of lying in bed and letting the limited time he had slip away. After rereading the two newspaper articles about the Lone Ranger, he put on his boots and went outside. As much as he would have liked, he didn't dare start drinking so early in the day. He imagined book company employees needed to maintain a certain decorum, but he had to get out of his hotel room. The Lone Ranger certainly wasn't going to come knocking on his door, and he didn't want to hang around in Tyler's Crossing much longer, since it didn't even have a newspaper he could place an advertisement in. The bartender hadn't been much help. If he didn't come across any trace of the masked man today, he'd head out tomorrow morning for the next nearest town.

Walking along the wooden sidewalk, he glanced across the street with some longing at the Rusty Spur. Hitched in front of the saloon he noticed a magnificent white horse. Garth paused and recalled how one of his newspaper articles mentioned the Lone Ranger riding a white horse. Garth knew there was more than one white horse in the West, but as he studied the magnificent stallion, the more impressed he became with the animal. A half-dozen other horses were hitched nearby, but the white horse stood taller and appeared more powerful than any of them. Garth crossed the street and ran his hand along Silver's flank, eliciting a resentful whinny from the horse. Garth pushed open the batwing doors and entered the saloon.

When the doors flew inward, they caught the Ranger's attention. He recognized the man immediately as the one Jim described, but his attention was drawn to something Jim had not mentioned. The man wore his gun low on his hip, the bottom of the holster bound with rawhide to his thigh—the exact way a man who used his gun for a living would wear it to facilitate a quick draw. The everyday inhabitants of towns like Tyler's Creek wore their holsters much higher, nearer the waist for comfort, and they depended on the weight of their rarely used gun to keep the holster in place. The Ranger wore his spare gun belt and holster high at the moment as part of his disguise. Clarence Witty seemed, on the surface, to be a man who knew something about guns.

When the two men's eyes met, they held for a moment. Garth approached the bar.

"Is that your horse outside, stranger?" he asked. "Beer for me," he added to the bartender.

"Which horse is that?"

"The big white one."

"Yes, he's mine."

"He looks like a fine animal."

"He's a very fine animal."

"Here in town for long?"

"No. On my way to San Antone. Got a job waiting there for me. Writing a book about the siege of the Alamo. How about you?"

Garth's eyebrows rose in surprise, and he took his two dime novels from his pocket.

"Small world. I'm in the book business, too," he said. "Looking for a masked rider known to be in these parts. Calls himself the Lone Ranger. My book company back East wants me to talk to him, maybe get information for a book. Books like these," he began, tapping the books he'd placed on the bar, "are mighty popular there."

"Are you a writer?"

"No, I just scout around for subjects to write about."

"Sounds interesting. I never heard of a masked rider in these parts."

"Oh, he's real. People have seen him. The bartender… Oh, it's not the same one. The bartender was in here yesterday knows about him."

"Well, good luck in your search."

"Thanks. Mind telling me your name?"

"Mind telling me yours?"

"Clarence Witty."

"Ned Buntline."

"A pleasure, Ned."

"I haven't touched this," the Ranger said, pointing to his glass. "It's yours if you want it. I have to be going."

"Nice talking to you, Ned."

The Ranger walked from the saloon, mounted Silver, and trotted down the main street.

Garth quickly downed his own beer and reluctantly left the other glass untouched. He dropped a coin on the bar and went outside. In the distance, he saw the white horse moving away at the edge of town. He watched it out of sight, then got onto his horse and set out after it.

When the Ranger reached Jim's, he went straight to the shack and removed his disguise before joining his friend inside the cabin.

"How'd you do, Ranger?" Jim asked.

"I met the man, Jim. Even talked to him."

"Clarence Witty, the book man? What'd you think of him?"

"He's no more connected with a publishing company than you are. I never heard of a book company sending someone so far away merely to look for things to write about. That's how Witty described his job. A writer would certainly research whatever he planned to write about, but I doubt he'd leave it to someone else to do, especially for the kind of books Witty showed me."

"The masked man books?"

"Yes. Consider this, Jim. I told him my name was Ned Buntline, and he didn't flinch. No glimmer of recognizing the name."

"Ned Buntline. Heck, even I know *that* name. He wrote them same kinda books, didn't he?"

"He did and still does. He's the man who gave Bill Cody his nickname in *Buffalo Bill, the King of the Border Men*. The book was very popular a few years ago. Anyone involved in books about the West would know the name Ned Buntline."

"So, you think this fellow's a fake?"

"I'm sure of it. He's hiding his real identity but for what reason, I wonder. Did you notice how he wore his gun? Low on his hip."

"I *did* notice that. Don't know why I didn't mention it."

"I'll sit tight until Tonto gets back, but I'm sure I know what news he's bringing."

"Let me whip up some dinner for us."

*

From the stand of trees not far from Jim's shack, Garth eyed the scene at the cabin. The white horse grazed in the small corral nearby, and a few moments earlier, a man in blue, his face hidden by a black mask, walked from a small shack to a cabin an old man had recently entered. Garth felt triumphant. If only his father could see him now. He'd found the man he was after. He hadn't seen the Indian, though, and he'd sworn to go back to his father with the news that *both* of them were dead. The identity of the old man puttering about the place was a mystery, but if the Indian and the masked man had to go, there was no reason to leave a useless old man behind to talk about it. Garth settled in to await the appearance of the Indian. Then, he would do what he came for.

Time passed and darkness arrived. The Indian did not.

*

When Tonto returned late the next afternoon, he brought the Ranger the news he expected. Beadles Publishing had never heard of anyone named Clarence Witty, and as they sat in the small shack behind Jim's cabin, the Ranger filled Tonto in on his meeting with

Witty the day before.

"What we do now, Kemo Sabe?"

"I'm not certain, Tonto, whether we should simply ignore this Clarence Witty or dig deeper and find out who he really is and what he's after. He's clearly not after information for a book."

"But him want you."

"Apparently, he wants both of us."

"Maybe someone send him find you for bad reason."

"Or he may be simply an innocent man with nothing much to do with himself."

"Me not think that."

"No, neither do I. We'd better find out what he really wants."

"How we do that?"

The two men sat quietly for a time, until the Lone Ranger said, "Jim can go to town and tell this Witty he's found me and you. He can invite Witty back here, and we'll deal with him when he arrives."

"Remember, him wear gun like gunfighter."

"I can't see him trying something with the two of us and Jim staring at him."

"That right."

The Ranger stood. He said, "Let's go and see what

Jim thinks of the plan."

*

Garth Cavendish had stayed in the trees the day before, watching the cabin and shack, not returning to town until nightfall. Sleeping in the woods held no allure for him, but he was back among the trees early next morning. Garth's watchful day moved by at a tedious pace, forcing him to rack his brain for some way to bring his vigil to an end. He could do nothing, though, until the Indian showed up. Twice, as he sat leaning against a tree keeping a casual eye on the cabin and shack, he nearly nodded off, but he snapped to attention when Tonto finally rode up and entered the shack. Twenty minutes later, the Indian and masked man paid a visit to the old man's cabin.

A short while afterward, the old man exited the cabin, mounted his horse, and rode in the direction of Tyler's Creek. The Indian and masked man returned to the small shack. Uncertain how to respond to what he saw, Garth ran through the events of the previous couple days. Having had a good look at the old man, he recalled seeing him in town while he explained to some of the town's citizens why he'd come to Tyler's Creek. Obviously, he was friends with the Indian and masked man, putting them up while they stayed in the area. The old man, having been in town the day before, surely reported to the masked man that someone named Clarence Witty was asking about him. The masked man then put on a disguise and came into town to take a look for himself. Garth gave a satisfied chuckle at the cleverness he displayed in figuring out the sequence of events. Following the stranger back to the old man's place, he saw him arrive looking one way and emerge from the shack as the very man he sought, the Lone Ranger, whom he was certain he'd come across to as a simple, harmless worker for a book company. Perhaps the masked man had sent the old man into town to let Witty know he was willing to be interviewed by the harmless man from the Rusty Spur. Garth finished his thoughts with a smirk on his face. He got to his feet and stared through the trees at the cabin and shack. The Ranger and the Indian rarely appeared outside, and he needed a sure way to get near enough to plug the two of them and not get plugged himself. He fetched his Sharps and found a spot to lie down, where he could maintain an unobstructed view of the shack. If he wasn't able to get a clear shot at the two men in half an hour, he'd take out after the old man and see what he had to say. If the old man offered an invitation back to his cabin, he would accept, then look for a moment of distraction by the three men, and in that moment of distraction, he'd have his gun out blazing. They wouldn't stand a chance.

*

The Lone Ranger and Tonto did not make an appearance until well over an hour later when they heard the approach of two horses. Tonto checked and reported that Jim approached, riding along with someone Tonto did not know.

"It must be Witty," the Ranger said, stepping into the light. "It is, Tonto. We mustn't take our eyes off of him."

"Me ready, Kemo Sabe."

"I found him, Ranger," Jim announced, dismounting along with his guest.

Garth walked up to the Ranger and extended a hand. Tonto moved to the side, his hand near his gun.

"I'm really glad to meet ya," Garth said, a wide, friendly smile on his face. "Do you know who I am?"

"Not really, but I know you don't work for a publishing company."

Garth's face dropped. "What do you mean?" he asked.

"I mean you're an impostor," the Ranger said. "I know it for a fact." He handed over the telegram Tonto had brought back from San Felipe.

Garth read it and tossed it back at the Ranger, who let it fall to the ground.

"I don't know what you're trying to pull," he said, "but I don't intend to be treated like this. I'm a hard-working man. I've come to help make you famous, but I see I'm wasting my time."

"Perhaps if you'd be honest with us…" the Ranger began.

"Forget it," Garth snapped. "I'll go back to town, and first chance I get I'll let my people know you're not worth writing even a *sentence* about, let alone a book." He spun away and remounted his horse. He threw the three men a dark look and rode off at top speed.

"You let him go, Kemo Sabe?"

"I don't think he'll be back."

For a few moments, the three men stood in the open discussing what had just passed. Suddenly, the crack of a Sharps came from the nearby grove of trees. The Ranger heard the whiz of a shell go past him. The men dashed inside Jim's cabin.

"I guess I was wrong," the Ranger said, sending three shots into the trees through Jim's open window.

The Sharps cracked six times, and the men heard the thud of bullets into the logs of the cabin.

Jim grabbed his Remington and said, "I'll blast that polecat outta them trees."

"Jim," the Ranger said, "stay under cover here inside your cabin and plug away at him to keep his attention. Tonto, I'll make a run for the corral. While he's attending to me, you go the other way and get to the rise." A small hillock rolled across the land to the right of and halfway to the stand of trees. "We'll have him at three angles, then."

"Me do."

"Rifle ready to fire, Jim?"

"Dang tootin'"

"I'll find cover behind the water trough." The

Ranger moved to the doorway and pushed the door open. Immediately, four shots struck the door and moved it in reverse. "Well, we know he can hit the broadside of door."

Jim stood near the window, ready to act.

"I'll go on your fourth shot, Jim. Ready, Tonto?"

"Me ready."

"Okay, Jim."

Jim began to fire. On the fourth shot, the Ranger bolted out the door, firing his own ivory-handled pistol toward the sound of the Sharps. He weaved, dove to the ground, rolled, rose and in seconds sheltered behind the water trough. Tonto, meanwhile, counted to three after the Lone Ranger ran for safety and set out in the opposite direction, coming safely to ground behind the hillock. Jim spent his sixteen cartridges, spacing his shots to coincide with the movement of his two friends. Now, he reloaded.

Garth cursed himself for missing his first shot. He hadn't relaxed enough to send a true shot into the masked man's head. He'd pressed the trigger too hard. He cursed again. Now he had the masked man to his right, the Indian to his left, and the old man pumping bullet after bullet his way. This was not how he'd seen it playing out.

A bullet slammed into the tree where he hid, six inches from his ear. He ducked low as panic set in. He duck-walked to his horse, vaulted into the saddle, and rode inside the trees for as long as he could before taking out across open ground, his spurs urging his mount on.

On his way to Tyler's Crossing, he'd passed a wide-spreading outcropping of tall cliffs and bluffs two miles off, where he could hide and feel safe. If the masked man and Indian chased after him, perhaps he could pick them off from there.

"Him escape, Kemo Sabe," Tonto called, running toward the corral.

"I see him. Here, Silver." Silver's saddle straddled the corral fence. The Ranger tossed it across Silver's back and fastened it. Tonto did the same with Scout.

"Me ready, Kemo Sabe," Tonto cried.

"Let's ride. Hi yo, Silver. Away!"

*

Garth had a considerable lead, but aside from the long, winding hillock which Tonto used for shelter, the ground stretched flat ahead until it reached crags and peaks which were Garth's destination. The Lone Ranger and Tonto kept their man in sight with no problem.

"Him head to mountains," Tonto called to the Ranger.

"Let's try to catch up with him before he reaches them. Come on, Silver. Faster, big fellow."

As rapidly as Silver and Scout crossed the plains, Garth's lead was too great, and the Ranger and Tonto had to rein up at the foot of the escarpment.

"Him find plenty places to hide in there, Kemo

Sabe," Tonto said, stroking Scout's neck.

"That means plenty of spots to sit in ambush," the Ranger agreed. "It'll be hard to track him on rocky ground like that."

"We keep going?"

"Yes. We need to find out why he shot at us and who he is."

They heard the shrieking whinny of a horse. The Ranger pointed, and he and Tonto moved slowly toward the sound. There was no path to follow, so they dismounted, drew their guns, and made their way as best they could between the boulders. Another whinny sounded, this one nearer.

"You go that way," the Ranger said, pointing. "I'll go this way."

The desperate whinnying continued as they climbed. They hadn't gone far when Tonto called, "Kemo Sabe. Me find something."

Moving carefully under cover, rock to rock, the Ranger saw what Tonto had found. A horse, its leg gruesomely broken, lay on its side, whinnying piteously.

"Witty must have tried to ride too quickly through here. The horse couldn't navigate the rocks at the speed Witty wanted, and this is what happened." Anger edged the Ranger's voice as he walked to the injured horse. "We can't leave this poor creature like this."

Two shots echoed into the mountains, and the horse lay still.

"Man on foot now. We find him."

A rifle cracked and rock splinters flew from a boulder to the left of Tonto. The two men calculated the direction of the shot and, without speaking, spread apart and began to home in on their enemy.

Tonto sent a bullet up the mountain and received a bullet in return.

"Are you all right, Tonto?"

"Me not hurt. Me see him. Him head to where rock stick out."

"I see. Witty!" the Ranger called. "Throw down your guns and come down the mountain. You can't get away from us."

A bullet sent more rock splinters flying, some brushing the Ranger's face.

"We're coming for you, Witty," the Ranger said, sending three silver bullets in Witty's direction.

"Him climb higher," Tonto called.

"Let's follow him," the Ranger answered back.

Garth had reached a narrow precipice requiring sure footing to navigate. He paused and sent six pistol shots toward the Ranger and Tonto before holstering his gun and sidling along the ledge, his stomach to the wall. The Ranger took careful aim ahead of Witty, hoping to prevent his progress and force him back toward them. He fired twice. Rock splinters sprayed into Witty's face. He instinctively reared back, causing him to lose his balance.

He still carried his Sharps in his right hand and his left could find nothing with which to steady himself. His left foot slipped off the precipice and he fell. A short piercing cry cut through mountain, ending in abrupt silence.

The Ranger holstered his revolver and joined Tonto. They wended their way to a safe spot from which to look down. Witty's motionless body lay far below, his Sharps in two pieces beside him. The Ranger studied the topography.

"I think I can get Silver down through there, Kemo Sabe," he said, pointing. "We'll take Witty's body to Jim's place for the time being."

While the Ranger went for Silver, Tonto retraced his path and retrieved Witty's saddlebags. He inspected his horse's gear for some clue to the real identity of the dead man, but the gear told him nothing; the saddlebags he tossed across Scout's back. It took the better part of an hour, but finally, the Ranger returned with the body. He also brought along the broken pieces of Witty's rifle, and Tonto tied them atop the saddlebags. They set out, and by dusk they were back at Jim's.

"You got him," Jim said. "Know who he is?"

"No," the Ranger said. "I went through his pockets but found nothing. Jim, you're going to have to take his body into town."

"I can do that."

"Kemo Sabe," Tonto said, his voice showing a trace of excitement. He walked to the Ranger, carrying the pieces of the Sharps. "Me find letters on rifle."

The Ranger inspected a roughly scratched "G C" carved into the rifle's stock.

"Here saddlebags me take from horse," Tonto said.

The Ranger opened the saddlebags and pulled out a set of clothing and two newspapers. After a quick glance through the newspapers, he said, "These are editions reporting on our capture of Razor Gilliam and Shark Lawson."

"That strange. Why him carry them?"

"G. C. The initials. Tonto, Cavendish has a son. Garth Cavendish."

"G. C.," Jim cried, slapping his thigh. "I think you got Cavendish's son."

"You may be right, Jim," the Ranger said. "I wonder why he would send his son after us all by himself."

"Maybe the kid did it on his own," Jim said.

"Perhaps. I have an idea," the Ranger said. "Tomorrow morning, Jim, take the body into town and turn it over to the sheriff." He lifted the newspapers he held. "These two stories made their way to Cavendish, it would seem. We need to put the story of his son into newspapers."

"You think a story about his son will get to him, too?"

"I think it might."

"You don't know for sure, though, that it is

Cavendish's son."

"You're right, Jim. We should make certain it's Garth Cavendish we've brought back. Tonto, you and I will head to Fort Davis with the boy's clothes and broken rifle. Shark Lawson is still imprisoned there. Maybe he can identify them. Afterward, we'll inform Sheriff Hosh of Garth Cavendish's death. Then we'll look up that young man, Hamil Peters, who writes for the *Bugle,* and ask him to put a story in the paper about what happened, making sure he mentions the Lone Ranger being responsible. We can hope the story brings Cavendish to us."

"Boy in newspaper office like plenty much write story about you."

"What do you think, Jim?"

"Could take some time for news like that to travel."

"If it brings Butch Cavendish to us, the wait will be worth it."

"When we leave, Kemo Sabe?" Tonto asked.

"First thing in the morning."

"Why don't you get that body off Silver," Jim suggested. "Poor horse don't want to be lugging that around all night."

"I'll put the body in the shack. Tonto and I will sleep outdoors tonight."

"I'll take things from there, Ranger. Don't worry about nothing. Go out and bring Butch Cavendish to justice."

Chapter 23

Hamil Peters

When the Lone Ranger and Tonto arrived at Fort Davis, one of the guards escorted them immediately into Captain Lawrence's office. Lawrence beamed a bright smile toward the two men, stood, and walked around his desk, his hand extended in greeting.

"Welcome back, masked man."

"Thank you, Captain. I have news for you."

"Sit. Tonto, welcome."

The three men arranged themselves.

The Ranger said, "I believe Butch Cavendish's son is dead." He went on to tell the story of Clarence Witty.

The captain listened closely, and when the Ranger closed with a request, he answered, "If you think it will work, I'm happy to do it. I'll handle it myself and do it right now. Let me have the broken rifle. Shark Lawson may not care to cooperate, though. We convicted him under army law for the murder of our soldiers. He goes before a firing squad in two days, so you got here just in time."

"I see," the Ranger said, somberly.

"Me get rifle," Tonto said.

"It's a one-shot Sharps, Captain. Accurate, but slow to use. Your soldiers still have them, I believe."

"They do. Ah, thanks, Tonto."

As the captain inspected the two pieces of the weapon, his face clouded.

"What's wrong, Captain?" the Ranger asked.

"Do you see this mark on the butt of the stock?" Imprinted into the wood, the Ranger saw a small symbol resembling an X.

"Yes, Tonto and I noticed that, but couldn't figure out what the X meant. We were more interested in the initials carved into the stock."

"It's quite worn down like someone tried to erase it, but the X is meant to be the crossed swords of the cavalry. This rifle was supplied to the U. S. Cavalry."

"Oh, I see," the Ranger said, understanding the captain's point. "You're saying Cavendish's son could only have gotten the rifle from a cavalry soldier."

"He must have picked it up after killing one of our men."

"It more proof him Cavendish boy," Tonto said.

"Let me do this anyway, masked man," the captain said. "Wait here. This won't take long." He carried the rifle pieces with him and headed for the stockade. The Ranger and Tonto stepped outside and watched him go.

When the captain reached the door of the stockade, he motioned for one of the guards to unlock it.

"Lawson," the captain barked.

Lawson looked up from his cot. "What do you want?" he asked

"You have a friend who's come to see you."

"What friend?"

"He got tough. Trying to break you out, maybe. We had to disarm him, and this is how his rifle ended up." The captain handed the stock of the rifle to Lawson, the scrawled initials on top.

Lawson glanced at the rifle piece.

"Garth! You got Garth?"

"Garth Cavendish? This is his rifle, then?"

"Yes. Wait. You said he was here."

The captain took back the rifle stock from Lawson and left the cell. He quickly paced the distance to his office.

"Come inside," he said. "Lawson saw the stock and asked if we'd captured Garth."

"That cinches it," the Ranger said, and he went on to explain his plan to draw Cavendish to him. "I'm sure you asked Lawson whether he knew anything about Cavendish's plans."

"As I said, he's not been in any mood to cooperate. This rifle surprised him, though. So, you're going into Corbin City from here?"

"Yes. We need to see the reporter from the *Bugle*."

"I have an idea that might help. Suppose I send a

message to Louderville. They have a telegraph office there. I'll have the story you want telegraphed and circulated to as many newspapers as possible. Telegraph offices respond pretty lively to requests from the U. S. government."

"Excellent idea, Captain."

"Write down the highlights, and I'll do it today. And if there's anything else I can do for you, send me word, and I'll have a troop of soldiers on the way to you within the hour. The army wants Cavendish even worse than you do."

"I'm not sure about that, Captain, but I appreciate the offer. Let me write the story for you, then Tonto and I will be off."

*

The Lone Ranger and Tonto made the office of the *Corbin City Bugle* their first stop and were greeted with an unwelcome surprise.

"The boy's in jail," said the man behind the counter when the Ranger asked for Hamil.

"In jail! What did he do?"

"If you ask me, he did nothing."

"You are...?"

"I'm Fred Holloway, editor and publisher of the *Bugle*. Hamil's worked here more than a year, almost two, actually. He's as steady and reliable and eager as they come."

"That's how he struck me," the Ranger agreed. "Why is he in jail?"

"Sheriff claims he stole a horse."

"What does the boy say?"

"He says he was only borrowing it to deliver an emergency message, but he won't say what the message was or who he was going to deliver it to."

"So, he stole the horse but never reached his destination?"

"That's right. He stole Sam James's horse from behind the bank. James runs the town bank. He saw Hamil through the window and went for the sheriff. Sheriff caught him, brought him back, and threw him in jail."

"When was this?"

"Only yesterday."

"Have you visited him?"

"I have. Says he wants to speak with Lucinda Pennyfeather, but the sheriff won't go and get her for him, and he won't talk to anyone else."

"Who is Lucinda Pennyfeather?"

"They're sweet on one another. She lives with her father about a mile out of town. They have a small ranch, a few head of cattle. Why don't you go to the jail and see him? Maybe he'll talk to you."

"I will, but first I have a story for your paper."

"Is it a good one?"

"Another member of Butch Cavendish's gang is gone. His son is dead. Fell from a height, trying to escape from Tonto and me."

"Hey, that should be some story. Sit right down and let me hear. I'll get it in tomorrow's edition."

"Tonto," the Ranger said, "go to the jail and tell Sheriff Hosh we'll be in to see Hamil soon."

A short while later, after detailing how he wanted the newspaper story to read, the Ranger knocked on the door of the jail and entered.

"Well," Sheriff Hosh said. "Welcome back, masked man. Pull up a chair."

The Ranger saw Hamil rise from his cot, come to the front of his cell, and grasp the bars with both hands. The Ranger nodded his way.

"Got any more of the Cavendish gang to hand over."

The Ranger filled the sheriff in on the fate of Shark Lawson and Garth Cavendish.

"You're really cleaning up that bunch of cutthroats. What can I do for you?"

"I'd like to speak with Hamil."

"Sure, go right ahead."

"May I speak with him in private?"

"Gotta ask for your guns… yours too, Tonto."

"That's not a problem, Sheriff."

The Lone Ranger and Tonto handed over their guns, and Sheriff Hosh put them into the corner safe.

"How long you think you'll need?" the sheriff asked.

"Maybe fifteen or twenty minutes," the Ranger replied.

"I guess that's enough time. I'll head over to the restaurant for some lunch. I'll be back in twenty minutes."

When the door closed behind the sheriff, Hamil spoke out. "You gotta help me, Lone Ranger. You gotta help me *today*. Tomorrow will be too late."

The Ranger and Tonto pulled wooden chairs near the cell.

"Sit down, Hamil, and tell us what's wrong."

"I'm always looking for good stories to write for the *Bugle.* Like the one I wrote about you and Tonto and Razor Gilliam. Mr. Holloway told me lots of other newspapers printed my story. It was exciting. Anyway, I'm friends with Lucinda Pennyfeather." Hamil's face reddened at the mention of the girl's name. "Her father owns a small ranch outside of town. He needs money to pay off a mortgage to the bank."

"The bank that Sam James runs?"

"Yes. Lucy told me he doesn't have it. She said he

gambles too often, and now if he can't get the money together by tomorrow three o'clock, he'll lose the ranch to the bank. She says he thinks the only way he can get the money is by gambling and winning it—a thousand dollars he owes, but the problem is, he's lost most of what money they have trying to win the money they need."

"A thorny situation," the Ranger said.

"But they're stuck now. Lucy says her father's convinced he has no other way."

"But why did you take Mr. James's horse? You did take it, didn't you?"

"I did. I was looking for a story, like I said. So yesterday evening after dark, I wandered over to Mr. James's bank because I saw a light on in the back window. You can see the window through the alley next to the bank. One horse was tied up in front of the bank, and I knew it wasn't Mr. James's horse. I walked down the alley and heard two people talking in the room. It was a hot night, and the window was open. I didn't get too close because the light spilled into the alley. I recognized Mr. James's voice. He was telling somebody he'd have enough money in two weeks at most to pay off the debt. Neither man mentioned what kind of debt. I didn't recognize the voice of the other man, but he asked Mr. James how he could be so sure. Mr. James laughed and said he had someone coming into town the next day—that would be today—and he'd be sure Lucy's father lost his money at the poker table. This man he had coming knew all the tricks, Mr. James said. Then he said he'd reclaim the farm, sell it for the bank, and have the money to pay the debt."

"How did he know Mr. Pennyfeather would be in to gamble tonight?"

"*Everybody* knows. He's there most *every* night. He's given up trying to borrow the money he needs. Everybody knows he gambles and isn't a good risk. He's got to pay tomorrow, Friday, and today is Thursday, so…"

"So, you took the horse…?"

"It was tied in back, so I had to walk through the light to get the horse and then ride down the alley through the light, and Mr. James saw me. I was going to ride to Lucy's and tell her not to let her father come into Corbin City. I was going to tell her to suggest to her father that he offer to pay whatever money he has and hope Mr. James would give him a little more time to find the rest."

"But the sheriff caught you and brought you back."

"He did. I don't ride much," Hamil said with some embarrassment. "I don't own a horse, and I never really go anywhere. Clem Hanson down at the livery stable lends me a mount sometimes to go visit Lucy."

"Why didn't you tell the sheriff all of this?"

"I wanted to tell Lucy. She's the only one her father'll listen to, but the sheriff wouldn't send for her. She probably doesn't even know I've been put in jail. Can you go and get her for me?"

The Ranger didn't answer. He glanced at Tonto.

"If the sheriff will let you out of jail…" the Ranger mused. "Tonto, I have a plan. It's the strangest plan I think I've ever had, but with the sheriff's cooperation, it might work."

"What me do?" Tonto asked.

The door opened and the sheriff entered.

"Had a quick bowl of soup," he said.

"Sheriff," the Ranger said, "I have a big favor to ask of you."

"Ask away," the sheriff said, settling behind his desk.

The Lone Ranger repeated the story Hamil shared with him. Then he went into the details of his plan.

"Masked man, that is about the craziest scheme I ever heard of," the sheriff said, removing his hat and scratching at his head.

"I don't see why it won't work," the Ranger said.

"Suppose the man Mr. James brings in isn't interest in playing with you," the sheriff asked.

"We'll have to rely on his greed and his desire not to pass up easy money."

"Your plan sounds like easy money all right… You sure you can pull it off?"

"Yes, if you allow Hamil to assist me. Let him out of jail. Both he and I will guarantee he won't be running away."

"I promise, Sheriff," Hamil interjected. "I won't run away. For Pete's sake, where would I go? I only want to help Lucy and her dad."

"Sheriff?" the Ranger queried.

"What'll I say if people ask why I let a horse thief out of jail?"

"Say the horse was returned immediately. Say there are circumstances which they're not aware of. Say the Constitution of the United States remains in force in Corbin City, and Hamil is entitled to bail. Say a masked man bailed him out and guarantees his appearance at any trial he might be involved in."

"I asked one question, you give me four answers."

The Ranger smiled. "Pick one, Sheriff. Will you do it?"

"Sure. I'd be pretty stupid not to trust a man like you."

"Thanks, Lone Ranger!" Hamil spouted.

The sheriff rose, got the cell door key, and let Hamil out.

He took a seat next to the Ranger, who said, "First, write a note to Lucy and tell her *not* to talk her father out of coming to town tonight. Say you have a plan to help him get the money he needs to meet the mortgage payment tomorrow, but she should say nothing about it to her father. Will she trust your judgment?"

"You bet she will!"

"Good. Tonto will take the note to her. Then you and I will go to the *Bugle* office. There's a story I gave to Mr. Holloway. I'm sure he'd like you to be the one to write it up. Sheriff, do you have a deck of cards?"

"I do. Things sometimes are slow around here, and I pass the time playing solitaire."

"Get them for me, please. After you write your story, Hamil, it will be time for you to learn a new game. Think you can master it in time for tonight?"

"Ready and willing, Mr. Lone Ranger."

"Tonto, I'm going to need a different disguise—I think an old man who's a little bit crazy would be the most effective. Someone any gambler would take for a fool and be happy to bet against."

"Me get what you need."

"So," the Ranger said, getting to his feet, "write that note, Hamil, and then we'll be off to the *Bugle* office."

Chapter 24

The Magical Playing Card

Later that night in the Lucky Deal, Sam James watched the poker table with satisfaction, as Rufus Pennyfeather tossed down his hand again and forlornly swept his palm across his brow. The four hundred dollars' worth of chips he'd begun the night with had dwindled to a hundred fifty. A fortunate stranger, who'd identified himself as Ace Martin, had taken crucial hands, hands whose stakes verged on giving Rufus Pennyfeather a leg up on his quest to build his pot to a thousand dollars—if only he'd won them.

The deal for a new game went around the table. The six men anted and play began. Soon only the stranger and Pennyfeather held cards. The pot had grown to nearly three-hundred dollars. Rufus found hope in what he held. Three kings. High cards and *three* of them. It could be the start of a lucky run, a run that would literally save his life. Ace Martin eyed his opponent's chips.

"I see you got fifty dollars left," he said. "Let's get this over with." He laid his hand face down on the table and counted out fifty dollars in chips. "All in."

Rufus stared at his cards, then at Martin. There was no way he could fold, not with three beautiful kings staring right at him. He pushed his every last chip into the pot.

"What do you got?" Martin asked.

"Three kings," Pennyfeather said, fanning his cards on the table.

"Hmmm." Martin laid down three deuces, and for a moment Pennyfeather's heart skipped a happy beat. "They got company." He placed two sevens next to them. "Full house. Sorry." He swept the chips his way.

Pennyfeather felt hollowed out. If three kings weren't enough to bring him luck, then he knew his luck had run out. In another few hours, he and Abby would be homeless.

"Ya call that gamblin'?" came a raspy voice from the edge of the crowd. A gray-bearded man wearing a low-hanging gun belt, moccasins, a floppy, tan hat, torn black pants, and a tan shirt missing two buttons made his way to the table. "I seen old ladies in rockin' chairs play more excitin' games than what you play. I got money, and I want to do some gamblin', *real* gamblin'."

"Sit down," Martin said, eyeing the stranger with interest. "This fellow's cleaned out; you can have his seat."

"I don't play no game like that three kings, two of this and four of that. Ain't no excitement in there. I got me a better game. I got me a hundred fifty dollars burning a hole in my pocket, but I gotta warn you, I bet big. Play my game and I'm in."

"What's your game?" Martin said, his interest rising.

"Game for two. Only two. Me and you? You look like the man for me. I see in your eyes, you're a real gamblin' man. You in?"

"Tell me what the game is first."

"Heh heh. Bet you ain't never played it. Listen up. I'll learn you. First, I lay down ten cards on the table, but let me warn you. I'm a magical man when it comes to cards. Yes, I am."

A tiny laugh went through the crowd gathered near the table.

"Magical, you say?" Martin asked, smirking.

"Ten cards on the table. Then, I go outside where I can't see nothin'. You followin' me?"

"So far." Martin crossed his arm over his chest in bemusement.

"Then you touch any one of them ten cards. Any one at all. The whole crowd'll see which one you touch. Then, my magical assistant… Did I say I need a magical assistant? Shucks, maybe I left it out." He looked over the crowd. "You there. You. Youngster."

"Me?" Hamil asked, innocently.

"Him?" Martin interrupted. "Ain't he the kid's been in jail all day? Don't guess there's much magic in him."

The crowd laughed.

"He looks magical enough to me. Come over here, boy."

The Ranger touched Hamil on the shoulder, the top

of his head, and over his heart.

"Yep, he's the one. He's plenty magical. He's got it in him. I can feel it. Now, lemme have them cards."

One of the men gathered up the cards, banged them on the table to even them up, and handed them over to the old man.

The Ranger riffled the cards next to his ear.

"Yep, these'll do. I hear magic in the cards. I'll shuffle 'em up."

The moment the Ranger started to shuffle the cards, they fell out of his hands, some landing on the table, the rest on the floor.

Martin rolled his eyes and laughed along with the crowd.

"Gather 'em up. Git 'em. Slippery fingers," the Ranger explained. "Happens sometimes. Let me have 'em. Give 'em here. Pay attention now. Everybody's watchin', right?" He laid out ten cards in the shape of an H. Four cards in the left leg, four in the right, the two in the middle arranged vertically rather than horizontally. Both he and Hamil breathed a relieved sigh at the appearance of one card in particular.

"Yep. Yep. These are magical cards," the Ranger said, passing his hand slowly in the air over top of them. "No one's allowed to touch 'em from here on out 'ceptin' two people. Anyone else touches 'em and the magic's gone. You hear me?" To Martin, he said, "When I step outside, you pick a card. Touch it. Touch it hard, touch it soft, don't matter. But touch it and step away. When I come back in, my magical assistant will touch each card three times starting with the top one here and then one after the other. I'll have my hand on his shoulder, and I'll feel the magical vibrations when he touches the card you picked. If anybody thinks there's some trick about it, they're wrong. It's magic, pure and simple. I got a hundred fifty dollars says I can pick the card you touch, and I can pick it every time."

"Let me get this straight," Martin said, putting his hands on his hips. "I pick a card. This no-account kid touches all the cards, but you'll tell me which one I touched."

"Hey, that's right! And I only had to explain it to you once. You're a smart fellow. You in?"

"A hundred fifty?"

"All the money I got. You got somebody in the crowd we can both trust?"

Someone called out that the sheriff was in the crowd.

"Where are ya, Sheriff?"

Sheriff Hosh stepped forward.

"Will you hold the money for us, Mr. Sheriff?" the Ranger asked. "Okay with you, stranger, the sheriff holds the money?"

"Fine with me," Martin answered, adding a sneer.

The Ranger handed his money over to the sheriff.

“If I see you cheating…” Martin threatened.

“Cheatin’! Me? How many people you see standing here? You got a million eyes on your side. You got the sheriff staring right at me. Cheatin’. I don’t need no cheatin’. You see anything you get the suspicions about, you sing out. You ain’t tryin’ to weasel out, are you?”

“Here.” Martin handed his money to the sheriff.

“Heh! Now, this is what I call *gamblin’*,” the Ranger said, rubbing his hands together like a fly. “When I get out the door, pick a card. Be back in one minute.”

“You,” Martin said, nodding at someone near the door. “Go with him. Make sure he ain’t looking in no window or nothing.”

Martin waited for the Ranger to step outside, then looked the crowd over and laughed. “Gonna be the easiest money I ever made. The old coot must be crazy. Drinks’ll be on me in about two minutes.”

A murmur of approval went through the crowd as Martin leaned over the table and touched the topmost of the two cards between the legs of the H, a six of diamonds. He straightened up and waited, a smug grin on his face. A moment later, the old man in the floppy hat backed through the batwing doors.

“Can I come in and turn around?” he called.

“You can. Well?” Martin asked the man he’d sent to monitor the gambler.

“Spent the whole time looking across the street.

Didn't look back once," the man reported.

"Okay, magical gamblin' man. Which card did I pick?"

The Ranger put his hand on Hamil's shoulder and said, "Boy, touch each card three times. Touch 'em anyplace. Don't matter to me. Three is magical. I'll feel the power. All you people. Keep an eye. Don't want to be accused of no trickery. Go."

The crowd grew quiet as the Ranger watched Hamil carefully touch each card three times, all in different spots. When Hamil reached the final card at the bottom of the right leg of the H, both he and the old man stood back from the table. The Ranger dropped his hand from Hamil's shoulder and closed his eyes for ten seconds. When he opened them, he said, "Ha! Easiest thing in the world. Felt the magic go right up my arm. You picked the six of diamonds."

The crowd burst into noisy disarray. Martin's eyes widened.

"How'd you know that? Anybody here see anything going on?"

"Ain't nothing goin' on 'ceptin' my magic. I'm ready to bet three hundred bucks!" the Ranger crowed. "I told ya. I told ya. I'm a magic man. I got three hundred to lay out. Go again?"

Martin angrily peeled off more money, and both men handed their stakes over to the sheriff.

Martin said, "Sheriff, keep an eye on this boy. I'm

watching you close, too, son. Don't try nothing you shouldn't."

"I just touched the cards anyplace I wanted," Hamil said, giving a defensive shrug. "You all saw. I didn't do nothing."

The ritual repeated. When the Ranger returned, he put his hand on Hamil's shoulder, and watched Hamil go through his routine, three touches to each card.

The Ranger closed his eyes at the finish, and when he opened them, he said, "You touched… the six of spades."

The crowd broke into applause this time. Martin slammed his hand down on the poker table.

"Were all of you watching?" he called. "Somebody must've seen something. The kid must've touched the cards funny. What did you do, kid?"

"Nothing. You watched me. I didn't do nothing wrong. Don't blame me."

Martin glared at Hamil, then at the magical gambler.

"Six hundred bucks I won," the Ranger crowed. "'Tain't enough. Not nearly enough. I'm a greedy man, and I got plenty more magic in me. I'm in for the whole six hundred this time. What say? You in? You a real gamblin' man? Come on. Don't bail on me now. Didn't I tell you this was more exciting than two of this and three of that? You ain't gonna tuck in your tail and crawl away from the table now, are ya? Not in front of all these people. You got a reputation to keep up."

Martin narrowed his eyes at the last comment. "Let me count what I got," he mumbled. He went through his table winnings and emptied out his pockets. "All right. I made it. Six hundred."

The sheriff held twelve hundred dollars.

"I'm stepping outside. Keep yer eye on me. I'm a magical man. Ya better send *two* men with me this time. Ya never know. Might have eyes in the back of my head."

Two men accompanied the Ranger outside. Martin chose a card, and for a third time the Ranger returned, and he and Hamil went through their act before the magical gambler chose the correct card. He received applause again, but this time, the applause lacked the element of surprise.

"What did you do?" Martin screamed, silencing the crowd. "I know you did something. You cheated me out of my money. I know you did! It's some kind of trick!"

"What! Cheated! A trick! With the sheriff and all your friends watchin' me? Not a chance."

"Give me back my money." Martin went for his gun, but before he could bring it to bear, the Ranger drew and fired. Martin's pistol flew backward into the knee of a man at the next table, who cried out, "I been shot!"

"You're not hurt, sonny," the Ranger said. "Weren't no bullet hit you. Only your gun. Didn't think to mention, but I'm a magical shooter too. Sheriff, gimme my money and arrest this fellow. Dang near tried to kill me. Everybody saw."

The sheriff cuffed Martin's wrists behind him saying, "You can't be drawing guns in a crowded place like this, mister."

"He shot at me," Martin argued. "I didn't even fire."

"Save your breath," the sheriff told him. "Everybody seen. You'll be in one of my cells for a while. You got anything else to say, magical man?"

"I do. I heard stories about you, Mr. Banker." Sam James produced a look of shock. "This man…" the Ranger indicated Rufus Pennyfeather. "…has a mortgage to pay tomorrow, or he'll lose his ranch to your bank. Ain't that right?"

Sam James, still astonished to be chosen from the crowd, fumbled to answer.

"Well," the Ranger insisted. "Yes or no."

"Yes, yes he does."

"And if he don't pay, the bank'll own his ranch at three o'clock tomorrow? Yes or no?"

"Yes."

"You there. Rufus Pennyfeather," the Ranger said.

Pennyfeather, wondering what in heaven's name was going on, could only stare at the magical stranger in astonishment.

"How much would pay off this here mortgage you owe to the bank?"

"It… it's a thousand dollars," Pennyfeather stuttered.

"Here you go, Mr. Banker," the Ranger said, counting off from his winnings. "I think you'll find exactly a thousand dollars there. You count it too. We'll have no mistakes here, Mr. Banker. Rufus Pennyfeather is paying off the mortgage to your bank here and now, right in front of all these witnesses. He'll be in your office tomorrow at three o'clock to pick up his receipt, his deed, and acknowledgement that his ranch is his free and clear. Understand? Yes or no?"

"Yes."

"You got time tomorrow to visit the bank at three o'clock, Pennyfeather?" the Ranger asked.

"I… sure. Of course."

"Good. So then, I wish everybody a goodnight."

The Ranger holstered his six-shooter, spun on his heel, and disappeared into the night.

*

The next morning, the Lone Ranger and Tonto ate breakfast in the same canyon camp where they'd come upon Silver.

"When sheriff come?" Tonto asked.

The Ranger chuckled. “He promised he’d be out here first thing. He wants to learn how the trick was worked same as you, Kemo Sabe.”

“How long you think before Cavendish come look for you?”

The Ranger’s mood changed abruptly.

“There’s no telling. Unless the newspaper story about his son makes its way to him, he may never show up.”

“He must wonder where son go.”

“Yes, no doubt he will, but unless he told his son to come to Corbin City, which is unlikely, there’s no reason for him to be anywhere near here, unless he sees that story. I’ll clean up from breakfast.”

“Me help.”

Twenty minutes later, they heard the sound of hooves approaching the canyon.

“You stay here. Me look,” Tonto said. A moment later, he returned. “It sheriff.”

The men greeted one another.

“Have you eaten, Sheriff? We can make something for you.”

“No, no. I grabbed scrambled eggs at the restaurant. That was quite a show you put on last night, Ranger.”

The Ranger smiled and explained, “That was a trick

my father and older brother used to drive me crazy with, until they finally let me in on the secret."

"Well, you gonna let us in now?"

"I still have the cards you gave me so Hamil and I could practice." The Ranger went for the cards. "Now, watch what I do."

He turned over ten cards in the H arrangement.

"Do you see that one of the cards I turned up is a ten?"

"Sure do," the sheriff said.

"That's the most important part of it. Do you see how the hearts on this ten are lined up in the same shape as the cards, four and two and four again, something like an H?"

"Sure do."

"Touch any card, Sheriff."

The sheriff chose the card atop the left leg, a seven of spades.

"Watch. I touch the heart on the ten of hearts located in exactly in the same spot as the card you picked—top of the left-hand side—and that tells me what card you choose. Simple, isn't it?"

"Well, I'll be…"

"Luckily, a ten turned up the first time I tried in last night's performance. Otherwise, I'd have had to do some mumbo-jumbo about the cards not falling magically and deal out another ten cards and hope for a ten to show up."

"What if two tens showed up."

"Then the first that came out would be the signal card. I taught Hamil all of this ahead of time in the newspaper office. He knew to go through a lot of hocus-pocus and touch each card three times in random places and make sure there was no pattern to his touches. The only touch that mattered was his first touch of the ten-card. He had only to touch the ten on the spade, club, heart, or diamond, which matched the position of the card the stranger chose, then touch it twice more anywhere and continue on with the other cards. What was the gambler's name, by the way?"

"Says his name is Ace Martin. Tonto, close your eyes. Ranger, pick a card."

The Ranger touched the bottom card of the right leg, a four of clubs.

"Okay, Tonto." The sheriff touched each card once, ending up on the appropriate heart of the ten.

"Ha, ha," Tonto chuckled. "Lone Ranger pick this card." He lifted the four of clubs.

All three men joined in a round of laughter.

"Mighty easy when you know the trick," the sheriff said.

"Most tricks are," the Ranger agreed. "Sheriff, make certain nothing goes wrong when Rufus Pennyfeather comes to town today for his deed."

"I'll be right there at the bank waiting for him. And before you suggest it, I'm taking Mr. James into his office right after and ordering him to explain about this debt he has to pay off. If it has something shady to do with the bank money, and I don't see how it don't, he'll have a lot of to answer for, and Ace Martin will have somebody to keep him company in my jail."

"Good, Sheriff. You know why I'm here. If Butch Cavendish or Montana Jenkins shows up or you hear anything about them, let me know. It could take a while."

"I'll be happy to let you handle them two critters, Ranger. I'll ride out here once in a while and see how you're doing."

"Thanks, Sheriff. I appreciate it. Tonto will be visiting town on occasion for supplies, and when he does, he'll stop in to see you."

"Good enough."

The sheriff got up from the ground where the card trick had taken place and mounted his horse.

"Dangdest card trick I ever saw. Good luck."

"Here, take back your cards and work on your solitaire. Adios, Sheriff."

Chapter 25

A Brother's Gift

Butch Cavendish rode out of his nearly two-month hiatus in Stony Creek, anger seething inside him. He'd originally expected to meet five of his gang in Coldstream, and these five men, *especially* these five men, were plenty to ride with. But Razor and Shark were gone. Done in by somebody calling himself the Lone Ranger. Now, added to that, he could not stop thinking about his son. Where was he? What had he accomplished, if anything? Was he all right? How long would he and Montana have to wait for him in Coldstream? He feared he'd sent his son off on a fool's errand—a job too big for him to handle. This Lone Ranger seemed to be a formidable enemy. To take down both Razor and Shark he had to be. Garth's best chance to succeed depended on his being unknown to this Lone Ranger and taking him by surprise. The Texas Rangers and the cavalry certainly knew his son rode with him, but Garth hadn't been riding with him for long. They'd never gotten a good look at him. Their ignorance could be his doorway to opportunity.

Cavendish had cleaned up, shaven himself to the skin, and bought new clothes. Always, there lurked a chance of someone, somewhere recognizing him. He trusted to his new, scrubbed, respectable image to prevent it from happening. After riding for days across the wide, Texas prairie, Coldstream loomed ahead.

The town looked bigger than Cavendish

remembered it. He'd last been there four, no, probably three years earlier when he and his friends made an unauthorized, late-night, withdrawal from its bank. On that night, the dark and empty streets offered no resistance, and his gang rode away slowly and silently from the bank; richer, too. Their deed hadn't caused the slightest stir.

The Coldstream Hotel looked the same as he remembered it. He'd taken a room there before the robbery under a name he no longer recalled, so he could study the town. He even opened a small account to get an idea of the bank's layout. Unable to restrain a smile as he rode, he recalled how he'd deposited twenty-five dollars in the afternoon and withdrawn eight thousand dollars the same night. As he passed through the town, he searched in vain for Montana's horse. After stabling his own mount at the livery stable, he walked to the hotel and got himself a room. He lay down in the bed, happy to rest his aching muscles after the long ride, and soon he fell asleep.

*

Later that day, Montana Jenkins approached Coldstream. He had three newspapers folded neatly in his saddlebags and wondered whether Butch already knew what the newspapers would tell him. Razor hung; Shark executed by a firing squad; his son dead in a fall. All three stories, all three deaths, touted the involvement of someone called the Lone Ranger. That any Ranger, lone or otherwise, had been involved in taking down his gang members would have sent Butch into a fit, but causing the death of his son… Montana hoped he wouldn't be the one breaking the news to him.

As he swayed gently in the saddle, Montana remembered the bank robbery of three years before. It brought a smile to his face, as it had to Cavendish's. He continued down the main street and hitched up in front of the hotel. He registered and asked whether Willy Parker had arrived yet. Room 28 he was told.

Butch was here.

For the briefest moment, Montana considered remounting his horse and heading to Mexico—he had plenty of money—but thinking of the Texas Rangers destroying the gang he'd been part of for years angered him. He could not let it go. Butch would demand vengeance, and Montana wanted to help him get it.

When he reached his room, he sat on the bed for a moment and re-read the stories about Razor, Shark, and Garth. When he left his room, newspapers in hand, he said a silent prayer, hoping he had nothing to tell Butch he didn't already know. Montana drew in a steadying breath and knocked on the door of Room 28.

Butch had awakened moments before, so Montana's arrival did not disturb him. When he heard the knock, he hoped he'd see Montana, and when he did, he let out with a big smile.

"At least you're all right," he said. "Glad you made it here. Come in. Did the news reach you?"

Montana felt a load disappear from his shoulders. He stepped into the room and tossed the newspapers onto the bed.

"I read about it. Looks like this Lone Ranger enjoys being in the headlines."

"He's gonna be in the obituaries when we get through with him," Butch promised.

"Got your sights set on him, do you?"

"I do. I sent Garth after him."

"I know."

"You know?" Butch stared at Montana, puzzled. "How could you know?"

Montana pointed to the newspapers on the bed.

"What? Garth got him? It's in the papers?"

Montana's stomach did a whirl. "You don't know, then?"

"Know what?"

Montana braced himself. "The Ranger got your boy, Butch. He's dead."

"Garth! Dead? No, no. Garth went after *him*."

"He found him, boss. Paper says Garth fell from some high rocks trying to escape this Lone Ranger."

"Oh, no. No."

Montana saw something in Cavendish's face he'd never seen before—weakness, sadness, regret.

"I'm real sorry, Butch. You want me to stay—"

"No, go. Go. Take those newspapers with you. I'll knock on your door when I can. Go."

"Room Sixteen. Want me to bring you some food..."

"I said go. I'll be all right."

"If you're wondering, Butch, I'm with you all through this. You can depend on me."

Butch gave a curt nod, and Montana closed the door behind him.

*

Linda Reid spent a great deal of time sitting on her porch, little Dan in a playpen next to her. She had not yet recovered from the loss of her husband and her brother-in-law, and she didn't think she ever would. She'd met her husband in Philadelphia when he was at school. They'd fallen in love and after his graduation, she followed him west. They married only a week after her arrival in Tyler's Crossing. When little Dan came along, she knew her life's fondest wish had come true. When her husband went out with the Rangers one day and never came home, she knew the dream had ended. Now, she planned to take the baby back to Philadelphia. She might return to the West someday, but for now, the memories were too raw, the surroundings too redolent of what she'd lost.

"Lokie!" she called.

A teenage girl stepped onto the porch. Lokie

Carol's parents had been killed in a robbery—a robbery undertaken by the same gang Dan had been chasing when he disappeared—the Cavendishes. Linda knew Lokie's family well and invited the girl in after the tragedy. When the baby arrived, both realized that Lokie's decision to accept Linda's offer benefitted each of them. Lokie also accepted Linda's invitation to go back East with her and continue on as a paid nanny for the baby. Lokie had become so attached to little Dan that if Linda hadn't suggested the arrangement, she would have suggested it herself.

"What is it, Mrs. Reid?"

"Please, Lokie. I've asked you so many times. Call me Linda."

"I keep forgetting."

"Please watch Dan for me. The lawyer brought me the final papers for Jim's property. I've signed them, and he should have them."

"When will we be leaving for Philadelphia?"

"Probably two weeks. We have longer if we need. The ranch hands here will keep the place up until the new owners take over. They've all been rehired so they're in good shape."

"I'm glad."

Linda went inside to change into clothing more appropriate for the horseback ride to Jim's cabin.

Jim had spent the morning in his mine, chipping away at the ore which supported him. Now, in the early afternoon, he sat in front of his cabin with his pipe. He waved a greeting to Linda when she drew near and helped her dismount.

"What brings you over this way, Linda?" he asked.

"These papers," she said, smiling. "My lawyer drew them up and brought them to me for a signature. This makes it all proper and legal. You have the deed for what you own now, and you own it forever." She handed the papers over and gave Jim a hug. "I don't know what I would have done without your help, Jim. With both Dan and his brother gone…"

"Now, now. You have a new life waiting for you back East." His heart and mind ached to tell her she hadn't lost all that she supposed, but the Ranger had explained why he needed to be a forgotten man—to keep her safe from the Cavendish gang's vengeance.

"I know. I know. It's so hard, though. Being alone in that big ranch house."

"You have little Dan to care for and Lokie to talk to. Can I cook you something? Make you coffee?"

"No, I still have packing to do. Protect those papers," she suggested with a chuckle.

"And you protect yourself and little Dan."

"I will."

She mounted and started back toward home, Jim wishing he could call out and bring her back for what would surely be good news.

*

When Montana Jenkins responded to the knock on his hotel room door later than night, Butch Cavendish greeted him with, "Let's go have a drink."

He and Montana walked in silence to the Saddle Horn Saloon.

"Two whiskeys," Butch said to the bartender once the men found a place at the bar.

"How are you feeling, Butch?" Montana asked.

"We're going to get that masked man, Montana. I swear to you he's a dead man."

Montana nodded. He picked up his newly arrived drink and held it up. Butch did the same. Their eyes met and they tilted their glasses toward one another. Then they drank.

"Who can he be, this Lone Ranger?" Montana asked. "If we knew who he was, we might be able to find him, but he's like a ghost."

"I'd like to know why he calls himself the Lone Ranger," Butch wondered. "Why Ranger? Why not the Lone Rider or the Lone Gunman or the Lone anything else?"

"And why 'lone' when he rides with an Indian all the time? You think maybe he once rode with the Rangers?"

Butch signaled the bartender, who brought over two

more whiskeys.

Butch repeated his question as if he hadn't heard a word Montana said. "Why does he call himself the Lone Ranger? Why doesn't he simply ride with the Rangers or join the Rangers?"

"Didn't you hear me, Butch? I said maybe he *used* to ride with the Texas Rangers."

"Maybe, maybe not, but I'm sure there's something in this Lone Ranger name."

"You could be right," Montana agreed. "What, though?"

"Let me think, will ya?" Butch snapped. He went over his encounters with Texas Rangers. "Collins said we killed those six Rangers in Bryant's Gap. I should've gone down to make sure myself."

"There was no time for that. The cavalry was on our trail then, too. You don't think one of them Rangers could have survived, do you? We filled their carcasses with bullets. None of them could have lived through that. Nobody got out of there, Butch. I would have seen something about it in the newspaper. It would have been a big story, boss, but, lucky for us, there's nobody to tell it."

Anger percolated inside of Cavendish.

"We never checked, Montana. We shouldn't't've left it to Collins. We've never been back there."

"I wonder whatever happened to Collins."

"Forget about him!" Butch snapped. "I think we should ride back to Bryant's Gap. If they buried the bodies there, we can count the graves. Make sure there's six. Maybe nobody even found the bodies yet."

"Oh, lord," Montana moaned. "You want to ride back and count bodies and graves?" Montana recalled something from the article about the death of Garth. Perhaps this would get Cavendish's mind off of Bryant's Gap. "Butch, you didn't read the newspapers I brought you. The one about your boy said this Lone Ranger was going to Corbin City to report to the sheriff there."

Cavendish threw back his drink.

"And you took till now to mention it me?"

"This is the first we walked, boss."

"With news like that, we got no reason to hang around this one-horse town," Cavendish argued. "I want to be sure Captain Reid and the other five Rangers are dead and in the ground. After we do that, Corbin City's nearby. We go look for this masked man and Indian."

"Butch, I think you're wasting your time. I agree we should look for this Lone Ranger, but none of them other six could *possibly* have survived what we did to them."

"But if one did, what would he be?"

"What would he be?"

"You heard me. If one lived through it, what would he be?" He gestured to the bartender.

Montana stared at Cavendish's profile. What was he driving at…? Then, he realized.

"You mean if one Ranger lived through the ambush, he'd have been… the lone Ranger to survive?"

"And maybe he calls himself that to taunt me—taunt me for failing to blast them all to kingdom come. Tomorrow, we ride back to Bryant's Gap."

Cavendish and Montana set out at sunrise next morning, and in the early afternoon, they trotted through the entrance to Bryant's Gap. They didn't ride far before six mounds of dirt with rocks piled at the head of each mound, indicated the graves of the six Texas Rangers they'd ambushed.

"Six graves, Butch," Montana said. "Looks like we got them all."

"Six graves don't mean six bodies," Cavendish growled.

"What? What do you mean six graves don't mean six bodies?"

Cavendish turned to his partner, a ragged scowl on his face.

Montana said, "You mean you think one grave is empty?"

"If six Rangers got shot up and one didn't die but didn't want anybody to know he didn't die, how many graves would you dig?"

"Butch, that's crazy! Who would come up with a

scheme like that?"

"Only one way to find out. Get the spades."

"What are we gonna do with them?" Montana asked, hoping for any answer other than the one he expected.

"You start at one end, I'll take the other."

"Butch, that's… that's crazy. Ghoulish."

"When did you get so squeamish? Get the spades," Cavendish said slowly. Montana obeyed.

"You want to take off your two six-guns, so they don't get in the way of your digging?" Cavendish asked.

"I'm not taking off my guns," Montana snapped. "You take off your gun if it gets in your way."

"Heh. Squeamish *and* sensitive. Start where you're standing."

Montana happened to be where Tonto had dug the final, empty grave. Cavendish started digging at the opposite end of the six graves.

After fifteen minutes, Cavendish stopped and said, "Something in this grave. I ain't going no deeper than I have to." He replaced the dirt he'd removed from the grave. "You find anything yet?"

"Only dirt, Butch."

"Keep digging."

Montana sighed in disgust, eager to get this grim

inspection over with. "Hey, you ain't digging," he said when he noticed Cavendish watching him. "Why'd you stop?"

"You should have come across something by now," Cavendish said.

"Well, I ain't," Montana spat.

Cavendish ignored the other graves and joined Montana.

"We dig till we find something," Cavendish ordered. "What's that?"

"What's what?"

"What you just threw behind you."

"Dirt. Just dirt."

Cavendish dropped his shovel and picked up a mud-caked, silver chain with a small round medal hanging from it. He rubbed the mud from the medal on his sleeve, and as he studied it, a sly grin crept onto his face. He tossed the medal to Montana. "Read it."

Montana turned his back to the sun. "Says 'From one Texas Ranger to another.'"

"Turn it over."

"Your loving brother, Dan."

"You remember the name of the captain of the Ranger troop Collins led here?"

"I do. Dan Reid. We had more than our share of trouble with him."

"Collins told me he had a younger brother in his unit."

"I remember."

"Seems Captain Reid," Cavendish began, sarcasm dripping from his tone, "gave his little brother a token of his admiration. Touching, eh?" His eyes went to the grave. "Let's keep digging."

They dug down three feet but pulled nothing but dirt out of the hole.

"What do you think of my idea *now*?" Cavendish asked when they paused to rest. "Tell me I'm crazy *now*."

"There ain't nothing in this grave. Jeez, Butch, you may be right."

"I *am* right. No maybe about it. So, the little brother didn't die that day, did he?"

"How do you know it's the younger brother? Could be Captain Reid survived."

"I don't care which," Cavendish said hotly. "It's one of the Reids. No question about it."

"Why'd he leave the necklace behind?"

"Sentimental nonsense. Think, Montana. This brother would be the only Ranger left alive, wouldn't he? He'd be the Lone Ranger."

"I gotta admit, boss. Makes sense. Didn't Collins say the captain was married, had a family?"

"He did. Had a family like I once had a son. A family with a big ranch near Tyler's Crossing."

"Yeah, yeah. I remember Collins telling us that too."

"Pack up the spades and give me that little present from one brother to another. I'm going to leave a little different present in the grave myself. Then we'll head to Tyler's Crossing. Someone there will tell us where to find the Reid ranch."

Chapter 26

Linda Reid

A few days later, Elijah Dobson, Linda Reid's foreman, stepped from the bunkhouse and stretched, taking a deep breath of the fresh, morning air. His sole responsibility today was to help Mrs. Reid pack for her long trip back East. She'd promised him a hearty breakfast, and this he looked forward to. Cookie prepared meals satisfactory enough to keep a hungry work crew happy, but he didn't cook like Mrs. Reid. As Dobson walked toward the ranch house, he sniffed the air, anticipating the first aroma of the promised bacon, eggs, and pancakes. He reached the porch, though, without detecting any cooking smells, and wondered whether Mrs. Reid had awakened yet. She'd told him to be there early, so he knocked on the door and waited a full minute.

"Mrs. Reid!" he called. After another, louder knock, he walked across the porch to the front window and knocked on the glass. "Mrs. Reid!" he called again. "Lokie."

He retreated from the porch and studied the house for a moment. At the top of his voice, he shouted, "Mrs. Reid. Lokie." Tension crept over him. He walked briskly back onto the porch and tried the door. Surprisingly, it opened. He took a few hesitant steps inside and called out again. The silence of the house heightened his discomfort. He sniffed the air. No bacon had been cooked recently, that much was obvious. Reluctant to be caught prowling through the house, he called out one last time but received no response.

Dobson thought of the horses. He left the house and headed for the corral, where he saw that both Lokie's and Mrs. Reid's horses were missing, but the buckboard sat in its usual spot. Where could they have gone, especially at this hour of the morning? And with the baby along, no less. It was far too early to go to town, and Mrs. Reid certainly wouldn't set out somewhere on horseback with little Danny in her arms. Jim's was the only possibility, although he couldn't imagine why she'd go there. Unable to think of anywhere else she might be, he saddled his own horse and set out at a quick pace for Jim's.

Jim stood alongside his cabin, shirtless, daubing himself with water from a rain barrel while singing a popular tune.

"Well, howdy, Elijah. What brings you over here this early?" he asked.

"Jim, morning. I'm supposed to help Mrs. Reid with her packing today, but neither she nor Lokie or the baby are in the house, and their horses are gone from the corral."

"Maybe she hitched 'em to the buckboard and went into town." Jim rubbed himself dry with a ragged, much-used towel. He threw the towel back over a nail driven into the side of his cabin and wriggled into his shirt.

"Nope, buckboard's still there."

"Hmm, funny. She wouldn't go riding with the baby strapped to her."

"No, she wouldn't."

"You look all through the house?"

"I went into the living room and called out, but I didn't go rummaging around the whole house."

"That's real strange. Let me saddle up. I'll ride over with you. I won't be so shy as you about what you call rummaging."

Jim had his mule Clarabelle ready quickly and they set out.

"You first," Dobson said, when they reached the front door of the house.

Jim opened the ranch house door and stepped inside. "Linda. Linda, are you here? Lokie?"

"Nothing, Jim. Like I told you."

As the two men moved slowly across the living room toward the kitchen, Jim eyed a folded piece of paper lying on a side table and noted, with concern, to whom it was addressed.

"Elijah, go on and look upstairs. I'll search around down here."

"You sure? I never been…"

"Go, go, go. Don't worry about it. I'm here with you."

When Jim heard Dobson's footsteps fade away up the wooden stairs, he grabbed the piece of paper. Written in clear block letters: "To: The Lone Ranger." He heard

Dobson calling for Linda and Lokie above him and pocketed the letter. No one but himself knew the connection between Linda Reid and the Lone Ranger. Who the devil could have left such a note?

"There's no one upstairs, Jim," Dobson said, stepping back into the room. "What'll we do?"

"Why don't you ride into town and see if they went there? I'll stay here till you get back in case they show up."

"Should I tell Sheriff Colson they've gone missing?"

"I guess you better."

Jim stood on the porch and watched Dobson ride off. He stepped back inside the house and opened the note. The first thing that caught his eye was the signature of the man who wrote it.

So Lone Ranger—Reid—yes, I know who you are. I want you to consider what you did to my family. Consider it closely. You killed my son. What do you think is going to happen now? I have no more family, but I have your family. Soon, I will have you. You left an empty grave in Bryant's Gap. That grave will soon have bodies in it. Three of them. I hope this letter makes its way to you. By the time it does, it will be too late, but I wanted to be the one to tell you that our families are now the same size. And you will be the next to die.

Butch Cavendish

Jim's blood ran cold. Cavendish had come in the

dead of night and taken Linda, Lokie, and little Dan, but he had no way to warn the Ranger or even contact him. He folded the letter and put it in his pocket.

*

Time hung heavy for the Lone Ranger and Tonto as they camped in the canyon where they'd tended to Silver after the buffalo attack. The Ranger especially felt the weight of the time and place, and Tonto noticed it.

"You heap quiet many days, Kemo Sabe," Tonto pointed out.

"Yes, I know I haven't been very good company."

"What wrong?"

"I'd like to visit my brother's grave, but I'm not sure how it would affect me. I'm not certain I could stand it. He's gone; Linda and little Dan are about to leave for the East. It's probably better if I close off that part of my life and simply wait to hear something about Cavendish."

"*Mmm*, now me understand."

The Ranger rose from the grassy patch where he sat and walked to the entrance of their camp. Tonto rose and followed him.

"If you want, me go with you to grave. You not go alone."

The Ranger turned to his friend. "Let me think about it."

By next morning, Tonto's offer had changed the Ranger's mind.

"I thank you for this, Tonto. I don't think I would have gone by myself. I realize now I should have asked for your help straight off."

"Me glad help you anytime, Kemo Sabe."

"I know, Tonto, I know. Let's ride."

The Ranger felt a deep change settle over him as he entered Bryant's Gap. His world had turned upside down since he last rode into this canyon.

"Tonto!" the Ranger cried. "The graves. Someone has disturbed the graves." He dismounted and ran to inspect the damage. "Who would do…?" He saw that his own false grave had been dug to a considerable depth. Inside the hole, kept in place by a rock, lay a folded oil skin. The Ranger dropped to his knees and drew out the oil skin. Inside, he found three newspapers and a folded note consisting of two words: Butch Cavendish. The top newspaper had been folded over to display the story about the death Garth Cavendish. The Ranger quickly looked over the other two papers, which were folded to the stories detailing the capture of Shark Lawson and Razor Gilliam.

"Tonto, Cavendish has been here!"

"How that possible? How him know about grave?"

"I don't know, Tonto. I don't know." The Ranger sifted through the pile of dirt which had been removed from the grave.

"Tonto, help me."

"What you look for?" Tonto knelt next to his friend.

"The medal; the medal my brother gave me. I left it in the grave."

"Oh. Me remember."

They searched thoroughly but could not find it.

"Somehow Cavendish learned what happened here. If he's found the medal, he doubtless figured out my identity. He knew I rode with my brother. He'll put two and two together and go after Linda and little Dan. I'm sure that would be his plan. They're in great danger, Kemo Sabe."

"What we do?"

"We must get to Linda before Cavendish does. Leave this as it is. Let's ride!"

*

The Lone Ranger and Tonto drove Silver and Scout hard, scarcely stopping to sleep or eat. Late on the second day of their journey, the Ranger, in a quickly donned disguise, and Tonto rode up to Linda's ranch house to be greeted by two ranch hands, pistols drawn, running toward them from the bunkhouse. One of the two men was Elijah Dobson, who challenged the new arrivals.

"Get down off them horses, you two. What do you want here?"

"I'm here to see Linda Reid," the Ranger answered, ignoring the demand to dismount. "I have reason to believe she's in grave danger."

The ranch hands exchanged a glance.

"Why do you say that? Do you know where she is?"

"No. Isn't she here?"

"I told you to get down off your horses."

"Isn't she here? Is she missing?" the Ranger demanded.

"She's missing, all right, along with her nanny and baby. Maybe you know something about it," Dobson demanded.

"I *do* know something about it, but not how you think. Have you checked at Jim Faraday's place? Perhaps she fled there."

"Fled? What did she have to flee from?"

"So, you know nothing about where she is? Have you told the sheriff?"

"We told him. He knows. He's looking for them. Now, I'm telling you for the last time, stranger. Get off those horses."

"Tonto, we have to go and see Jim. Get up, Silver."

"Hey, get back here you two," Dobson called after them.

"Who the devil were they, boss?" the second ranch hand asked.

"Damned if I know."

They holstered their weapons and walked back to the bunkhouse.

When Silver and Scout slid to a halt before Jim's cabin, the Ranger shouted Jim's name.

Jim stepped outside. "Ranger, am I glad to see you! Wait right there. I got something for you."

Jim hurried inside and a moment later handed the Ranger the note he'd found in Linda's living room. The Ranger read it.

"I knew it, Tonto," he said grimly.

"What it say?"

The Ranger handed the note to Tonto and said, "Cavendish has somehow learned my secret, Jim. He discovered the empty grave Tonto made in Bryant's Gap. He no doubt found the medal my brother gave me and figured out the rest of the puzzle from it. He took Linda, Lokie, and the baby. When were they taken, Jim?"

"Elijah rode over to get me only this morning. Said he couldn't find anybody in the house. I rode back with him and found this note. They can't have gone very far yet."

"Then Elijah knows my secret too?"

"He does not! I snatched up the note before he

could see it. I'm the only one read it till I handed it over to you. I didn't know where to find you. It's providential you showed up today."

"Tonto and I were in camp near Corbin City. I rode over to visit Dan's grave, but found my false grave opened and three newspapers left behind, all with stories about the end of Cavendish's gang and the death of his son along with a note that read 'Butch Cavendish'."

"Oh, lord," Jim moaned.

"How Cavendish know you ever visit grave or see note in Linda's house?" Tonto asked.

"He didn't. He left those newspapers and this note to taunt me after the fact. He thinks I don't know what he's up to. He thinks he has all the time in the world to do what he threatens in his note."

"If him head to Bryant's Gap, why we not see him? We come from there."

"I think the answer to that would be he has to travel by night and hide out during the day. He can't take a chance of anyone—maybe even a lawman or a cavalry troop on patrol—seeing him dragging along two women and a baby, women who could easily ask for help. Besides, the plain is often miles wide between here and Bryant's Gap. Even in the best of conditions, we could easily have passed one another unseen. But we know he can't travel fast in the dark. Tonto, we have to return to Bryant's Gap before he does. He beat us here; we must beat him there."

"Horses already plenty tired, Kemo Sabe," Tonto

pointed out.

The Ranger stroked Silver's neck. "I'm going to ask a lot of you, big fellow. This may be the hardest job you'll ever do for me."

"Scout plenty tired, but Scout plenty strong."

Jim said, "Ranger, let me cook you a good meal, and you turn your horses free in the corral. Let 'em eat and drink and rest. Get some sleep yourselves. First show of sun tomorrow, you and Tonto ride out on horses fresher than they are now. The night's rest will make a world of difference. I'm certain of it. Look, it's already sundown."

As Jim spoke, the sun lit up the sky with pinks and purples as it sank low in the west.

"I'd like to start back immediately," the Ranger said, "but you're right, Jim. If Cavendish is traveling only at night, and I pray he is, he'll be some twelve or fourteen hours ahead of us tomorrow morning but moving slowly. We'll count on Silver and Scout to make up the time."

"Silver and Scout go plenty quick, Kemo Sabe."

"All right, Jim. Start cooking. Tonto and I will take the horses to the corral."

Chapter 27

Return to Bryant's Gap

Again, with few respites to eat or sleep, the Lone Ranger and Tonto made the journey between Jim's place and Bryant's Gap, Silver and Scout maintaining a heroic, miles-devouring, steady pace. Late on the second day, as the sun dropped behind the crags of the Gap, the Ranger and Tonto directed their horses through the entrance, eyes keen for any activity. They reined up before the six graves.

"No one here, Kemo Sabe," Tonto said. "It look same as before."

"Yes, it seems we've arrived before Cavendish, Tonto."

"What we do now?"

"Cavendish has no idea we're onto him. We'll make camp and discuss how to deal with him when he gets here. When he does arrive, the advantage will be ours."

"Last time, him have advantage."

The irony of the situation was not lost on the Ranger, and he said, "He might be here as early as tomorrow morning. We'll camp out of sight near the entrance and take turns on watch for his approach. He'll be the one who gets surprised this time. Wait, let me wrap these newspapers up again and put them back into the empty grave along with this note. I don't want

Cavendish to have any idea we've been here."

The Ranger dismounted, tossed the oil skin package into the grave, and replaced the rock on top of it. He took a quick glance at the other five graves, then remounted.

"Let's find a place to camp," he said.

*

The next morning, in the growing light of dawn, Butch Cavendish led his group into Bryant's Gap. Montana Jenkins rode behind the two women. Linda clung tightly to her baby. Lokie's wrists were tied to the pommel of her saddle.

"I didn't think we'd ever get here, boss," Montana said, spurring his horse past the women to move abreast of Cavendish. "I can't see why we had to come all the way back here for you to do what you want. These women slowed us down real bad."

The eyes of the two women followed Montana, and their hearts sank at his words. Neither man had spoken to them the whole way, other than to bark an order. Very few words had passed between the women, other than Lokie asking Linda how the baby was managing.

"We're here, ain't we? We made it. Traveling at night's hard, but we done it before."

"Yeah, but when we done it before, we usually had our saddlebags full of money and were running away from a posse."

"We won't be here long."

"What place is this?" Linda Reid asked. "Are those graves?"

"That's right. And you know who's in one of them?"

Linda turned her face away.

"Heh, heh," Cavendish laughed. "Don't it make you feel better your family will be… what's the word? Oh, reunited."

Linda's head snapped back, and she glared hatefully at Cavendish. "Let Lokie go," she said in a steady voice. "Let her take the baby and go. I don't care what you do to me but let her take the baby."

"Nobody's taking away nobody. A relative of yours killed my son. Now, it's my turn."

"If my husband killed your son, your son deserved it," Linda snapped.

Cavendish jumped down from his horse. "Shut your mouth. I don't want to hear anything more from you," he said. "This won't take more than half an hour. Bring the spades, Montana."

Montana dismounted and took two spades from the gear his horse carried.

"No need to waste time," Cavendish ordered. "We can throw 'em all in one grave, the one already dug for them. We need to dig it a little deeper. Don't want them to be too crowded, do we? You two just sit on your horses and watch."

"My baby's awake. I have to feed him. I'm getting down."

Linda carefully nestled the baby in one arm and climbed down from the saddle. Lokie could only watch.

"You gonna let her, boss?"

"Dig, Montana. Anything to keep that brat quiet."

Linda stepped behind a shoulder-high rock and sank to the ground. A moment later, the wails of the baby subsided.

"I'll keep an eye on her. You dig," Cavendish said, and Montana went to work.

Cavendish leaned against the opposite side of the rock which sheltered Linda and the baby.

"What are you going to do to us?" Lokie demanded, shaking her hands, trying to free them from the pommel.

Cavendish ignored her. When, in time, Linda reappeared from behind the rock, Cavendish walked over to inspect the hole Montana was deepening.

"That's good enough," he said. "Climb out. Let me have that spade."

He took the spade and faced Linda, an unwelcome smile on his face.

"What are you going to do?" she cried, squeezing Dan tightly to her and turning away from Cavendish. She ran a few steps, and Cavendish pursued, the spade held high about his head.

Lokie cried out, "Don't! Don't you touch them!"

A shot rang out, and the spade in Cavendish's hands went flying. Cavendish stopped, struck immobile with amazement. Another shot broke the silence, and he heard Montana cry out, the gun he'd drawn falling nearby. When Cavendish checked, Montana lay writhing on his stomach atop the pile of dirt he'd dug out of the grave. Cavendish looked toward Linda, who had stopped running at the sound of the gunfire. A deep voice rang out from a wall of the canyon.

"You're finished, Cavendish. Throw down your gun or my next bullet is for you."

Cavendish sent six shots toward the sound of the voice, but the walls of the canyon so masked the direction of the voice that the shots were useless. He dashed for his horse, leaped into the saddle, and riding low over the horse's neck, raced toward the opening of the Gap.

Tonto hid just outside the entrance, Scout's and Silver's reins in his hand. The Ranger had given him strict guidance to leave Cavendish for himself, and instead, take responsibility for Linda, Lokie, and little Dan, both for their protection and to, eventually, find out what Cavendish had told them.

When, earlier that morning, Tonto alerted the Ranger to Cavendish's approach, the Ranger found a well-concealed perch on a small ledge of the canyon wall, not far from the graves. The shots that took away

Cavendish's spade and sent Montana to the ground were, for him, easy shots from his vantage point. Now, he left his lair and clambered rapidly down the canyon wall, as Linda and Lokie stared in disbelief. He whistled loudly, but Tonto had already sent Silver into the Gap. The Ranger and Silver met, and the Ranger leaped into the saddle as a shot rang out behind him. He spun Silver around as Tonto and Scout raced past him. He saw Linda, gun in hand, standing over Montana, who lay motionless on the ground. Leaving Tonto to attend to Linda, Lokie, and the baby, the Ranger drove Silver forward and set out after Cavendish.

When he burst out of the canyon entrance, his quarry appeared as an insignificant dot far across the plain, but Cavendish's horse was no match for Silver.

"Faster, Silver. Faster, big fellow," the Ranger cried, as he closed in on the man who'd murdered his brother.

Riding with desperate speed, Cavendish had no opportunity to reload his revolver. The six useless shots he'd randomly sent toward the echoing, threatening voice had left him vulnerable, and he realized it. Glancing back, he knew the strides of the great, white stallion would soon overtake him. All he could do was to spur and slap his horse forward, hoping for more speed. Soon, though, he heard the rhythm of Silver's hooves grow louder and louder. He dared not look behind, fearful of slowing his horse's pace.

Suddenly, a voice cried out, "Rein up, Cavendish. You murdered my brother, and I want you."

The Ranger gave the panicked rider a moment to decide, but when he saw him merely slap his horse harder and more often, he reached back for his lariat. He readied himself and cried, "Faster, Silver. Faster."

Silver put on a burst of speed until he rode nearly alongside Cavendish. The Ranger's lariat snaked out and settled over the outlaw. The Ranger pulled Silver to a halt, and Cavendish sailed backward out of the saddle into the dusty road.

The Ranger sprang to the ground as Cavendish staggered to his feet, grabbed for his gun and, in desperation, tossed it at the Ranger. Cavendish managed to wriggle from the rope and run, limping and frantic. The Ranger caught him easily, and the desperate man spun and lashed out with his fists. The Ranger stepped back, then waded in. He connected with a right, then a left, then a thunderous uppercut. Cavendish staggered but continued to swing his arms and fists blindly. The Ranger stepped to the side, and when he crashed a right to the left side of his foe's jaw, the man slumped to his knees. The Ranger pulled him to his feet again and swung a powerful left to the other side of Cavendish's jaw. The man went over backward, but the Ranger stalked forward and hauled him to his feet by his shirt front. He drew back his fist again, but before he could let fly, strong arms wrapped around him.

"Kemo Sabe, stop. You stop. Him finished. Stop, Kemo Sabe."

For the briefest of moments, the Ranger prepared to give battle to his new opponent but recognizing Tonto's voice tempered the flaming rage inside him. He pushed the beaten outlaw away and watched him collapse.

"Tonto, what you are doing here? How are Linda and Dan?"

"Them not hurt. Me tell them stay there, and me come back after help you."

The Ranger shook his aching right hand and caught his breath.

"Thank you, Kemo Sabe," the Ranger said. "I might have killed him with my bare hands if you hadn't shown up when you did."

"Him get justice now. You not worry."

Cavendish stirred and the Ranger pulled him to his feet.

"Me get his horse," Tonto said.

The Ranger got behind Cavendish and pushed him toward Tonto, who led Cavendish's horse to them.

"Mount up," the Ranger ordered. "Silver. Silver, come here, big fellow."

The Ranger had one foot in the stirrup when Tonto cried out, "Kemo Sabe!" and a shot rang out. The Ranger spun and saw a look of amazement on Cavendish's face as he slowly bent to his left and toppled out of the saddle. Tonto stood next to Scout, holding his revolver.

"You shot him," the Ranger said.

"See what him have in hand."

The Ranger went to inspect the body and lifted a derringer from Cavendish's right hand.

"A two-shot derringer," he said.

"Him pull from belt when you turn back," Tonto explained.

"You saved my life, Kemo Sabe."

"Him want shoot you, then try shoot me."

"His days of shooting people are over. Help me get him over his saddle."

When the body lay across his saddle, the Ranger asked, "What happened back in the Gap?"

"Linda heap brave woman. She take Montana gun from ground and shoot when him get to knees and pull other gun. Him dead."

"Do you know what Cavendish told her?"

"Me see her safe, then come after you. No time ask questions."

"I'll take the body to where you hid outside the Gap. Find out if he told Linda the truth about me."

"Then what me do?"

"If she knows about me, come and get me. There won't be any reason then not to see her. If she doesn't know, bring Montana's body out. I'll take both bodies to Fort Davis. Captain Lawrence will be glad to get them. Then take Linda back to the ranch, and I'll meet you at Jim's. Tonto, I almost hope Cavendish revealed who I am. I'd dearly like to see Linda again, if only to say goodbye."

"You wait. Me find out."

Tonto mounted and rode off at a gallop. The Ranger climbed onto Silver and set out for the appointed meeting place.

*

The Ranger paced the full hour, he bided his time waiting for Tonto to bring him the answer. When he heard the slow cadence of two horses approaching, his heart dropped. Tonto bringing him Montana's horse. He stepped out from cover.

"Well, Kemo Sabe?" he asked, already knowing the answer.

"Linda say Cavendish tell her your brother kill his boy. Him not mention Lone Ranger."

"She must have misunderstood. What are they doing now?"

"Me give them food. Them cook. After we eat, me take them back to ranch."

"Then I'll get started."

"Kemo Sabe, Cavendish gang gone. Why you not go back to ranch too?"

The Ranger's eyes met Tonto's. "I'll see you at Jim's," was his only reply. He mounted Silver and led the horses carrying the last members of the Cavendish gang toward Fort Davis.

Chapter 28

The Lone Ranger Rides Again

Tonto hadn't been long at Jim's when the Lone Ranger arrived. After the men greeted one another, Tonto said, "Linda and others safe. Little Dan happy him back at ranch."

The Ranger smiled. "Thanks, Tonto."

"What captain say when you bring in Cavendish?"

"He was surprised, to say the least." Captain Lawrence had lavished praised on the Ranger, praise he would not repeat.

Tonto said, "Linda decide to leave for East quickly. In two days. She send Jim to town get seats on stagecoach."

"Where is Jim?"

"Him at ranch, help Linda."

"Did Linda ask about…?"

"She ask who man with mask was. Me say you good friend. Mask on side of law. Tell her you take bodies to Fort Davis."

"Did she accept that?"

"She more worried about little Dan than man with mask. She ask no more questions."

The Ranger chuckled. "That's good."

"Kemo Sabe, I still not understand why you not go East with Linda. Or talk to her. Say goodbye."

"Tonto, Captain Lawrence did say something very important after I delivered Cavendish and Montana. He said you and I had made the West a better, safer place."

"That right."

"One day, Tonto, the West will be populated just as the East is with cities, real cities, families, schools, factories… This country has an opportunity to be unlike any other country in history. Now, though, the West is too violent a land. Law and order has yet to be respected or even established in many places. By bringing down the Cavendish gang, we've helped the West take a step in the proper direction, into the shining future I know is waiting. I want to continue to do all I can to help. One day, I'm certain the smell of gun smoke and the stain of bigotry, the might of the powerful being using against the powerless, will be replaced by tolerance and understanding. It's going to take time, but I cannot see my way to deserting the job we've entered on."

"Me hope see that day come too."

"Even if we don't see it, we'll rest better in our graves knowing we'd done all in our power to bring it about."

"There Jim," Tonto said.

"You're back, Ranger. How did it go?"

The Ranger reported and told Jim his plans.

"You're sticking with him, Tonto?"

"That right."

"I'll be here for you both, whenever you need. Making bullets and mining silver," he chuckled.

"We couldn't do it without you, Jim."

"Linda's leaving the day after tomorrow. It's a shame she don't know…"

The Ranger interrupted. "I've made up my mind, Jim. Linda will be safer, and I think happier, if she believes her ties to the West have ended."

"I'm glad you're not giving up *your* tie with the West. We need you and Tonto out here, Ranger." In a quieter voice he said, "It's a shame, anyway. Well, you must be hungry. I brought some supplies. Some fresh vegetables. I'll whip something up."

The Ranger walked off, leading Silver to the corral.

*

Two days later, the Ranger left Jim's place early. Tonto volunteered to accompany him, but the Ranger rejected the offer. He rode a short distance and brought Silver to a halt atop the peak of a hill. Below lay the road the stage would take. He'd been there no more than fifteen minutes when the stage rumbled into view. Inside it sat the only family he would ever know, beginning a journey of a thousand miles. For an instant, he indulged the fantasy of riding down to meet the stage and unmasking himself before Linda. The fantasy was pleasurable but could not be.

He watched the stage out of sight. His past had been erased. The West was his home. He'd made his decision. The Lone Ranger would ride again.

ABOUT THE AUTHOR

John Paulits lives in New York City and spent many years there teaching. He has written fiction for over forty years, novels for children as well as adults. His wife is a former banker; his daughter a psychotherapist. *The Adventures of the Lone Ranger* is John's first book with Two Gun Publishing and a second Lone Ranger novel, *The Lone Ranger Rides Again*, is in preparation.

To learn more about John's books, visit him at www.johnpaulits.com

Printed in Great Britain
by Amazon

22819529R00205